Murder Most Pemberley

An
Eliza Darcy
Mystery

JESSICA BERG

Murder Most Pemberley
An Eliza Darcy Mystery™: Book 1
Red Adept Publishing, LLC
104 Bugenfield Court
Garner, NC 27529
https://RedAdeptPublishing.com/

To those who, like me, wish Jane Austen's characters did, indeed, exist.

Chapter One

Sexy Underwear or Wool Socks?

I know not what to think of Pemberley. As a visitor, I knew my place.
As its mistress, I find myself quite out to sea. The housekeeper, although
kind, seems wary of me. I am content to deal with a mistrusting ser-
vant, as I get to enjoy the perks of this grand estate: my Darcy.
—Lizzy Bennet Darcy
Pemberley 1811

Sexy underwear or granny panties and wool socks? Who am I kid-ding? Eliza Darcy shoved wool socks next to her Agatha Christie novels. The last time she'd needed fancy undies... well, she glared at the tags dangling from the lacy material.

"*The Murder of Roger Ackroyd.*" Belle Knightley, Eliza's best friend, snagged the book from the top of the pile. "First of all, why are you packing books? Secondly, isn't summer in South Dakota also summer in England?" She plucked the socks out of the suitcase. "And who is this Roger character, and if he dies, why should I care about him, anyway?"

Eliza snatched the book from Belle's perfectly manicured clutch-es. "*The Murder of Roger Ackroyd* is one of Christie's best novels."

"And the first and second part of my question?" Belle threw a handful of frilly underpants into the suitcase.

Eliza replaced them with the socks. "I hear it can still be a bit chilly in England, especially during the evenings." Eliza collapsed in a heap on the bed, rolled onto her stomach, and rested her chin in her hands. "Oh, if truth be told, I need my socks and my books for comfort. I know only three people there." She tapped a fingertip against her lips. "I really should have waited until after this trip to break up with Seth."

"Have you heard of Kindle? And kindling a new relationship would be exactly what you need, too, and you won't find that with your nose stuck in a book. Besides, Seth is a twit and would have ruined your vacay. Come on." Belle smoothed Eliza's hair. "You've got this. This is not like you. Where's the girl who laughs in the face of danger?"

"Hiding in my wool socks?"

Belle rolled her perfectly lined eyes. "Now, let's pack for real and get you ready to impress the Darcy-Bennet clan."

Eliza peeled herself off her flower-sprigged comforter. "No wool socks?"

"No." Belle plopped the lace material back in. "And it never hurts to be prepared."

Eliza pulled her beloved books from her suitcase. It was silly to take them, given the surcharge on overweight baggage, but the crinkled pages and cracked spines were her comfort. She'd lost herself in those books, and maybe her ex-boyfriend, Seth, was right about her weird obsession with them. Even though his objection to them was because he was a male chauvinist pig who pouted when she didn't dote on him. No, that was unfair to pigs everywhere. Although maybe she was a nutcase, like he'd called her once. He was probably intimidated by her wit, something she'd had to deaden or else listen to him whine. She itched to hone it, but fear, a new concept, kept her sharp tongue as dull as a butter knife.

What better time to start a new chapter? She placed the books reverently on her dresser. *New chapter?* She was about to launch a whole new book. England and a family she'd never met awaited her. Maybe, just maybe, she would have a chance to let her inner Hercule Poirot or Miss Marple run free. Or maybe she'd sit and drink tea and eat crumpets all day.

"You should ban your cat from the closet. There's more cat hair than clothes." Belle's voice wafted from the depths of Eliza's closet, and sundresses, sleeveless tops, and shorts flew into the air and fluttered to the floor. "Why can't your parents go?"

"Can't" go? Eliza stifled a laugh. *"Won't" go is more like it.* If memory served—and honestly, it had never failed her before—something had caused her father to leave England, even going so far as to brush the dust from his shoes before getting on the one-way flight. She had tried to wheedle it out of him, but he had kept his lips sealed on the matter and spouted things like "Let sleeping dogs lie" and "Keep the past in the past." Eavesdropping on her parents like any good tween sleuth would do had never produced an answer. Apparently, even his wife was ignorant of the situation. But Eliza was twenty-six and above the art of eavesdropping. Sometimes.

Eliza huffed. "They have a pediatric seminar in Hawaii. Tropics over rainy English weather, I suppose."

Eliza's gaze flicked to Caesar, her large orange Maine coon cat, who peered around the corner of her room. He never dared share a room with Belle. He, at least, did not underestimate her hatred for cats. "And since the rest of my family has abandoned me, I will take Caesar. He is family. Where I go, he goes."

"You're taking your cat?" Belle's head poked out of the closet for a second, but it popped back in with what sounded like "crazy cat lady."

"Yes. You can take my books from me, but you can't take Caesar away. He's looking forward to the trip."

A grunt emanated from the closet. "Did you know you have a cute pair of wedges in here?"

"They hurt my feet." Eliza nabbed *The Murder of Roger Ackroyd* and stashed it in her carry-on, next to her encyclopedia of English slang words. A girl needed something to bide her time on the plane.

"Don't care." Out came the salmon-colored wedges, thunking on top of the bushel of clothes. Belle emerged from the closet, her blond hair standing on end, and dusted her hands. She smoothed her hair and studied the pile of clothes. "There, now we have a wardrobe to assemble."

"Are you sure you can't be my plus-one? Think of all the tea we could drink and the possibility of meeting Benedict Cumberbatch."

"First of all, I hate tea. Secondly, Benny would be blinded by our beauty and charm, and that would ruin his career. Then I'd feel bad, I'd eat Twinkies, and"—Belle slid her hands over her curvy hips—"my curves would become mounds. And that is not sexy. Thirdly, my new business can't run without me."

"So you're choosing flowers over your friend." Eliza blew her hair out of her eyes. One day, she would chop it all off, but too many people had complimented her black curls for her to take the plunge.

Belle took one look at Eliza and embraced her. "It's going to be okay. I'll make sure you have all the right outfits." She spun Eliza in a circle. "And you, my friend, are a fashionista's perfect model. Tall, slender, and—"

"No chest."

"That, I can't help you with. Now go gather all your toiletries and stuff." Belle dug out tags and tiny safety pins from her purse. "Remember, this is why you called me over. You'll be ready in no time."

"No time" took three hours, complete with packing and unpacking suitcases five times. Eliza hugged her friend goodbye, shut the door, and leaned back against the smooth wood. "Well, Caesar, that was fun."

Caesar blinked his multicolored eyes and stretched out his six-toed paw and licked it.

Eliza grabbed the gold-embossed, calligraphy-scripted invitation from the fridge.

"How does it feel being my plus-one?" She scratched between Caesar's ears. "I'm sure you'll be much better company than Seth would have." She swooped her cat into her arms and spun into the living room. "Watch out, England. Here we come!"

Caesar hissed.

"Keep that up, and I won't take you. You'll be stuck with Aunt Ethel. And we both know what happened the last time." She released Caesar, who saluted her with his tail and sashayed from the living room. "Drama queen," she taunted as the last of the orange fur rounded the corner.

She grabbed a pair of antique vases off the mantel then wilted onto her chaise lounge. The vases were gaudy little things, but she loved them. Three pink English roses stood out from the gilded vases. Two ornate handles, painted in gold as well, gave the impression that the vases had arms. They had belonged to her great-five-times-over-grandma, Elizabeth Darcy, a woman with whom she shared not only name but also, according to family legend, a personality. And the fact that the vases were sent on her twenty-first birthday from a nameless relative had her tingling with anticipation.

She fingered the emerald brocade fabric of the chaise and wished more than anything that she could travel back in time. The present, though, offered more mystery. She planned to find out exactly what had made her father run from his home more than twenty-five years ago. And maybe she would visit the Agatha Christie Gallery in Torquay, wherever that was.

"WE SHOULD HAVE COME two hours earlier." Eliza rolled the suitcase weighing exactly fifty pounds, jostling for position in the Monday morning Minneapolis-Saint Paul International Airport ticket line. Eliza and Belle had spent the night in a hotel, noshing on Chinese takeout and making a list of things Eliza *had* to do. She had secretly crossed off making the guards at Buckingham Palace laugh. Only tourists did that.

"You'll be fine." Belle scooted the strap of Eliza's carry-on on her shoulders and gave the pink bedazzled carrying case a jiggle when Caesar protested his mesh prison. "Oh, hush, cat. It's not my fault your aunt Ethel thinks you're a girl." Belle peered at Eliza. "Are you sure you want to take the cat?"

"The cat has a name. Maybe that's why he doesn't like you." Eliza grinned and moved in line, tripped on thin air, and rammed into the back of the person in front of her.

"Oh my gosh, I am sor—"

The man turned around and pinned her with an inquisitive blue gaze. She mentally fingered through the Rolodex of colors in her brain. She taught creative writing, for goodness' sake, and knew every name for blue, but at the moment, that was the only color to come to mind. Plain old blue. Belle nudged her.

"Yeah. Um, I'm sorry. I was walking and tripped over..." She glanced at the smooth tiled floor. "Over nothing, as you can see. I'm afraid I was never blessed with grace or agility or..." If only she could shut up. Her time with Seth had transformed her into a ninny.

Crinkles formed at the corners of his eyes. "No problem. I can't say I inherited those either. Overrated, in my humble opinion." He gave a crooked smile and turned around, presenting her with the back of his head once more.

Belle mouthed the word "Hottie" and fanned herself. For once, Eliza had to agree with her friend's assessment. She almost rammed into him again to see his chiseled and five-o'clock-shadowed face and to hear his lovely English accent once more. There were laws against those kinds of things. And she was a law-abiding citizen, unless the speed limit counted as an actual law. She gazed at the dark hair brushing the collar of English Man.

"Earth to Eliza." Belle wriggled her fingers in front of Eliza's face. "I think your cat needs to use the facilities."

Eliza ignored her and whispered, "I'm going to be single forever, aren't I? I'm going to be an English teacher spinster. Oh gosh, I'm the cat lady!"

"Calm down. We'll go on a double date when you get back. Me and Greg and you and..."

"See? You will marry and have a dozen children. That's fine, though. I'll grow to be an old maid and teach all your children how to diagram a sentence and conjugate verbs."

"That sounds dirty."

"Wait until I tell them to put their dangling participles back in their sentences."

Belle snorted. "Good grief! Sometimes I wonder why I associate with someone who knows a dangling participle is a real thing."

The blue-eyed stranger glanced at Eliza, a tiny smile touching his lips, as he left the ticket counter.

"Who knows," Belle whispered as Eliza placed her information on the counter. "Maybe you'll meet in London. He is English."

Eliza rolled her eyes. "Yeah, right. I think it's safe to say I will never see him again."

———

"LAST BOARDING CALL for Delta Air Lines Flight 3524 to London." The speaker voice clicked in and out, but Eliza got the message loud and clear and hoofed it through the airport to her gate. She had lost time in the duty-free shop and underestimated the distance between her shopping pleasure and her gate.

Caesar lay prone on the floor of his carrier, small mewling noises squeaking from his body.

"Hang in there, buddy."

She sprinted over the Jetway and nearly fell into the plane. "I'm sorry," she gasped to the airline attendant, who directed her toward her seat with an admonition about moving as quickly as possible. She sidestepped down the aisle, a long trek of shame, and tried not to pelt people with her purse. She shoved her carry-on into the over-head compartment and plopped into her seat before setting Caesar's cat carrier between her feet.

"That was a close—" She stared openmouthed at her seatmate. It was him—English Man.

"Hello again." A smile crinkled the edges of his eyes. He glanced at the kitty carrier and growling cat. "We have a world traveler on our hands, I see."

Eliza swallowed. Twice. "Yes. Um, this is Caesar. I'm afraid he's not used to flying or other people or the outdoors, for that matter. The vet said I should sedate him, but I thought he might want to en-joy the experience." Goodness, she sounded like an idiot. If humans had batteries, she would need to dig hers out and reboot. Not for the first time did she wish Seth a lifetime curse of scurvy.

The man's smile grew bigger, and he leaned down and talked through the mesh. "Caesar, it's a pleasure to meet you. My name is Heath." His eyes met Eliza's. "And your name?"

"Eliza."

"Nice to meet you." He flashed her a crooked grin and gave the flight attendant his full attention when the safety procedures were demonstrated. *Who does that?*

Desperate to hear his accent again, she searched for something witty to say, but only a jumble of nonsense came to mind. She didn't want him to think she was one of those annoying passengers who would jibber-jabber on about nothing for the entire flight. Instead, she placed her chin in her hands and studied Heath's perfect profile through her peripheral vision. Caesar peered at her from his kitty carrier, his eyes narrowing to tiny slits.

Eliza hissed, "Oh, quit judging me. I can already tell you're going to be a nuisance the entire trip."

"You talk to your pets too?"

"No?" She vowed to ignore Caesar the whole trip.

He chuckled, a lovely rumbling sound. "Don't worry. I talk to mine as well. A Saint Bernard would not fit in"—he glanced at the pink rhinestone-encrusted cat carrier—"one of those, so I must travel solo."

"Are you going home?"

"Yes. Visiting some old mates. I'm told it will be great. Apparently, there's someone I just 'have to meet.'" His fingers hooked air quotes. "I was also promised we'll have a right laugh. Or so I'm told. Probably end up being a damp squib."

Eliza pretended to understand the perfectly good English coming from his well-formed lips and steered the direction into smoother waters. "What do you do?"

"I'm a professor of archaeology." A soft smile curved his lips.

"Just like—"

"Don't say it. Not at all like Indiana Jones. Although I do hate snakes. My main work is in ancient Anglo-Saxon artifacts."

Eliza's inner English teacher fell a little bit in love. "It would be so awesome to go on a dig with you. To see the world of *Beowulf* and the ancient bards. What brings you here?"

"I'm on sabbatical and was visiting a mate of mine who teaches at the University of Minnesota."

With a jolt, the plane moved across the tarmac. She gripped the armrest.

"Are you okay?" Heath leaned toward her, his shoulder just centimeters from hers. "I hate this part too."

"I normally have my best friend's hand to hold. Don't suppose I could borrow yours?" *Holy crap! Did I just ask to hold his hand? What in the hell is wrong with me? He must think I'm an absolute idi—*

"I've always wanted to rescue a damsel in distress." He gave a cheeky grin and spread his hand, palm up, on their shared armrest.

She placed her hand in his, palm to palm, finger to finger. He never closed his over hers, but the warmth of his skin ignited her blood.

Risking a look at his face, she gave a shaky smile and lost herself in his blue gaze. *Why can't I come up with a better name for the color?* It didn't matter. His eyes were looking not at her but into her. Breaking the gaze, she looked out the window and said goodbye to the solid, steady ground as the plane jetted down the runway and into thin air. Hopefully, not too thin. Anything thinner than pea soup didn't seem logical to keep a behemoth contraption in flight.

Upon reaching ear equilibrium and no longer having the need to work her face into weird, unflattering positions to get her ears to pop, she grabbed for her purse and paused, knowing once she broke the skin-to-skin connection with Heath, she wouldn't get it back. But any further skin-to-skin time and he might call an airline attendant to toss her out.

Eliza broke contact. "Sorry about commandeering your hand."

"My mum always told me to be a useful little gentleman. This is me finally fulfilling her wish."

"Glad I could help make her dream come true." She tucked her hand in her lap. "I think I'll read for a while."

She ignored *The English Guide to Local Colloquialisms,* which she'd promised herself she'd read, and lost herself in the voice of Enya and the writing of Agatha Christie, yet her body seemed hyperaware of Heath's closeness.

"Eliza?"

She jolted to attention and blinked at him. His eyes, rimmed by long eyelashes she'd have killed for, twinkled with laughter. A slight spattering of freckles under his eyes—*cornflower blue*—and along his slightly crooked nose gave the impression that an impish boy lurked under the starched collar and English manners.

"Yes?"

"The flight attendant asked if you were ready for your meal."

Eliza cleared her throat and puffed out her chest slightly. "I knew that."

The flight attendant placed the food on the tiny seat-back tray. Spaghetti and meatballs with two breadsticks. Eliza snuck a peek at her English neighbor as she settled her napkin on her lap.

"Trying to decide if I'm an ex-con or something?"

She choked on her sip of water. "No! Well"—she blushed—"to be honest, I did learn some karate moves in case I meet some unsavory people."

"Let me guess. *Karate Kid*?"

"Where else can one learn the art of bonsai trimming, waxing a car, and killer karate chops?" She snatched a breadstick. "Imagine, if I had a sensei who taught me well, I could chop this thing into pieces."

Chuckling, Heath plucked it from her grasp and, holding the two sides between his fingers, leaned closer. "I dare you. Teach this breadstick a lesson it won't soon forget."

"Here?"

"Nobody's looking, and really, the breadstick won't complain too much."

After taking one last glance around her, she eyed the breadstick, raised her hand, and brought it down with precision. The seat-back tray rattled, her fork went flying, and a meatball rolled to the floor and across the aisle. Twenty heads swiveled in her direction. There on the tray lay the breadstick, whole and unscathed if not a little squished in the middle.

"Big fly," Heath announced to the rapt audience. "Huge. She got it, though."

"A fly?" Eliza's face burned.

"You told me you were an adept ninja, with skills to assassinate breadsticks. Load of codswallop, that. It was the best I could come up with at the moment."

A giggle formed at the back of her throat. She sipped some water, but nothing would dislodge it. The giggle burst out into the napkin she held tightly to her mouth.

"You are an absolute delight. I've had many transatlantic trips, but this one, by far, has been the most enjoyable."

She bit her bottom lip between her teeth. "What else do you take delight in?" She was flirting. *Finally.* It must be the air pressure resetting her Seth-ified idiocy. *About damn time.* She met Heath's eyes. *My flirting skills are as adept as my ninja ones.*

He pilfered the non-squished breadstick and took a bite. "Let's say I take enjoyment in little things, like uncovering an artifact that hasn't seen the light of day in thousands of years, making students' eyes glaze over in a lecture, or seeing a peng woman who can't even kill a breadstick."

Her heart vibrated in her chest. She rested her elbow on the armrest and leaned closer to him. "But that poor thing was innocent. I maimed it."

He glanced at the injured breadstick still lying prone in the middle of the tray. "It is your job as a merciful assassin to get it out of its misery."

"What happens if I need assistance? Who do I call?"

"I suppose I could be your sidekick. You'd look better in the cape, anyway." He jotted his number on a slip of paper and pressed it into her hand.

"I don't know. You could make spandex look good." She tucked the paper in her pocket.

"Tried it once. Children's theater. It looked ridiculous." He shuddered. "Couldn't get the bloody things off. Two of my mates had to pry me out of them. I'll leave the trousers to you."

During the rest of the meal, war stories about spandex morphed into chatter about her teaching job, students whose names she would no longer consider for her future children, her cat, and the weather, apparently a favorite English topic. After the trays were taken and the runaway meatball found, Eliza gathered her book once again, plugged in her earbuds so Chewy-Chewerton in the row behind her didn't get a smack to his gum-chewing face, and read. And fell asleep.

A cocoon. She snuggled in deeper. Hard yet comfortable, it was pliable yet firm. Her cocoon smelled like cinnamon and Irish Spring soap. She rubbed her head over the soft surface, her nose sliding along something smooth yet prickly. *Cinnamon?* Realization crept into her like a cat stalking a helpless mouse. No cocoon she'd ever come across smelled like Big Red gum.

She opened her eyes and saw a cross-eyed view of skin. Not any old skin but Heath's five-o'clock-shadowed skin. His Adam's apple bobbed when he swallowed, and his pulse beat in the soft shallow where his clavicles met. Embarrassment kept her immobile. All too soon, she would have to face reality and his piercing gaze.

A soft chuckle rumbled in his chest.

"How did you know I was awake?" She popped away from him, her book clattering to the floor, her right earbud ripping out and dangling.

"Your gasp of surprise gave you away, I'm afraid." His tongue clicked against his teeth. "If you are to attain master spy status, you must control your emotions when finding yourself in precarious situations."

"You are incorrigible."

"Many women find that endearing." He flicked the dangling earbud. "Do you?"

"No." At his cocked eyebrow, she stammered on, "Besides, it's not like I was hanging off a cliff or anything."

"No, you were burrowing into my neck like a—what you do call them around here?—a prairie dog."

She wanted to hate the twinkle in his eye and his twitching lips. *Is that a dimple in his left cheek?* Sure was. She stuck her chin out slightly. "I'm sorry if I caused you discomfort."

"Just a numb arm. Nothing a little time and massaging won't fix."

With a growl, she plunked her earbud back in and snatched her book from the floor, turned to a random page, and pretended to read until the airplane tires squealed against the London Heathrow Airport tarmac at four p.m.

Feeling *Dawn of the Dead*-ish, Eliza wished for a shower, a fresh set of clothes, a good tooth brushing, and a bed. Heath looked none the worse for wear and seemed to beam with a rosy glow. *Men!* An exasperated sigh escaped before she could squash it.

"Are you okay?" Heath's hand moved toward her face, seeming on a mission to place her wayward hair behind her ear. Her ear tingled in anticipation. Mission aborted, he plopped his hand back in his lap. "You look ready to escape out the window."

"Wouldn't fit." She'd already calculated the measurements.

"You'll feel much better once you get to your hotel room. Promise." As the row before them filed out, she gathered her cat, who was in a constant state of growling, and bumped her way to the front and out of the plane. The Jetway shivered as people plodded into the airport. Seeing her hotel room as the carrot dangling at the end of a long stick, she endured Customs, lived through a near mosh pit at the baggage claim, and withstood the rain as she and Heath waited for a taxi.

"Welcome to England." Heath placed his body in front of her as a protective barrier from people brushing past them, some apologetic, others brusquely businesslike in their shoving and displaying elbow dominance.

"I swear, if one more elbow touches me, I'm going to show these people how straightforward Americans can be."

"Not all mouth and no trousers, I see." He grinned. "You are a dangerous opponent. They wouldn't stand a chance."

"Budge up." A stranger growled from behind Eliza, and an elbow connected with her back, sending her sprawling into Heath's arms. His face was dangerously close to hers. He smelled of cinnamon. She wanted to punch Mr. Rude Elbow but had more important, and delicious, options. All she had to do was move an inch, and her lips would be satisfied, but before she could make a move, Heath drew back and glared at the man behind her.

"Hey, no need to be so pushy." Heath planted himself between Eliza and Elbows. "You owe this lady an apology."

Mr. Rude Elbows lifted his hands in surrender. "Didn't mean no harm, really. Just cack-handed is all." He mumbled an apology and pulled his raincoat tighter around him.

A taxi pulled to the curb. Heath put her luggage in the trunk—or "boot," as he called it—and settled Caesar into the back seat. "May I text you?"

She nodded, and her stomach twirled.

"I might need your number, don't you think?" His eyes glittered with laughter.

"Jet lag?" All the other options reeked of desperation: She wanted to spend more time with him; she wanted to kiss him; she was glad she had packed those frilly pieces of lace. She gave him her number and willed time to stop.

He bowed over her hand and kissed it. "Goodbye, Eliza. I look forward to when fate joins us again for our next adventure."

Before she could assemble a coherent sentence, he walked away, disappearing into the crowd.

Chapter Two
Welcome to England, Miss Darcy!

Tonight is a ball in my honor. Kitty and Mary will be in attendance, and I hope Lydia's influence over Kitty has loosened its grip. I feel as if I'll be on display tonight. Must I prove myself worthy of Darcy for the community? I do hope two things: that Mary will not want to exhibit her "talents" and that I will not fail my beloved.
—Lizzy Bennet Darcy
Pemberley 1811

"Welcome to London, miss." The taxi driver tipped his hat to her in the rearview mirror after he slid into his seat. On the wrong side of the car. "First time over here?"

She gave a little smile. "Is it obvious?"

"You'd be surprised how intuitive us taxi drivers are." He turned his attention to driving, and through the raindrops drizzling down her window, Eliza witnessed London, from the iconic taxis to the red phone booths. As the black cab maneuvered through congested London traffic, struggling for space on the narrow roads, she rested her forehead against the cool window. McDonald's and other American brick-and-mortar fast-food joints nestled between fish-and-chip shops and Indian restaurants. Her nose deceived her into thinking she could smell the essence of freshly roasted and ground coffee beans. Her stomach rumbled. She pinched her arm to make sure she wasn't dreaming, that she was still on Earth. She, Eliza Jane Darcy, was in London, and she had almost shared a kiss with an Englishman. If only stupid Seth could see her now. *Suck it*, her mind singsonged.

Upon reaching the hotel, the driver gathered her luggage and handed her off to a porter. Check-in went smoothly, the elevator to the fifth floor went glidingly, and the trek down the hall to room 525 went quickly. Key in, door open, luggage abandoned in the middle of the room, and Eliza stood at her window, London sprawling out as far as she could see. Which was not too far, as the fifth floor didn't offer panoramic or long views. The bed looked too good to ignore, and without even taking off her shoes, she popped open the kitty carrier, spread-eagled facedown, and fell asleep to the hypnotic, comforting purrs of Caesar perched on her backside.

Her phone buzzed and jiggled on top of the bedside table. She threw an arm out, sending it skidding across the carpet and under a corner chair. Its vibrations, though fainter, seeped out from under the cushioned furniture. Caesar flicked at it with his paw, his tail signaling the hunt was on.

"Coming," she mumbled, rubbing her eyes. After retrieving it, she glanced at the display. "Hello, Joy."

"Eliza!" Joy's clipped accent sang through the phone. "Charlie and I can't wait to pick you up from the train station tomorrow. I told Mum we should drive to London and get you today—"

"Jet lag" was all Eliza got in edgewise before Joy Bingley, well-known bodice-ripper romance novelist and one of the two cousins Eliza had met in her twenty-six years, began another tsunami of information and platitudes that strangely made her feel at home. Joy reminded her of Belle, and she snuggled that to her like a security blanket. By the time the conversation—if one could call it a conversation, as that usually required two people—was over, Eliza's ears rang. Energized by Joy's infectious energy, Eliza tore through her suitcase, grabbed her toiletry kit and pajamas, and headed to the bathroom for a much-needed shower.

"Caesar, do you want to order some room service? Binge on *Keeping Up Appearances*? I could use a little Hyacinth in my life right now." Eliza bounced from the bathroom, hair turbaned and body bundled in a pair of pajamas.

Caesar sat on the windowsill, his tail twitching and his jaw chattering.

"What do you see, buddy?" Eliza joined him at the window. "Ah, you have found English pigeons as intoxicating as I have English men." She plopped onto the nearby chair and cuddled Caesar to her chest. "Call me crazy. Strike that. I'm already crazy. I'm just nervous. What if they don't like me? What if they look at me and see the runaway's daughter?"

Caesar sniffed at her earlobe, sneezed, and jumped from her lap.

"You're right. I am a grown-ass woman and am perfectly capable of handling myself."

With that mantra going through her head, she ordered fish and chips, swirled her fork aimlessly through the extra side—a pool of mushed peas—downed a glass of wine, and fell asleep to the social-climbing techniques of Hyacinth Bucket.

A GOOD NIGHT'S SLEEP later, Eliza stumbled out the hotel doors, luggage, cat, and bags in tow. Her phone buzzed in her back pocket. She shifted her bags and grabbed it. The message light blinked.

Good Tuesday morning. How was your first night in London? Meet Benedict Cumberbatch yet? You promised me an autograph.

Oh, Belle. Eliza smiled. *London is a blur. Hotel was nice, and Caesar likes the view. Apparently, English birds are more exciting than American birds. No sighting of Benny, though. Will keep my eyes peeled. You can go back to bed now.*

Tired of squinting into the sun, she put her aviators on and waited next to the porter, who was doggedly waving down cab after cab.

After a few minutes, a cab pulled to the curb. Eliza slipped the porter a tip and slid into the back seat. "King's Cross Station, please."

King's Cross Station loomed before her as the taxi rolled to a stop in front of the brick building. Its clock tower kept steady time with massive hour and minute hands, and the large domed glass windows on either side of it gave the impression that a museum made up its innards instead of trains and tracks and travelers. After the cabbie assisted her with all her luggage, she paid and tipped him.

The interior of King's Cross was oxymoronic to the outside. A regal, royal entrance transformed into a sweeping ceiling honeycombed with a white lattice structure growing from the ground up and spreading itself upon the ceiling with a purple glow. Contemporary and modern, the station buzzed with life, energized by the sunshine streaming in through the skylights over the platforms and stretching to the ends where the tracks left the building.

She hunted for the correct platform as she cuddled Caesar's carrier to her chest and listened to his comforting purrs. *This is it.* Her pulse raced at the idea of meeting new people, people she shared a lineage and history with.

Her phone buzzed again. Her smile grew until her face hurt when she saw the number—Heath. *Good morning, Eliza! I hope London has treated you well so far. She can be a little feisty at times.*

Her fingers jetted over her screen. *London has been a perfect lady. Like me. ;)* She sat and stared at the text, her finger hovering over the send button. Time to make good on her promise to Belle and to herself. Kindle a new romance, turn a new leaf. With one tap of the send button, she turned that new leaf.

A perfect lady, huh? That's too bad. I like mine a little bit feisty.

Her insides flooded with warmth and tingles. Hearing the announcement of her impending train, she went with instinct. *I guess you'll have to find out!*

"Caesar, this could turn out to be a train wreck."

Several heads turned in her direction. It took several beats before her faced heated with embarrassment.

"Oh dear. I'm sorry. I didn't... I just—" She snapped her mouth shut and went for a winning smile. She got a few grins back.

On schedule, the train screeched to a halt, and its doors silently slid open, expelling people from its cars. Within minutes, Eliza had slid into a window seat. With a slight jerk, the train pulled out of the station. She settled back into her seat, stared out the window, and witnessed the cityscape morph from grimy Victorian buildings to Edwardian neighborhoods to suburban areas riddled with utilitarian architecture built during the twenties and thirties and finally got her first glimpse of the English countryside.

Rolling green fields separated from each other by natural hedgerows replaced the London skyline. An occasional small oak grove, majestic and ancient, shaded grazing red-and-white Hereford cattle and fluffy white sheep. Yellow fields of rapeseed swirled together with green pastures in a whirlwind of color as the train sped along the track toward the Darcy ancestral property of Pemberley. Eliza wiggled in anticipation of seeing it for the first time.

If she were to believe old family legends, she wouldn't be there if it weren't for an accidental meeting at the estate between her great-to-the-sixth-degree-grandparents. Supposedly, he had been blinded by pride and she by prejudice until the fated day when their paths crossed and the blinders were stripped away. Although, like in a storybook, scandal had threatened to wither their blossoming love. Something about a hussy sister and Grandpa Darcy's mortal enemy or something to that effect.

Jet lag won out over scenery, and before long, Eliza's eyes snapped open to the announcement that Lambton station was next.

Her phone rattled on the empty seat next to her. *How's my assassin spy ninja?* She pictured Heath's smile, his easy laughter.

Nervous. The train was slowing, and buildings became less of a blur.

You'll do great! Let me know when you get settled. Remember, if you need anything at all, ring me. Chat soon.

Before she could send a return text, the train jerked to a halt. She gathered her stuff about her and disembarked with a few other passengers. On reaching the platform, her fellow travelers, who seemed to know what they were doing, vanished, leaving her to circle around in search of a friendly face. Despite her searching gaze, all she spotted were the gingerbread-esque train depot, complete with eaves white enough to pass for frosting, and a parking lot scattered with cars of all makes and models. Fear of being stranded alone arrested her senses. Someone "yoo-hooed" across the platform, then a pair of hands clutched her shoulders.

"Eliza, I am so excited to see you again." Joy smiled with straight white teeth and hugged her.

Eliza returned the hug. "Hello, Joy. It's been a while. Twelve years."

"It seems like yesterday. I've tortured Mum for years, begging her to take Charlie and me back to the States, but she wouldn't hear of it." She slung a perfectly coiffed blond ponytail behind her. "Charlie couldn't make it. Girl issues, apparently, and sending everything all sixes and sevens." Joy peered at the pink mesh carrier. "This is your plus-one?"

"Trust me, he's cuter and better tempered than my original plus-one."

"Cats are much more resilient than men, that's for sure. Do you have your luggage?"

An answer obviously wasn't necessary as from then, Joy took charge, and in less than half an hour, she had packed Eliza, Eliza's suitcase, Caesar, and other accoutrements into a shiny dark-green Land Rover, and the quaint village of Lambton itself was a blur in the side mirrors.

Still stunned by the flurry of activity, Eliza couldn't reconcile the Joy of twelve years ago, who had given blonde jokes some validity, with the Joy of the present. She hadn't lost the ability to talk, but she had taken charge of the entire train station with such alacrity that, for a moment, it had seemed to bow to her.

"...invited some old mates from Oxford to meet you."

Eliza snapped out of her reverie. "I'm sorry. What?"

Joy patted her hand. "No worries. I only invited the most eligible bachelors. Once they found out I had an American cousin, they wouldn't leave me alone, and after I showed them your picture on Instagram, they all but demanded an invitation to Pemberley. I specifically invited one to meet you. He's an old ex of mine, one of my favorites, really. Lives in the States. I think you two will turn every head. It's a wonder you haven't met yet."

Eliza was about to inform her cousin of the millions of people who lived in the States and that the odds of her meeting said "favorite ex" were one in 328 million—give or take a hundred thousand or so—when Joy zipped around a car tiny enough to fit into the bed of a Ford F-150.

"Joy—car!"

"Got it."

By "got it," Joy apparently meant slamming on the Land Rover's brakes and driving into a hedgerow to avoid a head-on collision. Both the passed car and the almost-dead car honked at them. Unfazed and without a pretty blond hair out of place, Joy pulled back onto the narrow road.

Eliza patted her hand over her heart, which had yo-yoed between her toes and throat before settling back into her chest.

"Stupid drivers." Joy puffed her cheeks out and smiled. "Where were we? Oh yes. Men. You will love—"

"You shouldn't have." *Heath*. They had connected over flirty banter and a spaghetti dinner gone wrong. But even though they'd exchanged numbers and a few winky faces along the way, the odds of her seeing him again were slim to none. Meeting up later with a stranger met on a plane happened only in the movies. No need to starve herself of company while pinning her hopes on one individual man. She jammed her phone into her purse. "Thank you. I was contemplating my fated spinsterhood with my friend Belle before leaving. Looks like you might have saved me from that horrible fate. But I warn you, I have made a new resolution. I will not give the time of day to any more stupid men. Probably. Hopefully."

"I should make that my resolution as well. I've got more stupid-men stories than you could shake a stick at. Numpties, really, every last one of them. I'm sure Charlie will love listing off all the twits." She passed a slow-moving truck with a beep of the horn. Eliza gripped her knees and prayed. "Stupid lorries. Anyway, I figured you would feel out of the loop if you didn't have a date to the ball."

"A ball?"

"I told Mum to put it on the invitations. You don't have a dress, do you?" At Eliza's headshake, Joy squealed, "I love shopping, especially when it's not my money."

"Back to the ball. What ball?"

"Oh, it will be a riot. You'll see. Mum and I decided it would be top-notch to celebrate such a large family reunion with a ball." Joy danced in her seat. "Aren't you just dead pleased?"

As they were discussing a real-life ball with fancy dresses, tuxedos, and dainty little pastries that calories would never be invited to live in, Eliza assumed "dead pleased" meant something good. Not for the first time, Eliza regretted not cracking the cover of her English slang book. "Awesome" was all she could say as Joy waxed on and on about the plans, the food, the music, and the clothes.

Joy turned the Land Rover onto a wooded sun-dotted lane winding its way among the oak, beech, and willow trees. Sprinkled among the arbor giants, wildflowers of blue, purple, pink, white, and yellow carpeted the sides of the lane. Some of them she recognized: foxgloves, daisies, harebells, and forget-me-nots. She'd never been one for pressing flowers, but her fingers itched to preserve the delicate beauty.

"Are you ready?"

"For what?"

"This." Joy pointed out the windshield.

Eliza gasped. Pemberley surpassed even her imagination. Her father rarely spoke of the estate and had claimed it caused too much pain. The wild beauty of the surrounding woodland gave way to the massive honey-butter-colored brick structure, which instead of sticking out like a sore thumb, melded with nature around it. A snowy-white cornice capped off the top floor, and Roman Doric pilasters edged the corners of the mansion. Georgian vertical triglyphs, rosettes, and friezes, all depicting ancient Greek culture, separated the uppermost yellow bricks and the white cornice. Hundreds of windows, encased in six-gridded white frames, glinted in the sunlight. *Who's in charge of cleaning all of those?*

Rising gracefully from the banks of the stream snaking across the backside of the building, a manicured lawn sprawled across the vast estate, broken only by hedges walling off what Eliza assumed were gardens.

"What do you think?" Joy pulled to the front of the house, the Land Rover's tires crunching on the graveled drive. A young man immediately came to the door and opened it for Eliza.

Eliza tumbled out and gawked, openmouthed, at the redbrick archway towering over a stone walkway leading into the courtyard. "It's... it's... amazing."

Joy clutched Eliza's arm and waltzed through the archway. Eliza felt like Dorothy from *The Wizard of Oz*, but instead of Dorothy's ruby-red slippers clicking over a yellow-brick road, Eliza's tan half boots clomped over weathered, moss-stained stone. Ivy crawled the courtyard's inner redbrick walls, and pink and white roses bordered the walkway.

"Jonas will bring your luggage to the house. Come and meet everybody." As they passed a water fountain surrounded by sprigs of lavender, Joy leaned over and whispered, "I'm deliriously jealous of Fitzwilliam. Fancy living in this place. Of course, it doesn't hurt that he used to be a very successful venture capitalist. Oh, and being a baron does come with some perks."

Eliza rolled through her mental Rolodex of relatives. Ah yes. Somewhere along the line, a king or queen had bequeathed to a Fitzwilliam Darcy the title of baron. And the Right Honorable Lord Darcy, the fourth Baron of Pemberley, its vast estates and land—and her uncle—was a man she'd never met.

Butterflies fluttered in her stomach as she walked up the stone steps leading to the gleaming wooden double-door entrance flanked by white marble columns. Her namesake had walked up those very steps both as a stranger and later as its mistress.

A rotund voice stilled her butterflies. "Eliza, welcome to Pemberley." Her uncle, or the man she assumed was her uncle, stood before her, arms spread in welcome, his large frame dwarfed by the grand entrance. "I hope you enjoy your stay with us. I was hoping your parents would come as well."

"Prior engagements, I believe. It's hard to pass up Hawaii."

His keen eyes twinkled with intelligence. "Some pleasures are hard to forgo. And some, seeming sweet at the time, we come to regret."

Intrigued by the burly man with a set of salt-and-pepper muttonchops that would have made his namesake proud, she placed her arm in his offered one and walked through the doorway and into the entrance hall.

Her arms dropped to her sides, and her mouth hung open, but she couldn't help it. Knowing grand houses often fell out of repair due to the extreme cost of upkeep, she rejoiced that Pemberley had not shared the fate of its once-majestic counterparts.

"It's lovely... uh..." Instead of packing the stupid colloquialism book, she should have invested in a copy of Debrett's *Peerage & Baronetage*. If her uncle was a baron, she should address him as lord. *But is it my lord or Lord Baron of Pemberley and all the estates heretofore bestowed upon thee?*

Her uncle must have read her twirling thumbs and scuffling boots for the panic it was and placed his hand on her shoulder. "Eliza, here at Pemberley, we—I—don't put much stock in formalities or titles. Please call me uncle. Now, what do you think?"

"Well, Uncle Fitzwilliam, Pemberley is gorgeous."

"I'm glad you approve." He finally noticed the pink carrier and bent down, peering into the mesh. "And who do we have here?"

"Caesar. Aunt Sara said it would be okay. She's arranged for all the necessary cat... things."

"Of course. He might like it in the kitchen and the rose garden. Shall I give him to Jonas?"

Caesar could do with some exercise. "If you think he'll be safe and out of the way."

Uncle Fitzwilliam smiled and took the carrier gently and handed it off to Jonas, who was waiting silently nearby. "Make sure he gets a chance to go outside, please."

Caesar pressed his face to the mesh and stared at Eliza. She gave a tiny wave. He gave a pitiful meow as the stoic footman carried him away.

A movement on the staircase to the left appeared to catch Uncle Fitzwilliam's attention. "Ah, Nancy, my love"—he held out his hand to the elegant lady swathed in a sage-green wrap dress and silver heels and encircled his arm around her waist—"meet our newest arrival. This is Eliza Darcy, Andrew's girl."

Condescension dripped off Aunt Nancy much like the diamonds dripping from her ears. "Pleased," she purred with the friendliness of the Siamese cats from *Lady and the Tramp*. Eliza had always detested those cats. Now she knew what one would look like if it morphed into a human.

"You have a lovely home." Eliza had the urge to give a floor-sweeping curtsy but wasn't sure why.

"Was a cat in that carrier?" The question made it seem as if Eliza had smuggled scorpions into the house.

"Um, yes. I was told that was okay."

"I'm allergic."

If blushes could turn a person's hair red, Eliza was sure her black hair would have turned cherry. "I'm sorry, Aunt Nancy—uh, Lady Nancy—"

"It's Lady Darcy." Aunt Nancy's teeth clipped out the syllables with such force that Eliza feared the woman's pearly whites would shatter.

Uncle Fitzwilliam pressed a kiss to his wife's hair. "Nancy, you know we don't care about such things. Really quite ridiculous, I say."

Aunt Nancy's brow furrowed, and she wrapped her arms around her middle. Eliza imagined Nancy tightening a baroness's title around her instead of sloughing it off as her husband had his title of baron.

"I am sorry, Lady... Aunt Nancy, Aunt Sara told me I could bring Caesar."

"It's fine." Her uncle's hand rested softly on Eliza's shoulder. "We'll be sure Mr. Caesar stays away from our lovely lady here." His wink spoke wonders.

"Yes, well." Aunt Nancy sniffed and tossed her head, sending locks of auburn hair cascading over her shoulders.

"If you don't mind, I'll take Eliza to her room so she can get a good kip in." Joy stepped in and grabbed Eliza's hand.

With a smile to her uncle, Eliza followed Joy up the grand staircase and into a cavernous hallway.

"Two questions. What is a kip, and is this place haunted?" Eliza whispered both to respect the ghosts that might lurk in corners only to be awakened by noise and because the presence of Aunt Nancy had withered her ability to speak normally.

"A nap, and only if you count your aunt Nancy."

"Sadly."

"Only through marriage, though," Joy offered cheerfully.

"Small comfort." Eliza still clutched Joy's hand as they passed the gallery of people from the past gazing down at them. She paused and looked at Fitzwilliam Darcy. "Is it creepy to think your great-great-great-great-great-grandpa is attractive?"

Joy snickered. "Your secret is safe with me, although I do have to admit, your ancestor is fit."

Eliza assumed Joy meant attractive. "Where's Elizabeth's portrait?"

"Down the gallery farther." Joy pulled her along. "Here."

Elizabeth's eyes were what grabbed Eliza's attention. The artist had managed to capture the life and vivacity that family legend had claimed captured Darcy's heart. Elizabeth's face, rosier than those in the other female portraits, alluded to an openness, a vibrancy of personality. Her lips lifted at the corners with the smallest of grins. A grin with a secret. Maybe Darcy had been behind the painter, and that smile was for him alone.

Voices floated up the steps and echoed down the gallery. "Let's go before we have to face Nancy again."

Eliza didn't argue and all but fled out of the gallery and into another hallway. Joy stopped at a door about a third of the way down the hall and gestured grandly as she swung open the door. "Welcome to the Tulip Room."

"It's tulip-y." Eliza's finger traced a purple tulip embossed in the wallpaper. From the bedspread, to the curtains, to the carved tulips in the writing desk, tulips sprang from every nook and cranny. "I'll feel like Queen Titania from *A Midsummer Night's Dream* sleeping in her little bed of flowers."

"I wanted to call bagsies on this room, but Mum wanted this one to be yours. You're lucky you got this one and not the carnation room. Such drab little flowers." Joy plunked down on the tulip-bedazzled bedspread. "I'm glad you've come. Mum is in such a tizzy over this reunion, Nancy barely tolerates any of us. At least the rest of the family is nutty enough to make it all fun."

Eliza sank down next to her. "What's up with Aunt Nancy?"

"Besides the fact she's got a stick up her bum?"

Eliza choked on a laugh. "She should see a doctor about that."

"She despises everyone and everything that isn't, to her, 'top drawer.' That applies to most of your uncle Darcy's poorer, untitled relations, like me and the rest of the Bingley clan. Any of the Bennet sisters' descendants who aren't from Elizabeth's bloodline, she loathes. Except for the Wickhams. Which is odd, really."

"What right does she have?" Eliza's skin heated. "She simply married into the name—"

"It's all about the title. I imagine she calls herself 'My Lady' in the mirror every morning. No one else does, except for the servants, of course." Joy rubbed her fingers together. "Oh, and money. She attached herself like a leech to the Darcy name years ago and has done nothing since but sit there and suck on the prestige of it."

"But Uncle seems intelligent and kind. How has he been hoodwinked?"

"Love is blind?"

"How did your mother get permission to set up the reunion and take over control?"

Joy grinned. "She obviously didn't leave an impression on you."

No. It might have had something to do with the fourteen-year-old Eliza spending more time fishing her goody-two-shoes cousins out of their shell and Americanizing their sense of decorum. *Who doesn't slide down banisters?* "She seemed nice."

"Ha! You don't know my mother. She's a force to be reckoned with. Imagine a tornado that only wants to hug you."

Eliza knew all too well the force of tornadoes, and she had spent two weeks convincing her naive cousins that tornadoes were a daily occurrence in South Dakota.

A knock on the door interrupted Eliza's plans to prostrate herself before her cousin and apologize for past wrongs. "Come in."

Jonas, Caesar perched precariously on his shoulder and head, lugged her suitcase and accompanying bags into the room. "Miss, would you mind removing your cat from my head, please?"

Eliza eased Caesar off the man. "Thank you for taking care of him for a while."

Jonas smiled, revealing a gap between his two front teeth. "He and Mrs. Bankcroft are good mates already. Can't say the same for Gizmo, Mrs. B's pup. There was quite a faff with a bird, and I'm afraid he'll throw a wobbly when he sees a bird again." He sent Caesar a wary glance as the cat pawed at his leg. "Lord Darcy requests your presence whenever you have freshened up."

"Who's Mrs. Bankcroft?" Eliza asked when Jonas left.

"The head cook. Let's hope you don't make an enemy out of her. You'll have gross eggs every morning." When Caesar came to say hello, Joy rubbed a finger between his ears. "I'll leave you to it." Joy paused at the door. "Don't be nervous to meet the rest of the family. Even though most of them know the history of bad blood between your father and your uncle, no one tends to care anymore, except for Nancy, of course, but you've already been inoculated against her poison. She's only jealous." Joy's thin, porcelainlike face scrunched. "If I didn't know any better, I'd say she's afraid of your father."

After the door closed with a click, Eliza plopped onto her back and spread-eagled out over a field of flowers. Andrew Darcy wouldn't hurt a fly. He had even bought one of those silly contraptions to humanely trap a spider and free it in the wild. She'd tried it once, but the spider had freed itself from the entrapping bristles and ran up the handle, its mission clear: to eat her alive. Since then, she'd been perfectly fine squashing them, and she doubted she'd burn in hell for the murder of a few dozen—hundred—spiders.

She wished her childhood eavesdropping on her parents' conversations had produced more than a few uncomfortable images and an entire week where she couldn't make eye contact with them. Apparently, she hadn't been harvested from a cabbage patch.

Her phone buzzed, and her heart skipped a beat. Heath.

How's it going? Do you need me to rescue you yet?

She bit her lip. Maybe airplane strangers did meet again. Maybe that whole movie trope was real. On the slim chance that it was, she texted back: *Nope. I'm safe and secure in my tulip tower. Although there is a fire-breathing dragon you must slay if you want to rescue me.*

Seconds ticked by and turned into minutes. She tapped her phone, nudging it to give her Heath's response faster.

Fill me in later. Got to go. Oh, and there are a lot of things I want to do with you. Rescuing you is only one of them.

Tingling with anticipation at finding out Heath's plans for her, she launched off the bed and ransacked her suitcase for the perfect meet-all-your-extended-family-in-one-afternoon outfit, which Belle had clearly labeled with a tag safety-pinned to the shirt. She swiped her makeup case as well. An extra layer of mascara and lipstick never hurt either.

Chapter Three

Every Family Tree Has a Few Nuts. Right?

What a wretched way to spend an evening. Does one's family need to travel to visit their daughter so soon? Mamma could scarcely catch her breath with all the compliments and, dare I say this of my own mother, simpering. Poor Darcy. I hear his footsteps. I think I shall invent ways of making up for Mamma's social gaffes tonight.
—Lizzy Bennet Darcy
Pemberley 1811

"Breathe," Eliza whispered. If she could make it to the drawing room without snagging a heel and falling headfirst down the steps, she would dance a jig. If it had been up to her, she'd have worn ballet slippers, but Belle had disagreed: "A girl who doesn't want to make an ass of herself does not wear slippers to a lunch shindig." Eliza pulled a face at her friend's echoing reminder.

"Ah, Eliza, you look refreshed and ready to conquer the world. Much like your father if I remember correctly." Uncle Fitzwilliam, looking regal and handsome in pressed khakis and a mint-green button-up shirt, greeted her when she reached the bottom step. She took his proffered arm.

"I'm also a good actress." Eliza sensed a connection with her uncle that was more than her hand on his forearm. He reminded her of her father, and homesickness produced an abundance of honesty. "I want to run back to the tulips and hide under the bed."

He stopped next to a gilded vase sprouting lilies and lavender. Taking both her hands in his, he whispered, "I often find myself wanting to hide in my study too." He squeezed her shoulders. "Your secret is safe with me. Besides"—he took her arm again—"most of these people want to approve of you. They won't be looking for blemishes. You belong to the infamous Andrew, defector from England. You, my dear niece, are quite the attraction to our little gathering."

The open drawing room doorway proved her uncle had a skewed view on crowd sizes.

"Little?" she squeaked.

"Considering the number Sara Bingley invited, this is indeed rather tiny."

Bolstered by her uncle's presence, Eliza entered the room, her head held high, chest slightly puffed out, and stomach quaking.

"Good afternoon, everybody. May I introduce you all to Eliza Darcy, Andrew's daughter."

Eliza wanted to add she was also Pamela's daughter, but as no one in the room had ever met her mother, that factoid would fall on deaf ears.

"Eliza?" A tiny woman packaged in a hot-pink polyester pantsuit and white tennis shoes squeaked over to her, dragging a shuffling octogenarian behind her. The white-haired lady laid a warm, papery hand on Eliza's cheek, tears swelling in her eyes. "You look like your father. Oh, William"—she glanced at the old man next to her—"I can't believe this day has finally come." The dam of tears burst and slid down the woman's wrinkled face.

Uncle Fitzwilliam placed a hand on the weeping woman's shoulder. "Eliza, this is William and Iris Darcy, your great-uncle and -aunt."

"Do forgive me, Eliza." Her great-aunt's hand slipped from Eliza's face only to latch on to her hand. "I've prayed for years that someday I would look upon you, Andrew's child. It is amazing to finally meet you. Your mother has been sending us Christmas cards, on the sly I think, but pictures aren't the same."

Great-Uncle William nodded in solidarity with his wife. "We miss him terribly, you see. How long has it been now? Some thirty years, I'd say." His eyes reminded Eliza of her father.

Anger sizzled inside her. *How many hearts did my father break when he left?* The weeping woman before her was only one of them. More than ever, she wanted to figure it out. Maybe her father would come back and make amends.

"Aunt Iris, you must let Eliza breathe." Uncle Fitzwilliam gathered Great-Aunt Iris into a sideways hug. "I must have Nancy take Eliza around the room for introductions."

Great-Aunt Iris snorted a grand harrumph. "Sorry"—she smiled sheepishly—"but might I have the honor?"

He pecked Great-Aunt Iris's cheek. "Go and introduce your great-niece, Aunt Iris."

Great-Aunt Iris clutched Eliza's arm as they walked away and whispered, "I couldn't let that woman introduce you."

Eliza didn't have time to ask for details. The rounds had begun. Her great-aunt's fingers dug into her arm, but she didn't care. She was her great-aunt's lifeline to the past, to her nephew, and if Eliza could serve as a conduit for that, she would. Between the punch bowl and the chocolate fountain, Great-Aunt Iris came to a stuttering stop. Her fingers dug a little harder.

"Margery. Nice to see you could come. I was not aware you and your sisters"—she paused and looked about the room—"and the whole Wickham clan would be able to attend."

Margery looked like Eliza's childhood cello teacher—tall and husky and with a few chin hairs sprouting from various pores. What she assumed were Margery's sisters looked like carbon copies, all lined up neatly in a row.

"Hello, Iris." Margery's tenor voice seemed to boom across the room, but no one else seemed to notice or care, so Eliza concentrated on the chin hairs. "We did send our RSVP."

"Must have been lost in the post."

"We are family." She nodded to her sisters, who silently bobbed their heads, their support implied rather than stated. "Didn't think we'd need an invite." Margery pinned Eliza with a stare. "This is the American relative?"

The disdain in her voice took a few seconds to hit home as Eliza was lost in the ditty from "The Three Little Pigs" and was in the middle of "Not by the hair of my chinny chin chin." At her great-aunt's prodding, Eliza stuck her hand out. "I'm Eliza. It's nice to meet you."

Margery sniffed the air as if she smelled something foul. "Pleased, I'm sure. These are my sisters, Lucy and Gertrude." Before the women could speak for themselves, Margery set a half-eaten pastry on the white-clothed table behind her. "Iris, the lobster canapés are slightly dry this year, don't you think?" And without further ado, she gathered her sisters to her like a robe and paraded through the room, people scrambling to give her a wide berth.

"That woman is odious and always has been. Her brother, Samuel, used to be the estate manager years ago, but he dare not show his face around here. Can you believe he embezzled from the estate? Complete imbecile. Sadly, that doesn't keep her away." Great-Aunt Iris glared at Margery's back then peered at Eliza. "You survived your first Wickham experience, then?"

"Why do they come if no one likes them?"

Great-Aunt Iris grabbed a lobster canapé and chewed thoughtfully. "These aren't dry. She's the dried-up old... well, no more of this foolishness. We are all family, and every family tree needs a few nuts, don't you think? Grab a canapé, my dear. You'll need your strength for the rest of the introductions."

Eliza nabbed a canapé or five and hustled along after her great-aunt, who introduced her to Kitty's descendants. Kitty had married a barrister named Whitechapel, supposedly a love match, although according to family records, either their first child was premature, or they had preempted their wedding vows. As Eliza laughed and joked with newfound relatives, ones she'd had no idea existed, her brain mapped out family trees for each of them. Even though last names and an ocean separated them, these were her cousins, people she shared a blood tie with, who shared a claim to five sisters who had lived together, fought together, and loved together, an experience she'd never had. Being an only child was a lonesome affair.

Ushered along at the insistence of her great-aunt, she encountered Mary Bennett's descendants cloistered in the corner, far removed from the rest of the gathering. According to family history, Mary had married late in life and, having realized spinsterhood looked better on paper than in reality, married an equally boring vicar named Deering and somehow created five children. Eliza stifled a giggle. Sometimes generations weren't enough to remove certain genetic qualities or defects. Her great-aunt must have noticed her glazed eyes and interceded when Eliza was asked for the fifth time her theological viewpoint on global warming.

"Eliza, I am thrilled to see you again. It seems like forever." A musical voice chimed from behind Eliza, and slender arms squeezed her in a hug. Sara Bingley's blond hair, having escaped from a chignon, tickled Eliza's nose. Sara had not aged a day since Eliza last saw her. She fought the itch to rifle through Sara's toiletry kit for the fountain of youth.

"Mrs. Bingley, it's great to see you too."

"First of all, call me Sara, and secondly, you look a little pale. Where's the spitfire girl from twelve years ago?"

"She's still contemplating hiding under the bed until everybody leaves." She snatched from a passing tray a tiny pastry filled with something that looked edible. "Joy says you've put in a lot of work on this reunion."

An eye roll accompanied an unladylike snort. "It's been ghastly. But despite certain mean old hags who shall remain nameless, I've had the time of my life and have no right to whinge." Any further enlightenment on that subject died upon the arrival of Charlie Bingley.

"Hiya, Eliza. Lovely to see you again." Charlie's dimples winked at her when he smiled. The years had been kind to him. With his athletic build and his mother's blond hair, there was no doubt he was the honeycomb and England's women were the bees. "Come. I'll introduce you to the cooler"—he smirked at his mother and Great-Aunt Iris—"and younger crowd." He led her away and leaned in conspiratorially. "Have you met all the relations who are off their trolley?"

"Do Margery and her sisters count?"

"Don't waste your time on them. Spiteful old cats, they are. Oh, and Garrison, their nephew, is a complete tosser. Joy has nothing for him. Speaking of Joy, she said we're to meet her out on the lawn. Keeping with my mother's blast from the past in celebration of the 'good old days,' a game of croquet is in the works along with my sister's potty matchmaking schemes. Whoever you choose, don't choose Willoughby. He's an ass."

Head spinning about how the word "potty" dealt with matchmaking, Eliza followed Charlie out the door and down to the lawn, where young people, especially young men, milled around like cattle.

"Bingley, is this your cousin?" A man with wavy chestnut hair, a straight nose, and high cheekbones sauntered over to them.

"Willoughby, this is Eliza Darcy. Eliza, meet Jack Willoughby, gentleman by day, rogue by night. You have my fair warning."

"Bingley, thanks for making me look a right twat in front of her." He punched Charlie in the shoulder. Charlie sent one last warning look to Eliza before trotting down the hill and joining the others.

While Eliza played the new rhyme of "twat" and "hat" through her mind, Willoughby took her hand and bowed over it, his gray eyes smoldering into hers. When Heath had done the same thing just days ago, her heart had thudded. But with this dandy simpering over her, she had to fight an eye roll. Two could play that game, so she gave in and sank down into a curtsy.

"Ah, I like American sarcasm." He took her arm and led her down the hill.

She snuck a glance at his profile.

He turned his head toward her and smiled at her blush. "Looking for my apparent roguishness? It doesn't manifest itself until after sunset. You're safe until then." His lips pulled back in a grin. "Want to partner up for croquet?"

"I suck at it. You might regret your decision."

His hand brushed the air as if aiming for an offensive fly. "Just knowing my mates will be cheesed off that I got to you first will appease even the worst loss."

Jack Willoughby's charm and good looks should have tempted Eliza, but Heath stuck to her thoughts like flypaper. She couldn't douse the flicker of hope that someday she would see him again and maybe, just maybe, they would continue where they had left off. Warmth pooled in her middle. Heath had somehow lit a sleeping fire inside her. Instead of hiding in her books as she had planned, she thirsted for a new life, to set fire to the old Eliza, whittled down by Seth's insecurities, and rise like the phoenix, a love goddess from the ashes of a once-burned bibliophile.

She held her hand out for the mallet, not moving when his fingers brushed hers. "Let's go lose big. Make it worth your while."

"Eliza, wait up." Joy's voice sailed over the lawn from the house. Eliza shielded her eyes from the invading sunlight. She really should have grabbed her shades. For a second, all she could make out was Joy's blinding blond hair. But then another figure looming behind her cousin caught her attention. Tall, dark, handsome. Her heart raced. No. It couldn't be. *Could it?*

Jack muttered, "Bloody plonker," and sulked away, mallet dragging across the ground.

"Good riddance to bad rubbish, I say," Joy called out none too softly and came to a gasping halt, her hand clutched around Tall Dark Handsome's wrist. Or if Eliza wanted to use first names, Heath.

"Eliza?" His deep voice echoed with confusion, and his eyebrows quirked in question.

"Heath?" Eliza's confusion twinned with his.

"Wait one bloody minute. You two know each other?" Joy's head swiveled from Eliza to Heath and back again.

"We just met—"

"On the plane." Eliza finished Heath's statement then lost herself in his blue gaze.

A grin spread over Joy's face. "This is brill. I mean, I couldn't have planned this better. Just wait till I tell Charlie." Joy took Heath's hand and shoved it in Eliza's. "Poor Willoughby. He's going to whinge on about this for days." Joy scurried away and weaved through the group, apparently spreading the surprising news from the swiveling necks and inquisitive gazes.

"Well"—Heath switched their grips, his hand holding hers—"what are the odds?"

"Apparently better than getting struck by lightning or getting eaten by a shark or winning the lottery." Eliza's arm hairs quivered at his warm touch, and even in the warmth of the summer sun, goose bumps exploded over her arms.

"I like our odds much better. Seems less perilous."

She couldn't stop grinning. Didn't want to. "That's too bad. I like adventures." And if anything foretold adventures, it was innocent freckles sprinkled over a slightly crooked nose on a grown man. She handed her mallet to him. "Here's to our first adventure."

"And what would that be?"

"Losing at croquet, of course."

Heath completed the action he had started on the plane and caressed a piece of her wayward hair behind her ear. "A noble mission. I accept."

Eliza, her hand still gripped in his, traipsed down the hill, the flames of desire licking away the last dregs of the old Eliza. She waltzed past Jack Willoughby. She didn't need a tiny dandy match to light her fire when she had a blowtorch.

"YOU AND HEATH SEEMED cozy this afternoon at the sixth hoop."

Eliza's hand stilled midbrush of her hair, wishing her insides would quit going squishy at the mention of Heath's name. His face. His laugh. She cleared her throat. "You have an overactive imagination, Joy."

"With your fine eyes and raven-black hair, you have all my old uni friends in a tizzy over you. It's no surprise Heath's taken a fancy to you. Jack will pout about it for days. I can't wait."

Eliza continued brushing her hair and pulling the side strands to the back before securing them with bobby pins. "I didn't think men got into tizzies."

Joy harrumphed from where she lay on her stomach on the bed, chin resting in her palms. "Well, whatever blokes get, they have it."

"So you and Heath were an item?" Eliza slid a glance at Joy.

"Of course." Joy huffed as if Eliza had stated the earth was round. "Well..."

"We dated about two years, and—"

Eliza choked on air and sputtered, "Two years." She could never compete with Joy's blond *Sports Illustrated*-swimsuit-model look.

"And when I broke it off—"

"You broke up with him?" *Great, just great.*

"It was probably one of the biggest cock-ups of my life, but I've made my bed. Without Heath." Joy launched off the bed and hugged Eliza. "Heath doesn't belong to me. Not anymore. He's yours for the taking. You better call dibs on him before anyone else does."

"Seriously?" When Joy rolled her eyes, Eliza added, "Because if you still have a thing for him, I won't even spare him a second of my time." The words tasted bitter on her tongue.

Joy clutched Eliza's shoulder and gave her a small shake. "I broke it off because we didn't fit anymore. We were more together because we thought we should be, family expectations, all those bits and bobs that keep a couple together longer than they should. Now we're good chums. That's all."

Eliza wanted to believe it. She gave one last brush to her black hair, grabbed a cardigan, and threw it over her sleeveless red top. "Aren't we going to be late for dinner?"

"Late, shmate. I don't care if Nancy gets her knickers in a twist. I need to know."

"Know what?"

"You." Joy's hand circled the air. "And Heath."

"Isn't it a little too early to tell?" But she knew—knew she was crazy.

Joy tapped her temple. "I have a sixth sense about these things."

"I'm going home in three weeks." *How expensive is it to change a return flight?*

"Mm." Joy cocked her head to the side. "What's the big deal with flirting with Heath? It's part of being on holiday, anyway."

"You're right."

"I'm always right." Joy's eyes gleamed.

"I don't know if I trust your judgment."

Joy grabbed her hand and led her out the door. "That's your first mistake. Now, go and stake your claim on Heath."

"That's exactly what Belle would say."

"She sounds brill."

When they entered the formal dining room already packed with people, there was no Heath. Hiding her disappointment, Eliza sipped champagne and listened half-heartedly to Jack and Joy flirting shamelessly, which sounded more like a battle of wits than sweet nothings. *Different strokes for different folks, I guess.*

By the time Eliza was three champagne glasses in, twilight had settled upon Pemberley, and the scent from the thousands of roses adorning the estate trickled in the open patio doors. Eliza itched for a walk in the garden. To be kissed in a garden surrounded by moonbeams and roses defined romance. She excused herself from the J-and-J flirt fest and escaped into the cool evening breeze. Slipping on her cardigan, she traversed the stone steps and paused at the bottom, contemplating which rose path to take.

She spun around at a footfall behind her.

"Waiting for someone? Scandalous, I say." An unfamiliar male voice wafted through the dark. A heavy cologne smell followed the voice.

She stepped back. "Nonsense. I'm enjoying the night air."

"Alone?"

"This conversation might go better if I knew who I'm speaking to."

"Name's Wickham. Garrison Wickham. You can call me Gary. All my mates do. I believe we're, like, sixth cousins and all that, so if you want to—"

"Nice to meet you, Garrison."

Silence hovered between them. "Right. I just arrived and heard the infamous American cousin was milling about. Wanted to make your acquaintance."

She wrapped her cardigan tighter about her. "Brisk, isn't it?" Not waiting for an answer, she sprinted up the steps and back into the overcrowded room. Seeking Joy, she found her by the chocolate fountain, dipping strawberries in a glass of champagne then dredging them with chocolate.

"I don't need your judgment. You left me alone with Willoughby." Joy plopped a booze-infused fruit into her mouth. "My blinding plan of not falling in love with him is going all to pot." She latched on to Eliza's arm with a free hand. "You must keep me away from Willoughby before my dodgy heart does something stupid."

"You're actually *in love* with Willoughby? Jack Willoughby. The one guy I've been warned against a dozen times?"

"Yeah, horses for courses, I guess." Joy nibbled on the last strawberry, her eyes rounding as she looked across the room. "Charlie once clouted Willoughby's face—"

"He what?"

"Punched. In the face. After catching us snogging. Oh, bugger. Never mind. I have to rescue him from a curvy redhead."

More like rescue her from him. Eliza rolled her eyes and sailed out the door and up the steps to seek the solitude of her tulips. At the top of the steps, she paused, one foot midstride.

"Who knows what he's told her."

"Keep your voice down." Wickham's voice sliced through the darkened gallery.

A strained whisper taunted Eliza's ears. She backed down the staircase and planted her bottom on the fifth step from the top.

That time, the woman's voice was distinct enough. Nancy's voice bit out, "But we have to be sure. Did you make a good impression?" Eliza could picture her aunt's piercing gaze, a gaze that could surely kill if given hands and a weapon.

"I made an impression."

"You made a cock-up of it, didn't you?"

"I'll earn her trust. No worries, Aunt Nancy."

Aunt? Eliza's ears perked. Nancy Darcy couldn't be Garrison Wickham's aunt. Cousin, maybe, through marriage but not an aunt. Their family tree might be ginormous with branches every which way, but to her knowledge, it wasn't twisted and gnarled back upon itself.

Their voices were getting closer to the stairs. Faster than she thought herself capable of, Eliza scampered down the steps and made a show of leaving the dining hall.

"Ah, there you are, my dear." Aunt Nancy held out a bedazzled hand. "You have met Garrison already, I understand."

Eliza's skin crawled at her aunt's smile and the use of "my dear." "Yes, I have. Please excuse me. I believe today has been too much. Headache." She rubbed her temples.

"If you need anything, don't hesitate to ask." With a pained parting smile, Nancy, Garrison in tow, entered the dining hall, leaving Eliza alone in the foyer.

"What I need are answers." Eliza clambered up the steps and sprinted to her room before locking the door and vaulting herself onto her bed. Caesar hopped on the bed, sniffed at her face, swiped his tongue across her nose, and kneaded her cheek. She scratched between his ears.

A knock sounded at her door. Hoping it wasn't Nancy come to claw her eyes out, Eliza opened the door a crack and peeked through the opening.

Heath smiled at her. "All right?"

She stepped into the hall and clasped her hands behind her back. "I think so. Just tired is all."

"You sure? You look like you've seen a ghost."

Eliza glanced down the fully lit hallway. "There's a high probability of that, actually." Then she speared him with a glare. "Where were you, by the way? My evening was full of an icky cousin and some sort of odd foreplay between Joy and Jack."

He chuckled, a deep, rumbling sound. She wanted to cuddle up to his chest and maybe even purr. "Got caught up in a poker game with some of the men. When Lord Darcy asks you to play, you play. When they finished fleecing me, I looked for you." He tucked a rogue strand of hair behind her ear. "If Pemberley has ghosts, they've been rather silent. No sightings. But if you want to go searching for some, I know a bloke who'd love to join you on your expedition."

"How about we choose a less creepy maiden mission?"

"How do you know I'm the guy? Maybe I meant Willoughby."

She aimed a playful punch at his shoulder only to be stopped by his quick hands. He untangled her fist and planted a kiss to her palm. "I came to say good night. If you need anything, I'm only a few doors down. Next to Garrison's, actually."

"Don't you mean Gary?"

"Only his mates call him that." Heath grinned. "Have yet to meet anyone who calls him that." He released her hand. "Sleep tight, Eliza."

With her heart beating its wings against her rib cage, Eliza closed her door and locked it for good measure against ghosts and Garrisons. Her first day at Pemberley was one for the history books. Besides having an amazing start to a holiday romance, she would get to do what she'd always wanted to do: make like Hercule Poirot or Miss Marple or even Sherlock Holmes and get to the bottom of Aunt Nancy's rude behavior and even stranger connection with Wickham. And maybe, if she were lucky, pin all the nasty family history on nasty, horrid Nancy.

Chapter Four
Let the Mystery Race Begin

*Jane and Charles have come for a visit. I missed them dearly, especially
my Jane. We played charades tonight, and I don't think I've ever seen
my sister look so radiant. I think she might have some news to tell me,
as she blushes exceedingly and pats her belly frequently.*
—Lizzy Bennet Darcy
Pemberley 1811

Arose thorn embedded itself in Eliza's backside.

"Ow." She slid farther into a natural alcove created by rosebushes. If caught, she had her excuse ready: birdwatching. It worked
in all the old mystery novels and movies, so it had to work in real life.
The Wednesday morning sun filtered through the greenery as she dialed her father's cell number.

She squirmed away from a too-inquisitive rose branch. The dial
tone joined in the orchestra of birds chirping feet away from where
she crouched.

"Hello?"

"Hey, Dad. I've got a question for you."

"Eliza, how are you?" Bass notes thumped through the phone,
accompanying her father's tenor voice.

"What is that sound?"

"Sorry, dear, your mother and I are still at a conference party." He
must have stepped out of the room, as the thumping had dissolved to
a pitter-patter of bass. "Sorry, now what's your question?"

"Dad, could Nancy be an aunt to anybody on the Wickham side?"

"No. Has she been unkind to you? If she has, I'll—"

"No, not really. I was curious. She seems to dislike me, though. Not sure why."

"Eliza..."

Silence and birds and her own breathing filled the small leafy alcove.

"Leave her alone, enjoy your trip, and leave the past where it needs to stay. The past." He cleared his throat. "How is everyone, by the way?"

"Good. Great-Aunt Iris has not stopped regaling me with stories of you as a child."

"Don't believe any of them."

"Not a chance. They're too good not to be true."

"What about Fitz? Has he said anything?"

"Not really, but I can tell he is pained by your estrangement. He wants to make things right."

A heavy sigh came. "Yes, but some things need more than an apology and a handshake."

Having witnessed the hurt in the eyes of those who missed her father, Eliza went in for one more fool's mission. "But I don't understand. What happened that made—"

"Drop it, Eliza." Her father's voice scraped her raw. "Sorry. I shouldn't have taken out my anger on you. Forgive me?"

"Yeah." Eliza's eyes stung. "Have fun in Hawaii and remember to wear sunscreen."

"Should have reminded me yesterday. Now, please be careful. Don't do anything stupid."

"When have I done that?"

"You want me to make a list and send it?"

"Nope. I'm good. Have fun and give Mom a hug for me."

"Will do. Love you." Her father's voice clicked off into silence.

"What on earth are you doing?" Willoughby hovered over her, his eyebrows almost touching his hairline.

"Bird watching." In solidarity, the birds surrounding her chirped in agreement.

His eyebrows still did not budge. He held a hand out, and he hauled her to her feet, her chest ramming into his. His arm snaked around her waist. "I do hear that gardens are convenient for two things."

Eliza squirmed from his hold. "And what would those be?"

"Bird watching, for one." His gaze flicked to her eyes. "And kissing, another."

She dipped out from his aim. "Um... ah... I've got to go and... water my cat." She stumbled out of the garden in search of Heath.

She never found him, only a gaggle of pink-cheeked gossiping cousins a generation older than her. Their plump bodies roamed the entire estate.

"You look lost."

Drat. Wickham. "Someone is only lost when they are looking to be found."

"Is that a hint for me to leave?" His bushy eyebrows wiggled at her.

Yes! "Of course not." She continued to walk. "Do you know many people here?"

"Quite a few. Neither of my parents could make it, but I have several first and second cousins here and a few aunts and uncles."

"Really? Who are your aunts?"

He rattled off the names of Margery, Gertrude, and Lucy, but Nancy's name was never mentioned. Eliza's brain cut and pasted ideas like a wackadoodle toddler who had pilfered scissors and glue. Her outcome was just as messy, nothing but smidgens of conspiracy theories lying jumbled together.

If only she had a pipe to smoke or a set of impressive mustaches to preen or even a sweater that needed to be knitted. But alas, she was no detective, professional or amateur, so she settled for chewing on her bottom lip and rubbing her thumb and middle finger together. How that would inspire her, she had no idea, but she couldn't just gape at Wickham in curiosity.

"Aunt Nancy seems to adore you."

"Ah yes, she has always been kind to me, ever since I was a young boy. She sees potential in me."

Eliza was sure that if he'd had a waistcoat, he would have tucked his thumbs in between the buttons. As he had no buttons nor a waistcoat, his puffed-up chest did the job.

"Yes, she seems like a wise woman."

"You, my dear cousin, are a keen observer of human nature."

"So I've been told." Her gaze flicked to the grand house. "If you'll excuse me, I need to snag something from my room. Toodles." She waved at him and dashed off to the house.

With everyone outside enjoying the morning activities, only the echoes of staff and caterers rumbled down the hall from the dining room. It would soon be lunchtime, and various leaves from the Darcy and Bennett family trees would overrun the house.

Her father would take his secrets to the grave, so she searched for the room where all secrets hid themselves in books and movies: the library. Maybe somewhere in the dusty, brittle pages of books, she would find clues, hints, and if lucky, a straight answer. Maybe before leaving, her father had stashed a note in a farewell to his only sibling. Maybe she would find his journal hidden among the tomes of war strategy. Meeting her extended family had ignited the need to fix her father's past, to knit two brothers back together, to mend the broken bridge.

The library door swung open, revealing floor-to-ceiling bookshelves. Her fingers itched to trace the bindings, to crack open the leather-bound novels and almanacs, to lose herself for hours among new friends. She pulled a leather-bound copy of *The Canterbury Tales* from its spot and opened it to the first page, wishing she had time to lose herself in the world of Chaucer.

"Looking for something?"

She screeched and dropped the book to the floor. Puffs of dust erupted from the leather surface.

"Uncle Fitzwilliam, I didn't hear you," she stammered, brushing off the abused book.

"I noticed." He smiled as he took the book from her hands and turned it over, studying the cover. "You may use the library anytime." His eyebrow quirked. "Is there something specific you're looking for?"

"No. Yes." She took in his furrowed brow and pursed lips. "Never mind. I was curious as to the history of the place."

He held an arm out. "Would you like the grand tour?"

"But I was already given a tour by Joy."

"She doesn't know half of what this place has to offer."

She took her uncle's proffered arm. "I only expected to look at dusty books today."

"You are in for quite a surprise." He walked over to an alcove in the bookcase and flicked an intricate carving of a lion's head. Something clicked. He motioned toward the back of the alcove. "Go ahead. Push."

She applied pressure to the paneling. A crack appeared, and the paneling shifted to the left. Dampening her rising excitement, she nudged the panel farther into the slot. "This is so cool."

He chuckled. "Yes, cool it certainly is. Here." He pulled out a flashlight from a drawer. "You'll need this torch."

"Me?" she squeaked. "By myself?"

"You wanted an adventure, didn't you?" His kind eyes smiled down at her. "No. I'm coming with you." He patted her hand. "Don't worry. Pemberley doesn't have any ghosts or goblins."

The repeated reassurance didn't quell her queasy stomach. "Where does this lead?"

"That, my dear niece, is the adventure. This leads out into several rooms in the house." He gave her an encouraging smile. "Ladies first."

She paused, her hand clutching the bookcase. *Is he planning on killing me, burying me alive inside the walls?* She shook her head to clear her fevered thoughts and clutched the flashlight. Sometimes her imagination was a little too healthy for her own good. One step. Two steps. Three. And then total darkness except for two beams of light shivering in the blackness. Her uncle had slid the paneling back into place, killing whatever meager daylight had seeped through. The walls and floor were smooth. No dripping water, no dungeony smells. Just stale air and a few cobwebs swaying in a minuscule breeze.

The passage was wide enough for her and her uncle to walk side by side. Muted laughter and clinking of silverware and glassware seeped through the walls.

"This goes behind the dining room. The caterers must be setting up." Her uncle rested his ear against the wall, too, and whispered conspiratorially, "Should we take a gander?"

"Can we do that?"

He slid open a little door and moved to the side, allowing her access to the small portal. An army of caterers tackled the battle of setting up glassware, plateware, and silverware to the high standards of the militant head caterer, who was barking orders and signaling with rigid gesticulations.

"I feel like a spy."

"So did I as a child. Your father and I spent countless hours in these passages. We gleaned some cracking information too."

She giggled at the mischief in his voice. "I'm sure you two didn't stoop low enough to blackmail people."

"How do you think I paid for my Cambridge education?"

Eliza giggled and took her uncle's arm and for the next hour explored the tunnels winding through the grand house. On coming to a dead end, her uncle pressed the wooden surface, and it sprang open, belching them out into a room resplendent in drop cloths and dust.

"It pains me for you to see the less-opulent parts of the house, my dear, but"—his eyes twinkled—"I believe you will love this room in spite of its less-than-glamorous appearance." He opened the curtains, letting sunlight pour in. Dust motes danced in the sun's rays.

She trailed her finger along a bookcase and came away with one cobweb in her hair and a finger quilted in dust bunnies. Her eyes widened as her uncle uncovered the cloth-laden furniture. "Oh, my goodness. Look at these treasures."

Settees upholstered in rich fabrics, a Regency-period writing desk, and a few cabinets and side tables dotted the room. Protected from the elements, they looked brand-new and ready for display in a museum. Her uncle joined her next to a rosewood settee clothed in rich maroon velvet. "It is rumored this was your namesake's favorite room"—he trailed a finger along the settee, leaving a light streak along the dark fabric—"and favorite furniture."

Her own living room suddenly seemed provincial, mundane, and American. That room and its elegant yet simple furnishings captured her imagination. She could almost see Elizabeth Darcy penning a letter at the writing desk in the corner or relaxing and talking the day over with her beloved Fitzwilliam. Sitting on the couch, she closed her eyes and drank it in, dust motes and all.

Uncle Fitzwilliam opened a set of cupboard doors and held out two gilded vases identical to the ones she had at home, except yellow roses adorned the china.

Eliza traced her fingers over the cheery flowers. "These look like mine back home."

"I know." He smiled sheepishly. "Elizabeth had a matching set of four. I sent you the pink ones for your twenty-first birthday. It was important you have something from her the year she became a Darcy."

She threw her arms around his neck. "Thank you. I never knew who sent them, but I've cherished them. Very much."

"I kept the other two safe and sound, hoping someday, the quartet would join together again."

"I'm glad you did." Her heart somersaulted in her chest at one mystery solved. She gestured to the other items in the room, lonely and dejected. "Why is this furniture not out in the main part of the house?"

He gave a small smile. "The current lady of the house prefers a modern touch." He heaved a sigh and clapped his hands. "Shall we? We'll be late for lunch." He led her down a hall that flowed into the main passage through the house. "Do you know where you are?"

"We are in the east wing, right?"

"Quick learner and excellent navigator, it seems. If you were to take a right here and go up the steps, you'd be at your room. And this room up ahead is my study."

"Does it ever get old? Living here, I mean?"

His eyes twinkled with delight. "No. I'm afraid I am a boy at heart and still delight in this old rambling place." He released her hand as they came to the doors of his study. "I need to see to some things before lunch. Are you okay finding your way from here?"

"I won't get lost too quickly. If you can't find me in the dining room, you might want to send a search party."

He chuckled as she walked away. Her feet wanted to go faster than propriety and her age allowed. Skipping probably wasn't even allowed. *More importantly, can I still skip?* She would find out only one way.

"Are you barmy?"

"Joy!" Eliza stopped midskip and laughed. "It's a good thing you're the one who caught me and not Aunt Nancy or Wickham. They give me the heebie-jeebies."

"Wickham"—Joy shivered—"is an arse. He informed me we were far enough removed on the family tree that if we wanted to... you know... our children wouldn't be born with only one eye or something."

"Oh, like the Cyclops in *The Odyssey*. You know, I always kind of felt sorry for Polyphemus. It's not his fault he was ugly and unloved. Hey, did you know those cases happened in Ancient Greece? You see, women would—"

"Eliza. I. Don't. Care. Not about cyclopes and not about some guy named Polymus."

"It's Polyphemus," Eliza muttered and followed Joy, who came to a standstill. "What's wrong?"

Joy yanked her into an alcove covered with a heavy curtain.

"What the—"

"Shh!" Joy hissed. "It's Wickham."

Eliza peeked through the curtains. Garrison's hair stuck up in uneven waves, and a look of panic had whitened his face, leaving only red blotchy marks.

"Look"—his voice cracked—"I don't know what's going on, but I don't appreciate the threats. No, you listen here, you... What?" He stormed past the alcove, phone plastered to his ear. He stopped and turned and stomped the other way, only to march back again.

"What do you mean you know it all? No, you listen. If I hear you have breathed a word of this to people, you will hear from me."

Eliza wasn't sure how threatened the other person felt as Wickham's voice squeaked at the end, but she gave him props for attempting to sound dangerous.

"That was interesting." Joy dusted off the back of her black slacks as Garrison stomped off, his curses fading.

Eliza plucked a dust bunny from her cousin's hair. "What do you think Garrison has got himself into? He looks terrified."

Joy snorted. "Wickham has always been a wet blanket. I was relieved as a child when he and his parents stopped coming to reunions. It was rather awkward, knowing his father had broken a tenuous truce between the Darcys and Wickhams. Fitzwilliam puts on a nice face for nasty Margery and her equally nasty sisters. Why Garrison still shows up, I have no clue." Joy shivered. "And how he hangs upon Nancy is a bit naff to say the least."

"I'm surprised Margery and company still come. It must be embarrassing knowing your brother embezzled from the very person opening his home to them. Is that why Margery is so angry?"

"She was a dried-up old prune before the embezzling. She had to have been born with chin hairs."

Eliza choked on a laugh. "I wonder if they jiggle when she laughs."

"I don't think she does. We're safe from seeing that travesty." Joy wiggled her fingers from her chin. "Speaking of travesty, if my aunts treated me like Garrison's aunts treat him, I would look for new aunts, ones who like me."

Eliza chewed on her lip and worried her fingers together. Something was cooking. Something hot and spicy, and she couldn't wait to sink her teeth into it. "They are his only aunts?"

"As far as I know. Why?"

Eliza snaked her arm through Joy's. "I overheard Garrison call Nancy his aunt."

Joy blinked. "Doesn't make any sense. Why would Wickham call Nancy 'Aunt'?"

"And refuse to name her as one when I asked him earlier today?" At Joy's questioning look, Eliza explained, "After Jack almost kissed me in the rose—"

"What?" Joy squeaked. "Repeat that."

"Jack almost kissed me. In the rose garden."

"And?"

"And nothing. I don't want *his* kisses."

"I will have a little chat with that twit. The only person he's supposed to knock off kisses from is me."

Eliza waved away Joy's tantrum. "Does he know this?"

"He should just sense it."

"Anyway, can we get back to the mysterious and creepy connection between Nancy and Garrison?"

Joy cast her a sideways glare.

Eliza ignored her. "According to Garrison, Nancy adores him. But if that were truly the case, why doesn't she proclaim her supposed nephew's greatness from the rooftops?"

"The only way for Nancy to be Garrison's aunt would be if she were a Wickham herself."

"Does Uncle keep a record of all the family branches?" Eliza stopped midstep.

"He does. It's in the library."

"Let's go." Spinning on her heels, Eliza dragged Joy away from the dining room door and to the library.

"Aren't we going to grab some munch? I'm starving."

"We will, but I need to figure this out."

Joy rolled her eyes but grabbed a large book off the shelf and plunked it down on a table situated in front of a window. Eliza gazed out as Joy paged through the book. Sunrays played off the windowpanes, and the roses in the garden nearby swayed in the gentle breeze, beckoning Eliza to come out and play. She was about to when Joy punched her in the shoulder.

"Oi! Bob's your uncle." Joy stabbed a finger on a page where someone had spelled out *Wickham* in calligraphy. "Here's Lydia and George Wickham, the first Darcy enemy."

"And a spoiled young woman for a sister-in-law. Poor man." Eliza trailed her finger down the list of names tied to the infamous Wickham and Bennet flirt. "Here we go. Digory Wickham married Cecily Plathe, and the stork visited four times, delivering Samuel, Margery, Gertrude, and Lucy. No mention of a Nancy, though." Eliza scratched her temple. "This doesn't make any sense. In order for Garrison to be Nancy's nephew, she has to be listed here."

"All this mystery makes me hungry. I heard Mrs. Bankcroft made a trifle. Shall we?"

"But what about Garrison and Nancy and—"

"We won't figure anything out by looking for Nancy's name. Besides, you can't force me to work on an empty stomach. It isn't done."

Eliza's stomach rumbled in agreement. Outnumbered, Eliza followed Joy to the dining room.

"You're late."

Eliza's spine stiffened. "Sorry, Lady—Aunt Nancy. We got caught up in the library."

Nancy's gaze roamed from the top of Eliza's head to the tips of her black flats. The once-over lasted all of two seconds, and by the time Nancy's eyes drilled into hers again, Eliza felt as if she should be thrown out with the trash. "The library? Whatever would hold your interest there?"

"You do know I am an English teacher? And Joy is an author? Where else would we be?"

Nancy spared Joy a glance. "I know what she writes. You will not find that smut in the Darcy library."

"I say—"

Nancy held up a finger, stemming Joy's outrage. "We have a dining room full of guests, my dears. We must be cordial." She smiled for the crowded room. "Please, find a seat."

Eliza rested her hand on Joy's quivery shoulders. "Take a few deep breaths."

"I want to smack her arrogant little face in." Joy punched her own hand.

"Ditto." Eliza sought the only face she wanted to see and pulled out a chair next to Heath.

He nudged his knee up against hers. "Thought I would have to rescue you two from Nancy—"

"Isn't that Lady Darcy to you?" Eliza faked a British accent, held up a teacup, and stuck her pinky finger out.

Joy snorted and slathered a tablespoon of butter over a bun. "Like I said, no one calls her that when she's out of earshot."

Heath saluted them both with his water glass. "That is beside the point. I'm just glad I didn't have to expose my superhuman alter ego in saving you two damsels in distress."

"And what would that be?" Joy asked. "Finder of Old Things, Mind Trap of Useless Information?"

Heath grinned. "Don't be all in a pet. You didn't stick around long enough to find out." He winked at Eliza and squeezed her hand under the table. "Maybe some lucky woman will eventually dig out all my secrets."

Joy snorted and waved her bun dismissively before biting into it.

Eliza's insides had turned to goo. And instead of relishing the feeling, her brain mutinied and snapped to attention. *The book.* "Oh, we should put the book back, don't you think?"

"And risk Nancy's wrath?"

"Sissy," Eliza hissed. "I for one am a grown-ass woman and will not be intimidated by Nancy. I'll be back." She tapped the back of Heath's hand. "Quack, quack seat back."

She scanned the room for her aunt. Not seeing the punctuality police, she darted from the room, slid into the library, and skidded to a halt.

"Aunt Nancy?"

"Interested in the family tree?" Nancy's fingernails tapped the page dedicated to the Wickham branch.

Eliza imagined those long nails drilling into her. She swallowed. "Yes."

"Does the Wickham branch intrigue you?"

Something in Nancy's tone made Eliza pause. "That's where we ended before Joy's stomach intervened."

Nancy's scarlet fingernail traced the loop-de-loos of the fancy lettering. "I see. Well, the Wickham name has a notorious history among certain people here. I'd hate for you to get the wrong impression of this branch. I'd be careful who you talk to."

Like you. Eliza clamped her lips shut. "Thank you, Aunt. I get your point loud and clear."

"Do you?" Nancy spun on her spiky heels and clipped out of the library.

Eliza released a pent-up breath and closed the book before setting it reverently back in its spot. Her appetite for food had vanished only to be replaced by her hunger to find out her aunt's secret. If Nancy's secret was tied to Eliza's father's self-exile, that would be dessert, and Eliza hankered for very sweet, very decadent justice.

Chapter Five
A Welcome Party with a Side of Death

It appears married life agrees with Darcy, as he complained this morning that his waistcoats no longer fit him. I told him to blame the cook. And to get some exercise. Which we both took part in. Quite exhilarating. I like my husband's idea of exercise. Apparently, it makes my "fine eyes" even brighter.
—Lizzy Bennet Darcy
Pemberley 1811

"I told you to keep your mouth shut."

Eliza stopped and nearly tipped herself and her champagne glass into the thick foliage at the edge of the rose garden. A man's voice, angry and clipped, stabbed the air and filtered through the greenery.

"You idiot!" a woman's voice responded with equal vehemence. "Keep your voice down, Piers. Who knows who could be wandering by with this ridiculous reunion going on?"

"Like you care. All the more for you to get your grubby little hands on." The sound of a slap reverberated through the bush, making Eliza wince. "Oi! You slag!"

Another slapping sound was followed by a vicious curse and a woman's whimpering. "Please"—the woman's voice shook—"I didn't say nothing. Mum's the word. I'm not dead from the neck up."

"I can't do this anymore, play her little game. She can take her money and stick it up her arse. Make sure you stay quiet, and don't get all airy-fairy about it." The man's voice faded, and Eliza tucked her head in between the hedges to get a better look in the darkness, but all that greeted her was a startled squirrel and a large spider. She swallowed a squeak.

"I thought I'd find you here."

Eliza whirled around. "Heath, you scared me half to death." She steadied her champagne glass in one hand and placed the other over her heart.

"Forgive me?"

Eliza worried she would forgive him anything. Better he not know that. Yet. "For a price."

"Anything. Just name it." His eyes darkened.

A kiss in the moonlight among the roses. "How about another glass of champagne?"

His smile slipped a smidge. "That's peanuts. Let me know my punishment when you've cooked up something truly horrid." He held out his hand. "I've been sent to find you. Your aunt Nancy seems concerned about your whereabouts." He assisted her over a hedge. "Now that I found you, where do I take you? Back to your aunt?"

"Not if you even kind of sort of like me. She treats me like I might make a mess on the carpet in the middle of a tea party."

"That is usually frowned upon in this country." His teeth flashed in the soft illumination of hanging Chinese lanterns swaying gently from tree branches. His hand still encased hers.

She ignored his joke. "Still, I'm not a child, and I'm not two. And the fact that she—" Eliza stemmed the angry words and snuggled her cardigan closer about her. Her aunt had given her a death glare when Eliza had shown up to the garden party in khakis. Apparently, one did not wear khakis to an evening garden party. And when Eliza had pointed out that another woman, a nut from Mary's branch, was wearing khakis, Nancy directed her attention to the woman's propensity to drink heavily and wear a unibrow the size of a caterpillar. Eliza had changed into black slacks immediately.

"Enjoying the party?"

He chuckled. "You mean the posh party you're missing? Splendid. I believe Callum and Jasper are about to entertain us all with their karaoke skills."

"Who?"

"Gertrude's boys." At her blank stare, he brought the back of her hand to his lips. "Gertrude and Margery, the mean one, are sisters."

"How do you know these people?"

He grinned against her hand. "Simple. I pay attention." He guided her around a family of ceramic rabbits and back into the graveled path meandering through the gardens.

Eliza pressed up against Heath's side as they strolled through the rose garden illuminated by lanterns and moonlight. That was what dreams were made of, but instead of gauzy reality, a fine-looking, charming Englishman actually held her hand.

"Eliza, what were you doing out here in the dark, anyway?"

"Research." She wasn't about to admit she'd been practicing the art of eavesdropping, a skill every sleuth honed to razor-sharp accuracy.

"And what were you researching?"

"A lady never tells." But she was mystified about the conversation she had overheard. The heated conversation had been tinted with the same tone of fear as Garrison's phone call that she and Joy had eavesdropped on. She couldn't tell if the voices behind the shrub had been staff or family members, but she would bet on the staff. Her inner sleuth salivated at the idea of another mystery to solve. Making a mental note to watch the staff members closer and to hide her valuables, she walked on. "How well do you know the Darcys?"

"Well"—Heath scratched the back of his neck—"you know Joy and I dated. Long time ago. Right? Yeah... and Charlie and I attended the same university, chummed around a bit, so I'm usually invited to Pemberley when they're around. Your uncle strikes me as a kind man. He does a vast amount of charitable work in the area."

"He reminds me a lot of my father in that sense." *In all aspects, really.* "What of Nancy?"

He grimaced. "I don't want to talk rude of the hostess of this gathering, but I'm not sure what your uncle sees in her."

They approached the patio and the open doors into the ballroom. "Sadly, I agree. She doesn't like me very much."

"She doesn't like anybody." Heath squeezed her hand. "I hate to leave you, but I promised Callum and Jasper help with the setup. Wait until you hear their rendition of 'Ice, Ice Baby.'"

"I can hardly wait." Eliza went in search of Joy and found her and Great-Aunt Iris.

"Eliza"—Joy clamped her shoulders—"Aunt Nancy has asked about you every two minutes." She gestured across the room, where the subject of their conversation raised a glass of champagne in their direction. "She doesn't like you."

"Funny. I said the exact same thing about her." Eliza beamed a sugary smile back at her aunt and snatched a flute of champagne offered by a server.

Great-Aunt Iris laid a warm, papery hand on her cheek. "Want me to take her down for you? I have experience in such things."

Eliza choked on her sip of bubbly liquid. "Dear Lord, Aunt Iris."

"Oh dear, do forgive me, Eliza. Your great-uncle tells me I have to think before I speak, but really, what's the fun in that?"

"No fun at all. Keep not thinking."

"I knew I liked you."

Eliza was leaning down to kiss her great-aunt's wrinkled cheek when a crash shattered the subdued chatter.

Garrison Wickham and another man Eliza didn't recognize were rolling around on the ground in a stew of broken glass, spilled punch, and chocolate éclairs. Wickham rammed his fist into the other man's face. The whole room gave a collective gasp.

"That's Piers," Eliza heard people around her whisper. If that was the same Piers from the vicious conversation she'd overheard thirty minutes ago, it made for quite the violent evening for him.

Another punch, another grunt from the victim, another gasp from the crowd, and that time a scream. The shock worn off, several men, including Uncle Fitzwilliam and Heath, waded into the mess and pulled Garrison off his victim.

"I swear to God, I will kill you. Do you understand?" Spittle flew from Wickham's mouth. "If you touch her again, hell, even if you look at her, I will beat you to a bloody pulp!"

Piers leaned back, lost his balance, fell, and inchwormed away. "I didn't do anything."

"Bloody liar!" Garrison roared. Eliza feared his head would explode.

"That's enough!" Uncle Fitzwilliam's voice cut through the cursing. "Take Piers to the kitchen. Mrs. Underhill can tend to his wounds."

Eliza rummaged through her memory. *Ah yes.* Mrs. Underhill was the housekeeper.

"Aunt Iris, who is this Piers guy?"

"Oh dear. I believe he's a groundsman, but I'm not sure." A twinkle in her eye took ten years off of her. She patted her perfectly permed silver hair. "Shall we go snoop and see what we can learn?"

The last thing Eliza saw as she followed her great-aunt out of the ballroom was Wickham shoving people out of the way and stumbling out of the double doors and into the darkness.

Her great-aunt paused outside the library door, pressed her ear to it, and grinned. "Come, come, dear." With what Eliza swore was a skip, her elderly aunt entered the room and went directly to the secret passageway. Eliza sucked in a gasp.

"Ah, you know about this, do you? Good. Then you aren't scared of the dark."

Eliza didn't want to ruin her great-aunt's perception of her, so she didn't contradict. "Why are we using the tunnel?"

"Because you can hear everything from the tunnel." Great-Aunt Iris pushed the doohickey, the latch clicked, and in they were, flashlights shedding beams of light. "If memory serves me correctly, the kitchen is this way."

"How do you know of the tunnel's existence?"

Great-Aunt Iris chuckled. "Those silly boys. They never could figure out how all their plots went all sixes and sevens."

Eliza matched her great-aunt's mischievous grin with one of her own.

They took off in the opposite direction of Eliza's first trek through the tunnels. Every so often, Aunt Iris would pause and listen, or open a peephole, and speed away down the dark tunnel.

Not wanting to lose her elderly aunt or, more accurately, have her aunt lose her, she contemplated taking her arm or something, but Great-Aunt Iris kept trucking down the tunnel, her white tennis shoes nearly glowing in the beams of light.

"Ah, here we go." Aunt Iris laid a finger to her lips and opened the peephole. Murmured voices became clearer as Eliza brought her ear against the opening.

"I don't know what came over Garrison." A weepy woman's voice shook.

Eliza placed her eye to the hole and peered in but saw only cheery yellow paint and a few pots of herbs nestled along the window above a huge utility kitchen sink. *An elephant could bathe in there.* The sound of a man's voice piqued her interest.

"Clearly protecting you. Piers is a bloody wanker. He deserves more than a punch to that ugly mug of his," a gruff and gravelly voice responded.

"I can take care of myself. Besides, we weren't doing nothing in the garden." The weeping had turned into petulance.

"Whose handprint is on your face? I'm telling you now, that lad needs to be taught a lesson."

Eliza blinked at the sound of a fist punching a hard surface. She wished she could see the woman she had overheard in the garden. Piers had threatened her, accused her of stealing, had even slapped the mystery woman. Eliza shimmied to the side and twisted her head in awkward positions but to no avail. The woman's identity remained a secret. And the voices had stopped entirely. *Drat*!

Aunt Iris tugged at her arm and motioned for her to move aside. How she would reach the hole to peer into the other room, Eliza had no clue. "Hoist me up."

"Excuse me?" whispered Eliza.

"I weigh all of seven stone. I'm as light as a feather."

Eliza conjured up the odd facts she still remembered from her British literature classes: a stone equaled fourteen pounds. But her math skills, rusty as ever, kept her from completing the equation. Her great-aunt did look light enough, though.

"All right. Are you sure about this?"

"Girl, I was an ambulance driver during World War II and killed at least twenty Nazis when the situation called for it. Now, do as I say and lift me up."

Eliza bent at the knees, grasped Aunt Iris's waist, hoisted her up, and settled her great-aunt's feet on her bent legs. It was like a squat but worse. Much worse.

"I can't see anything," her great-aunt whispered. "Pretty paint, though, and I do love those herb pots. I have a friend who crafts. I should take a picture and send it to—"

"Do you see anything else besides the decor?"

"Oh, sorry, dear. Are your legs starting to hurt? They don't feel as stable."

"I think you might weigh eight stones."

"I did eat quite a few chocolate éclairs. I'm glad I got some before those silly boys ruined them all."

"Aunt, please."

"Quite right." Great-Aunt Iris went back to peering through the hole. "Nothing. They must have left."

Eliza settled her on the floor and creaked back to a standing position.

"You're a good girl. And fun too. This is going to be the best reunion ever. Most of the time, they're damp squibs, but this time"—she pinched Eliza's cheeks—"this time, something big is going to happen. I can feel it."

Eliza had no doubt her great-aunt felt things and worried they might be heart palpitations, but she kept her thoughts to herself and followed her out of the tunnel.

ELIZA WOKE TO A SCREAM. It curdled her blood and made her want to hide under her covers, but no sleuth worth her weight did that. After sliding her feet into her flip-flops and wrapping her robe around herself, she slipped out the door.

"Eliza." Heath jogged down the hall. "Are you okay?" He traced her right ear with his finger. His dark hair, tufted and askew, begged to be smoothed, and his white undershirt revealed roped muscles hidden under his habitual dress shirts.

"Yeah. I think my heart's in my toes, but I should survive that."

He grabbed her hand, and together they followed the sounds of commotion down the hall, the steps, and into the foyer.

"Did you see who did it?" A maid, still in uniform, grabbed Eliza's arm.

"No." Eliza glanced at Heath. "We heard the screams seconds ago."

"Oh. I saw someone in the hall a little while ago, and I thought I saw... well... it doesn't matter." The young woman held a tissue to her dripping nose. "Oh, miss, he's dead."

"Who? Who's dead?"

"Eliza!" Uncle Fitzwilliam's voice resonated through the dimly lit foyer. "Are you all right, my dear?" Her uncle's arms enfolded her in a swift hug. He spoke gently to the maid, still sniveling into her tissue. "You should go back to your room, Greta. I will let you know if something more comes to light."

"Thank you, Lord Darcy. I'm sorry. I should have known. It's all my fault. It's all my fault." With a fresh onslaught of tears, she rushed off and disappeared down the stairs.

Eliza's thoughts clicked into place. Greta's voice. She was the one in the garden. She was the thief. And Piers had threatened her. It had been too dim to see a handprint, but Eliza bet one was branded on the woman's face.

"What's going on, Uncle?" Eliza peered around her uncle's sizable frame.

He studied her for a moment and flicked a glance at Heath before leading them out the door and to the fountain. A man's body floated facedown in the fountain's still, red water. The back of his head was crushed and matted with blood.

Bile roiled in Eliza's stomach. "Who is he?"

Heath steered her away from the sight.

"I can't be sure, as we haven't touched the body to turn it over, but it might be Piers." Her uncle massaged the back of his neck.

"The guy Garrison beat to a pulp?" Heath hugged Eliza to his side.

"Yes."

"So"—Eliza looked around at all the people huddled in robes—"where's Garrison?"

"I have no idea. He's usually the first piranha to sniff out scandal or gossip. I'm surprised he hasn't made an appearance yet." Uncle Fitzwilliam's frown gave him wrinkles she hadn't noticed before.

Sirens and whirls of lights preceded a cavalry of police cars speeding up the drive.

A smile cracked Fitzwilliam's frown when the first car came to a stop and the door opened. "Wentworth."

A man of medium stature, his dark-blue, gray-pinstripe suit fitting him with military precision, shook Uncle Fitzwilliam's outstretched hand and cut his gaze to Eliza and Heath.

"Allow me to introduce my niece, Eliza Darcy, and a family friend, Heath Tilney. Eliza, Heath, this is Detective Chief Inspector Finn Wentworth."

Wentworth grasped her hand in a firm shake, his white teeth flashing against his dark-brown skin. "It's nice to meet you. Quite the welcome party, aye?"

"I could do without these types of parties, to be honest, Detective Chief Inspector." Eliza wormed closer to Heath's side. She would never forget the sight of bloody water and a lifeless floating body.

"Sorry. Police humor. And it's just Wentworth. No sense in bandying about with a title longer than my leg." He turned his attention to the nearby constables. "Let's go, boys." He headed off with his "boys," even though a third were women.

"Wentworth and I serve on the parish council." Uncle Fitzwilliam saluted the man's retreating form. "He's a steady chap."

Said steady chap barked a few more orders and demanded the gawking guests "get back in the bloody house, for the sake of everything good and holy."

Uncle Fitzwilliam herded Eliza and Heath inside. "Come on. Let's do what he said. The police will be a while."

"I can't go back to bed." Eliza averted her gaze when they passed the fountain. She knew what floated in its once-pristine waters.

"Shall we find some tea? I'm sure we can convince Mrs. Bankcroft to slice us some cake as well. What do you say?"

"It doesn't seem right to eat cake when someone's floating in the fountain. Dead." Eliza swallowed around a lump in her throat.

"It's two in the morning, my dear, and honestly, we Brits hide our emotions behind discussions about the weather and food. A little tea and cake will go a long way to settling your nerves. I'm afraid you'll need them later."

Exhaustion seeped into her body, and she wasn't sure she would be able to even chew cake, but the idea of going to bed, alone, with only Caesar for company, had her stomach quaking. She leaned harder into Heath, his arms strong and steady about her.

"My oh my, Lord Darcy. What a to-do." When they entered the cook's domain, Mrs. Bankcroft's cheery red face warmed Eliza. Mrs. Bankcroft's riot of white curls, pinned under a nightcap, attempted to spill out from the frilled edges. A pink gingham housecoat spread over the cook's ample body like a queen's robe. She sat Eliza and Heath down at a kitchen table, poured them a "proper cuppa," and placed a china plate complete with chocolate cake in front of each.

"Now you tuck into that cake, Miss Darcy. We don't want any more mishaps or fainters." She slammed her hands onto her hips. "I never could understand fainters. Me? I've never fainted a day in my life." Mrs. Bankcroft next settled Uncle Fitzwilliam with a cup of tea and cake. "Food. That's what people need. Food. Many girls go on diets nowadays and starve themselves. And faint."

Heath nudged Eliza's knee. "I don't think we have a fainter on our hands, Mrs. B."

The cook eyed him. "Been a while since I've seen your face, Mr. Tilney. Thought you and Miss Joy were on the quits?"

Heath cleared his throat and fiddled with the cake on his plate. "We are. Were. Just good chums now." He slid a glance at Eliza.

"I ain't no curtain twitcher. Just asking, that's all."

Uncle Fitzwilliam laid a hand over the cook's calloused one. "Mrs. Bankcroft, how are you doing?"

"I don't know how such a horrible thing could happen here, Lord Darcy. This is Pemberley. Not some red-light district in a penny dreadful." The cook used the edge of her housecoat to dab at a tear. "How do we know we're not next?" She whipped a gaze around the room as if searching for a hidden murderer.

"There's no need to worry, Mrs. Bankcroft. I'm sure the police will catch whoever did such an evil thing. Wentworth is a capable DCI."

Mrs. Bankcroft crossed her arms and grunted. "No offense, Lord Darcy, but I'm still sleeping with a kitchen knife under my pillow."

Exhaustion won out over cake. Eliza's eyes refused to stay open. The continuous chatter of Mrs. Bankcroft droned on as she complained about everything from the dullness of the kitchen knives to a new nick in her favorite rolling pin, but it all soon turned into white noise against the black emotions creeping into her. The kitchen's warmth seeped into her bones, heating them, melting them...

Warm, soft hands patted Eliza's face. She shooed them away. Again they patted her, that time not so softly. Eliza's eyes flew open and saw the world sideways. Mrs. Bankcroft's face popped into her vision.

Her eyes peered owlishly into Eliza's. "Oh dear. Did you faint? I was promised you weren't a fainter." Mrs. Bankcroft cut a glare at Heath.

"Nope." Eliza peeled her face off the table. *No, no, no.* Not the table but her piece of chocolate cake. "I fell asleep." She clawed cake off her face. "In my cake, apparently."

Heath grabbed a napkin and wiped off the remainder of cake and frosting. His kind eyes were as gentle as his hands. For a few blissful seconds, she had escaped from the reality of death, of murder. In the coziness of the kitchen, Piers's dead body had disappeared, but then reality struck. Someone had killed a man. A man who had been alive enough to slap Greta and fight Garrison. Eliza gripped Heath's hand as he wiped the last of the cake off her face. He quirked an eyebrow. Garrison had threatened Piers hours before his death. And Garrison was missing.

Eliza finished her lukewarm tea and glanced at the clock. Three in the morning. She was too tired to think. "I suppose I should go back to bed."

"The cops will be hours yet, and we'd only be in their way. It's best if you get your rest. Heath, will you escort Eliza?" Her uncle looked up from gathering the dirty dishes to the tune of Mrs. Bankcroft's scolding that the master of the house shouldn't do dishes.

"With pleasure." Heath gathered Eliza in his arms and left the kitchen, Uncle Fitzwilliam's rumbling voice—stating that as master of the house, it was his decision whether to do the dishes—diminishing as they walked away.

In silence, they made their way through the myriad hallways, the glare of numerous headlights from the emergency vehicles parked outside seeping through the windows. The kitchen had been like a cocoon. Cozy, protected, hidden. Just like the books she'd grown up on. The murders in their pages had been trapped in the book. But her present situation was not a book. She was the main character, a murder had occurred, and she couldn't snap the book shut and end it all. There was a body and blood, and the killer could still be in the house.

"What the bloody hell?" Heath muttered.

"What is it?" Eliza latched on to his hand. The brave man didn't even wince.

He jerked his head down the hall. A figure stood just outside Garrison's door, hand on the doorknob.

"Excuse me. Can we help you?" Heath asked.

A slim maid in a starched black-and-white uniform whirled around. Eliza guessed the woman measured only five feet when wearing heels. The woman's body might have resembled a fourteen-year-old's, but her face was etched with the trials and tribulations of a careworn forty-year-old.

She sniveled into a convenient tissue. "No. I knew Piers would die. What about the rest of us?" The whites of her eyes shone in panic.

"We will be fine. The police will figure it out—" Eliza knew she should be empathetic, should have wanted to lay a comforting hand on the woman's shoulder, but her hand stayed where it was, clutched in Heath's grip.

"No. They can't. They mustn't."

"Slow down. What's your name? We haven't met." Heath spoke as if he were calming a wounded animal.

The woman darted looks behind her, her auburn ponytail swinging violently. "Poppy."

"Nice to meet you, Poppy. I'm Eliza." She paused. "Why aren't you in bed?"

"I was looking for Garri—Mr. Wickham." Poppy jumped at a creak on the stairs. "Please. You didn't see me, okay?" She latched on to Eliza's arm, bringing with her a whiff of cigarette smoke. "Please. Don't tell Theodore." Poppy slipped the tissue into her uniform pocket with a metallic clink and backed away, her eyes cutting through Eliza.

"Since when do tissues clink?" Eliza eyed the keyhole and tested Garrison's door. "Locked."

"Ones stuffed with keys might." Heath laid a comforting hand on the small of Eliza's back. "Allow me to walk you to your room?"

Eliza shivered as Poppy rounded a corner and disappeared. "Please."

"Want me to stay? I can sleep on the floor." He brushed her hair from her eyes.

Eliza stared into her room. Caesar, who peered at her with luminous bicolored eyes, did not look pleased at having his beauty rest interrupted. *Probably not.* "No. I'll be fine. Remember, I'm a—"

"Grown-ass woman." He kissed her hand. "I believe our croquet adventure has been outdone."

"Yeah, by murder." Eliza wished Heath a good night, clicked the door shut, and flicked the lock into place before she ended up begging him to stay.

After falling into bed, she pulled the covers over her head for protection and prayed the murderer wasn't also skilled at picking locks. And didn't have a key.

Chapter Six

A-Hunting We Will Go... for a Wickham

I have not been feeling well of late. This morning, on my usual walk over the grounds, I had to stop and rest more than I'd like to say. I shall have to hide my exhaustion, or Darcy will think me ill, and he already has so much to manage. According to Betty, Wickham visited just the other day. I had wondered why Darcy seemed preoccupied.
—Lizzy Bennet Darcy
Pemberley 1811

Roses smelled better with dew on them. Eliza plucked a red rose and tickled her nose with the velvety petals. The Thursday morning sun barely peeked over the horizon, and the thick woods bordering the property kept even that light from dispelling the gray gloominess. Eliza had awoken at five. Actually, she hadn't slept at all after hunkering down in her blanket fort, but sleep was overrated, and roses at five thirty in the morning did smell better. Especially after the strange rustling sound she'd heard outside her door before she'd opened it. Not wanting to meet with any unsavory characters, Eliza had listened breathlessly and had heard the faint click of a door down the hall.

It was good to be out in the garden where she could see hidden enemies, know what was coming before—

Eliza tripped and nose-dived into a rosebush. She cursed and wrestled out of the thorny thicket.

"I hate roses." She freed herself and studied her hands. Turning to go back to the house, she tripped again. "What the—" Eliza scooted closer to the body on the ground and prodded it with her index finger. "Garrison?" No sound. She poked harder. "Wickham?" That time, a grunt leaked out of the prone figure. Or at least Eliza hoped it was a grunt.

She leaned over and yelled in his ear, "Garrison Wickham, are you or are you not dead?"

"Not." He peeled his face off the ground, tiny bits and pieces of grass clinging to his dewy face. "Maybe." His head fell to the ground with a thump.

Not wanting to touch him again, as he smelled like a whiskey-drenched dog, she nudged him with her foot.

"Ow."

"That didn't hurt, you big baby. And at least I know you're alive."

"That's too bad." He burped.

"Good Lord." Eliza backed away. "You stay here. I'll be back." She jogged to the house, not sure who would be awake at that time besides herself and a semiconscious drunk in the garden.

Tash, the butler, met her at the door. "Good morning, Miss Darcy." His heavy-lidded eyes studied her over a protruding hawklike nose.

"Oh, good morning, Mr. Tash."

"It's just Tash, ma'am."

Eliza smiled. "Then it's just Eliza."

The butler's lips twitched into a smile, making his craggy face seem homey instead of homely. "What can I help you with this morning?"

"I found Garrison. In the rose garden." She held out her war wounds from the rosebushes for inspection. "I wanted to get my uncle. I found Garrison."

"Right away"—Tash's eyes twinkled, and he tapped a finger to his nose—"Eliza."

She whiled away the time by studying a bust of Margaret Thatcher. The woman looked as formidable in hardened clay as she did in pictures.

"Eliza?" Uncle Fitzwilliam placed a hand on her shoulder. "Tash informs me the lost has been found."

"In the rose garden." She led him to the garden and through the maze of roses. "Here he—"

Nothing. Eliza peeked under the bushes. Nope. She shook her head and spun in circles, getting her bearings. It was a maze. Maybe she was lost. Maybe Garrison was lost. Her mother had always asked if Eliza's belongings had grown legs and walked off. Garrison's newly functioning legs must have walked off, taking the rest of him with them.

"I swear, Uncle, he was here." She pointed at the dented rosebush. "See, here is where I fell into the bushes after tripping over him."

"I'll inform Wentworth. He'll want to know." He scratched his muttonchops. "I'm afraid Garrison is top of the suspects list. It doesn't look good for him."

Eliza frowned. "That doesn't make any sense. If he truly killed Piers, why would he come back to the estate and pass out in the rose garden?" She added that mystery to her ever-growing list. So far, her sleuthing skills would have had Miss Marple stabbing her with knitting needles just for being incompetent. She didn't want to imagine what Mr. Poirot would say.

Her uncle placed her hand in the crook of his elbow and walked her to the house. "Shall we breakfast and go on the hunt for our missing relative? Annoying though he may be, he is blood, after all, and I don't think he could kill. Probably."

By his tone, Eliza guessed her uncle wouldn't care if Garrison Wickham disappeared into thin air and never returned. Maybe he suspected something illicit about Wickham's relationship with Nancy. The questions spiraling through her head should have diminished her appetite, but they acted as spices, making even the kippers taste delicious.

"WHAT ARE WE DOING?" Joy whispered as she and Eliza crept through the rose maze an hour later.

Eliza crawled down the length of one arm of the maze, peering under the bushes. "I know he was here." She stopped midcrawl and twisted her neck to look at her cousin. "Hurry up."

Joy scowled. "Just so you know, I'm wearing a short dress for the ball. If my knees are calloused and unsightly, I'll blame you."

"Ice them later."

"I don't think that works." Joy screeched. "Bugger it. A grown man couldn't fit under these bushes even if he tried."

"But what if he didn't place himself there on purpose? What if someone did it for him?"

Joy blanched. "You think someone killed him?"

"There's already a killer on the loose, and killing once makes it easier to kill again."

"Personal experience?" Joy plucked a thorn out of her hand and flicked it at Eliza.

"I read it somewhere. Piers was the first. The killer now has a taste for blood. What if Garrison was the second? Or he could have been an accomplice and was just a loose end to clip off."

"Garrison could be the killer."

Eliza rolled that theory through her brain. "No. If he was going to kill Piers, why make a big deal of everyone seeing him fighting?"

Joy grunted and after a few seconds squealed. "Blimey! Eliza, look."

Eliza sprint crawled over to Joy. "What is it?"

"A button." Joy reached for it.

"Don't touch it with your fingers." She ignored Joy's quizzical look. "It could be evidence."

"Or it could be someone's missing button."

Eliza brought out a tissue she'd stuffed in her pocket for just such a moment and tucked the blue button in the tissue.

"What in the devil are you two doing?"

Eliza and Joy squeaked. Charlie and Heath stood over them, their arms across their chests, their eyebrows raised.

"We were just... ah... we were..." Eliza's tongue stumbled to a stop.

"Gardening." Joy hopped to her feet and hauled Eliza up with a tug.

The men's gazes traveled down the length of them and, when they got to Eliza, stopped midleg. Her cold knees told her she'd ripped her knees out of her pants.

A smile tugged at the corners of Charlie's mouth. "Can't Darcy afford gardeners? Are you looking for an internship?"

"Oh, piss off, Charlie." Joy slapped his arm and huffed her way past them to the house.

Eliza stuck her nose in the air as she stalked past Charlie and Heath. "While you two"—she gave Heath a little smile—"have been lazing around, wasting the morning, we have been in search of Garrison. And a killer. Have you seen Garrison? Or the killer?"

Charlie poked around in a rabbit topiary. "Nope. No Garrison."

"You are an idiot." Eliza stomped off in the direction of the house, the men tagging along.

Charlie laughed. "You might want to lose the attitude. DCI Wentworth is here for a visit. He wants to see you."

"Me?" Eliza pulled up short. "Why?"

"He's been questioning everyone in the house." Heath wrapped his arm around Eliza's shoulder and gave her a squeeze. "Staff, family, and guests."

"So they don't think it was someone from the outside?"

Heath shook his head. "Apparently, the last person to see him was Poppy, one of the maids. Mrs. Underhill had put her in charge of bandaging him up in the kitchen. No one saw him again until he was found in the fountain. Access to the grounds is pretty tight after the gates close."

Even though the chill of the morning was gone, Eliza shivered. Even Heath's arm around her didn't dispel the coldness seeping into her bones. The killer was still on the loose and probably in the house. She replayed the strange run-in with Poppy the night before. She was reportedly the last one to see Piers alive. More importantly, she'd been roaming the halls, jiggling the door handle of Garrison's room at three in the morning.

Eliza fingered the tissue-wrapped button in her pocket and made a mental note to look into the maid. "Have they found the murder weapon?"

"I don't know. I stopped eavesdropping when I had to come and find you." Charlie opened the door to the study. "I have found her. She was"—he gave her a sideways glance—"gardening."

She forced an innocent smile. "What can I say? I like roses."

Uncle Fitzwilliam and DCI Wentworth rose as she entered. The former cocked his head to the side, and the latter studied her kneeless pants.

Heath released his arm from around her, his fingers trailing her waist. "Don't bottle it. Just imagine them all in chicken suits." With a last supportive smile, he and Charlie left her to her own devices.

"Have a seat, dear." Her uncle motioned to a brown leather chair opposite the ones he and Wentworth had settled into.

"Miss Darcy," Wentworth began.

"Please call me Eliza." Eliza crossed her legs then uncrossed them. She wasn't sure how to sit when being questioned by police. Foreign police, for that matter.

He gave a small smile. "Tell me what you remember from last night."

"Well, there was the party, and everyone was having a blast when all of sudden, there was a crash. We were all startled to see Garrison and Piers going at it like cats and dogs." She paused and pursed her lips. "Although really, Garrison was pummeling him. Anyhoo, the fight was broken up, Piers left to get doctored by Mrs. Underhill, and Garrison stalked out. More like stumbled out."

"And then what?" Wentworth paused, his pen poised in his hand. "Go on."

"Oh, right. After that, Aunt Iris and I used the—"

Uncle Fitzwilliam cleared his throat. "Aunt Iris is a little frail, and I'm sure Eliza assisted her to her room. Right?"

"Yeah." Eliza avoided her uncle's gaze. "Um, then I went to bed only to be awoken by a scream."

"Did you see anybody?"

"Heath and I ran into a maid. What was her name?" She snapped her fingers. "Gertrude? No. Ah..."

"Greta," her uncle said. "She was talking to Eliza when I encountered them in the foyer."

"What did she say?" Wentworth clicked his pen.

"She asked me if I saw somebody and said it didn't matter and kept repeating it was all her fault."

Wentworth's face scrunched as if in concentration, his tongue peeking out between his lips as he scratched the last of his notes on his notepad.

"And then there was Poppy, another maid. She was acting all strange too. Was fiddling with Garrison's door. And that night, in the garden, I overheard an argument—"

"Did you see them?"

"Um, no."

"Recognize their voices?"

Eliza dug her fingernails into her palms and said nothing.

Wentworth clicked his pen. "Darcy, how many guests were at this little shindig?"

Uncle Fitzwilliam steepled his fingers and rested them under his chin. "Around a hundred or so. You'd have to ask Nancy for the guest list."

"But I don't think they were—"

"Thank you, Miss Darcy." At her frown, he smiled. "We will interview everyone on the guest list and speak to the staff. We'll see if someone else heard this argument who *can* recognize the voices." He snapped his notepad shut.

"Have you found the murder weapon?" Eliza asked.

DCI Wentworth studied her for a while. "Something tells me, Miss Darcy, you will not just sit and stay quiet."

"But I could help."

His smile was gentle and kind. "Sometimes, my ten-year-old wants to help as well, and I get stuck having to undo everything he did and do it myself."

Tears burned at the back of Eliza's eyes. She bit her lip to keep them leashed. "Excuse me, please." She rose and fled from the room and bowled into Nancy, who had obviously been eavesdropping.

"Eliza, how surprising." Nancy preened and fluffed her hair. "I was about to ask Lord Dar—your uncle if he's seen Garrison."

"Ah, he's busy now with the detective chief inspector." Eliza was about to reveal what she knew about Nancy's precious secret nephew, but something in Nancy's eyes shut her mouth. *Worry? Fear?*

Nancy's smile nearly cracked her face from the force of it. "I'll just come back later."

Eliza sprinted up the steps and skidded to a halt in front of Garrison's room. The sudden interest in him piqued her curiosity. She jiggled the handle. It turned. *Odd.* It had been locked last night. Groaning, she slapped her palm to her forehead. *Duh! The police already searched his room.* After they had searched her room and every other room on that floor. Heavy footsteps clomped around the floor above, proving the police were diligently searching every room. The coast clear in the hallway, she poked her head into Garrison's room, made sure it was empty, and crept in. Going through someone's room grated on her conscience, but either Garrison was in danger, or his killer needed to be found. Maybe the officers had missed something, something that would point her in the right direction.

The room, decked out in lilacs, made her question her choice of purple as her favorite color. Garrison had obviously never learned to pick up after himself. Avoiding the strewn bikini briefs on the floor, she opened every drawer, unzipped every pocket in his suitcase, and even checked under the mattress. And came up empty-handed.

If the phone call she overheard meant anything, Garrison had secrets. Secrets that had him running scared. Or lying dead somewhere. And from his violent argument with Piers, he could be the killer.

Eliza conjured up the plots of Agatha Christie's books. *Where would someone who wanted to keep something hidden hide it?* She stepped to the bed to inspect the mattress again, and the floorboard squeaked. Sweeping away blue-and-green-checkered underwear, she eased to her knees and ran her fingers along the board. As far as she could tell, it was solid.

Footsteps sounded down the hallway. Eliza eyed the bed, calculated some quick measurements, and darted under it, her hind parts catching on the bed frame. As the door opened, Eliza tucked in her butt and slid the rest of the way under. She peeked through the dust bunnies and saw two feet clad in a pair of heels—Aunt Nancy's heels. They clicked about the room, pausing for several seconds to the tune of slamming dresser drawers. A pair of flying socks rolled under the bed and thudded against her hand. She prayed Nancy didn't care about wayward socks.

"What did he do with it?" The venom in Nancy's voice seemed to splatter the entire room. With a curse, she slammed something shut and stalked out of the room.

Eliza choked on the swirling dust. What Garrison wanted hidden obviously wasn't in his room. She swiveled out from under the bed and sat on the mattress. Nancy's voice seemed to echo through the room, her venom seeping from the wallpaper. Eliza gulped. She had stumbled upon something big. Bigger than she could probably handle. She leaned forward, taking deep breaths. If Garrison was involved in Piers's murder, that could mean Nancy was as well.

Not wanting to do the math to figure out what time it was in Hawaii, she tapped out a quick text to her dad: *Tell me all you know about Nancy. And don't even think about being as vague as before. I'm onto something big! Your loving daughter. Oh yeah... don't forget sunscreen. And tell Mom hi!*

Brushing herself free of dust, she exited Garrison's room. It was time for reinforcements, but she wasn't sure her slightly batty great-aunt and her cousin were all that reinforcing.

Chapter Seven

Aunt Iris Lets One Slip... a Secret, That Is

My aunt Gardener came for a visit. She and Uncle were visiting old friends in Lambton. I so enjoyed our time. Darcy took Uncle fishing, and Aunt and I caught up on all the gossip. It seems as if my sister Mary has herself an admirer. I do so wish it's another Mr. Collins, as I miss his wit and constant referrals to Lady Catherine de Bourgh. Oh my, I must call her aunt, mustn't I?
—Lizzy Bennet Darcy
Pemberley 1811

Rain wept down the windows of the library. The weather, in solidarity with the tensions of the household and the fear that stalked the hallways, kept the family prisoners in the grand house. The weather had dissolved the cricket game between the gentlemen holed up in the billiard room. All the gentlemen except for the missing Wickham. Eliza plucked off a stray dust bunny still clinging to her pants from her adventures under Garrison's bed earlier that morning and drummed her fingers on the armrest of the chair she was currently curled up in, a book draped over her knee, her hands cupping a warm mug of hot chocolate. She had hoped the book would bring her comfort, help her forget the awfulness, the sense of dread hovering over her, but no. For once in her life, books were useless. She needed to make sense of the jumbled pile of clues in her head.

Setting the book down, she sighed. "All right, ladies." She spoke to her great-aunt and Joy, the former sitting straight-backed in her chair, her eyes bright. Joy, in the exact opposite position, slouched in the chair, her legs tucked underneath her. "What do you know about Nancy?"

"She's a social-climbing tart," Great-Aunt Iris quipped, nodding to emphasize every word.

Joy coughed on a piece of scone. "I like a lady who knows how to tell it as it is."

Aunt Iris closed her eyes briefly. "From the beginning, I knew she was trouble. After the death of your grandparents left two orphans, William and I raised Fitz and Andrew. They were a comfort after my own little John passed away." She patted the corners of her eyes with a napkin. "For the longest time, I thought we'd lose poor Fitz too. He was such a sickly little thing. Wouldn't know it looking at him now, though. Poor thing. Almost died on his twenty-first birthday."

"What about Nancy?" Joy attempted to put Great-Aunt Iris back on the right track.

"Oh yes, Nancy seemed to pop out of nowhere and soon had Andrew so wrapped around her finger—"

"My father?" Eliza's heart dipped.

"Yes. That's what I said. You young people, never listening." She aimed a pointed stare at Eliza then continued. "It pained me to see Andrew and then Fitz being manipulated by that... that..."

"Tart," Joy reminded her.

"Yes, thank you. Old age is starting to set in and all that. Why just the other day, I—"

"Wait? What about my dad?" Eliza perched on the edge of her seat.

"Caused quite a to-do." Great-Aunt Iris stared off into the distance, seemingly lost in thought.

"Aunt Iris?"

Aunt Iris blinked several times. "Yes, quite a to-do. Some feathers were ruffled, but after the dustup, everything seemed back to normal."

"What to-do? What dustup?" Eliza held on to the arms of the chair to keep herself from catapulting onto her great-aunt.

"Don't quite remember the particulars. Doesn't much matter now. I can tell you Fitz had hearts or something dancing in his eyes and didn't see, or refused to see, what everyone else saw."

"Saw what?"

"Greed. Lust. You name it, she had it. And Fitz wouldn't hear anything against her." Her wizened gaze speared Eliza. "Relationships were destroyed."

"But why couldn't he see it?"

Her great-aunt closed her eyes as if in pain. "Oh, Nancy had the capacity to make people believe whatever she wanted them to, I suppose."

Eliza finished her hot chocolate. "Why would Garrison refer to her as his aunt?"

"He wouldn't." Joy yawned. "That's not possible."

Great-Aunt Iris studied her. "Has he?"

"Yes." Eliza set her cup down with a clink. "I overheard the two of them in an argument, and he called her that."

"Well." Her great-aunt's mouth dropped, snapped shut, and dropped open again. "That throws a spanner in the works."

"Who's her family? Where does she come from?" Joy abandoned her aloof posture for a straight back and alert gaze. "She can't have just popped out from the fairies."

"That's an option I never considered." Great-Aunt Iris stared out the window. "They even work in rain, apparently."

Eliza walked to the window and pressed her nose against the cool glass. Police officials wearing slickers traipsed across the property. She shuddered. They were looking for signs of the killer. The hairs on the back of Eliza's neck told her the killer was still inside the house.

One of the officers turned and caught her eye—Wentworth. He nodded at her. Whether in salutation or as a reminder to keep her snoot out of police business, she wasn't sure. She waved back.

"Okay, ladies, let's make a list of clues. Who has a pen and paper?"

At their blank stares, Eliza grabbed her phone, swiped the screen, and opened her memo app. "Shoot."

Joy ticked off on her fingers. "One, we all heard Garrison threaten Piers hours before Piers was found dead. Two, anyone had the opportunity to do it. Staff or family members. Three, Poppy was the last to see him."

Great-Aunt Iris piped up, "Four, Garrison is missing. Innocent people don't run."

Eliza finished typing the clues on her phone and filled them in on her snooping adventure and Nancy's interruption. "The sudden interest in Garrison is odd. Poppy. Now Nancy. She's looking for something. And upset she can't find it."

"Is she in on the murder of Piers?"

"You sound a little too excited, Joy. But her veneer has cracked. Did you see her at breakfast? She could barely keep her fork from trembling to the table. Something is not right in Nancy's world." Eliza turned her attention to the lawn. Police still scoured the property.

"They must be searching for the murder weapon," Aunt Iris chirped from Eliza's side. "I hear the hole it made was ghastly. And done by something metal. Although, from what I hear, the boy deserved it."

"Aunt Iris! That was not nice." Eliza's blood rushed from her head to her toes. "How do you know?"

"I have my ways. Besides"—she gave a blinding smile that Eliza didn't trust for one minute—"I'm an old lady, and no one pays attention to old ladies."

Brilliant. Eliza had a secret weapon at her disposal. And it was time to deploy her.

GREAT-AUNT IRIS MARCHED off in the direction of the kitchen. Indeed, it was quite the march. A large handbag almost bigger than she was slung over her shoulder and stuffed with goodness knew what, but it was all vital and lifesaving according to the little lady who toted it around. Joy had been dispatched to flirt information out of the first constable she met.

Eliza's project was currently in the tulip room.

"Oh, hello, Greta." Eliza sailed into her room and quirked an eyebrow at a mousy-looking man standing behind Greta.

Greta gave a yelp and jumped, clutching Eliza's pillow to her starched uniform. "Hello, miss, I was just tidying your room a bit." She fluffed the pillow and set it against the headboard. "I... ah..." She glanced at the man. "We were just about to leave." She gave a whisper of a curtsy. Bruising from Piers's hand stained Greta's cheek.

"You don't need to leave. I was escaping the family for a bit, if you know what I mean." She outstretched her hand to the man. "And you are?"

His thin lips twisted, awarding her with a glimpse of yellowing teeth. "Theodore. One of the footmen." His eyes flicked to Greta, who twisted her hands in her apron.

So that was Theodore. Short and stocky, he could be an extra in a hobbit movie. "Tell me, do footmen usually help make the beds?"

Greta's gaze flicked from Theodore to the still-unmade bed and glanced at him again. Wilting slightly, Greta moved to the bed. "I couldn't say, miss."

"Really? How long have you been in service at Pemberley?"

Again, Greta looked at Theodore. "A year."

"And you, Theodore?"

"Three years."

"It must be hard on you, losing a coworker. How have you been holding up?"

A pillow dropped to the floor. Greta snatched it and stammered, "Fine, miss."

"It's been an ordeal for the family too." She pretended nonchalance. "Did you know Piers well?"

Greta's face flushed crimson, and her hands shook as she smoothed out the comforter. "Not really."

Liar, liar, pants on fire, hanging by a telephone wire. "Oh well, I've heard he was an outstanding young man and will be sorely missed." Eliza put on her best pouting face and hoped it didn't look as if she were having a stroke.

Theodore placed a hand on Greta's shoulders. "Piers was a dear friend to us all and will be greatly missed. Especially by Greta."

The starchily pressed maid in crisp black and white seemed to grow redder. A tear slipped down Greta's cheek. She swiped at it as if it burned. "Sorry, miss."

"It's hard when a friend dies." Eliza placed a hand on Greta's shaking shoulder.

Greta tore away. "He had no friends." She ripped herself out of Theodore's grasp and tripped out of the room, not bothering to shut the door behind her.

"She's a bit barmy right now." Theodore slid a hand through his hair. "The maids are a bit tetchy after Piers's murder. Superstitious lot."

"Including Poppy?"

His cheeks reddened, and his gaze darted to the door. "Is there anything else I can do to be of service?"

"No, thank you."

He inclined his head and left.

What an interesting turn of events. She couldn't help envisioning Theodore as the puppet master and the other staff members merely puppets. Nancy had to know about the tyrannical Theodore. That meant that either she had no control over the beast, or she had no intention of reining in his beastly qualities. And the way he evaded her question about Poppy only added to the juicy clues swimming around in her head, but nothing made sense. Not yet. But she would figure it out. Eliza wanted to do a victory dance in the middle of her room, but instead, she skipped down the steps in search of her great-aunt.

"YOUR GREAT-UNCLE WILLIAM often says I'm deaf, but what he doesn't know is I only pretend to be deaf." Eliza's great-aunt perched on a bench in the rose garden, her large bag of tricks at her feet, Caesar on her lap.

"What did you find out?" Eliza nibbled at a tiny cake Mrs. Bankcroft had sent out as a "snack." Eliza eyed the treats and mentally added on a few pounds or maybe even a whole stone. She stuffed the cake into her mouth. Vacation calories didn't count.

"Well," Great-Aunt Iris stage-whispered, "I had a little chitchat with old Giles Winfield, Greta's father and the head gardener. He's known to take tea in the kitchen with Mrs. Bankcroft, so I pretended to be lost." Her aunt twisted her lips. "Why do people assume elderly people are always lost?" Eliza didn't have time to answer the question before her great-aunt swept on. "Anyway, Giles offered me some tea, as the cook had stepped out to have a word with Mrs. Underhill."

Eliza eyed another pretty pink pastry. "And?"

"The gossip I heard about Piers was true. He was hated. By everybody, apparently. Even more so by Giles." Great-Aunt Iris stopped, nabbed a cake, nibbled on the edges, and offered some to Caesar.

"Aunt?"

"Oh yes. Sorry, my dear. Age and all that. Speaking of age, Giles is a doddering old fool, and I as much as told him so."

"What did he say to that compliment?"

Aunt Iris brushed crumbs from her bosom. "He agreed with me. Apparently, he misplaced the key to the garden shed and had to resort to using the spare. Doesn't want your uncle thinking he's senile or going dotty in the head." She flicked a stubborn crumb off of Caesar's mane. "Although, if you ask me, it's too late, poor man. Almost put salt in his tea instead of sugar."

"What did he say about Piers?"

"Ah yes, that naughty boy." She paused and whispered, "Isn't it unchristian to speak ill of the dead?"

"We're not gossiping, Aunt. We're investigating a crime."

"How fun, then! According to Giles, Piers had been bothering Greta for some time and even got violent with her a few months ago."

"And in the garden the night of Piers's murder." The conversation Eliza had overheard from the kitchen made sense. Giles must have been the male voice comforting his daughter.

"I suppose that would make any father hate someone."

Aunt Iris shooed Caesar off her lap. "I'm not sure there's a father in the area who hasn't had his daughter messed with."

"I see you ladies are enjoying a lovely little chat."

Eliza spun around and shrank under DCI Wentworth's gaze. "Hello, Detective Chief Insp—"

"I see you didn't take my meaning last night." He came around the bench, a scowl creating ridges in his face.

She bit her lip against a retort and hoped a few rose thorns were embedded in his backside. "I'm sorry, sir, I just—"

"With all due respect, Miss Darcy, my warning was clear. Stay out of this. All of it. For your safety."

"No need to be so blinkered, Wentworth." Aunt Iris hauled all of her five-foot-one-inch self to her feet, her white Velcro-strapped shoes a perfect foundation for her quivering frame. "My niece here has a snappy brain, and she's figured some cracking information out. Haven't you, my dear?"

Eliza wished the roses would turn carnivorous and end it all. She knew she resembled one as her face heated with embarrassment. "That's okay, Aunt. The detective chief inspector here is just doing his job."

Her great-aunt let loose a stream of air. "He's doolally if he thinks he can stop you."

Eliza wasn't sure who had just been insulted, and from Wentworth's twitching lips, she assumed he was in the same quandary.

DCI Wentworth cleared his throat. "Tell me, Miss Darcy, what have you found out?"

"Now you listen here. Eliza is my niece, and you will treat her with the respect she deserves. She will inherit all this someday, you know."

Eliza's mouth dropped open, and her heart skipped not one but two whole beats. "What?"

"Oh dear. I've gone and done it again." Aunt Iris frowned, compounding her wrinkles upon themselves. "You didn't know? Well, the best kind of prize is a surprise." She giggled and stared unblinking at the still forms of Eliza and DCI Wentworth. "Tell him, Eliza."

"Um... sorry. My mind's a little boggled." *Holy shi—*

"I believe she's lost the plot," Aunt Iris whispered to DCI Wentworth, whose chest seemed to have difficulty drawing in air.

"I'm not crazy, Aunt Iris. Simply stunned is all." Eliza didn't need to take her pulse, as she could feel her blood roaring like Niagara Falls through her veins.

"Tell him what you've found out." She gushed to DCI Wentworth, "It's the bee's knees!"

Afraid of what her aunt would say next and wondering if bees had knees—*odd*—Eliza told her tale, starting with the fight between Greta and Piers, the fact that Piers was abusive, the odd little Poppy, and she even snuck in that Nancy was Garrison's aunt. "And that, sir, is the extent of my..."

"Investigation?" Wentworth provided.

"Yeah. But I figured out who was arguing in the garden."

He spared her a glance and ground out words of praise between gritted teeth. "Nice work, Miss Darcy. Greta refused to name her attacker. I'll be sure to question Mr. Winfield closer." He scratched a batch of whiskers sprouting from his dark cheeks. "Funny business about Nancy and Garrison, you say? I'll check that out further as well."

Aunt Iris jumped to her feet again. Well, creaked to her shiny white shoes was more like it. "We used the secret—"

"Aunt, didn't you say you had to take your meds?"

"I'll have you know I'm as healthy..." Aunt Iris's voice trailed off at Eliza's exaggerated wink. "Now that you mention it, your great-uncle will be ready for his kip, and he hates to sleep alone." She waddled off, leaving Eliza with a huffing detective chief inspector staring down at her.

"Miss Darcy, I'm not some gormless constable who hasn't figured out how to tie his boots yet. How did you find out your information?"

"Will I have to stay at Her Majesty's pleasure if I don't answer your question?"

Wentworth barked out a laugh. "Blimey, Miss Darcy, but I haven't met with a more stubborn woman besides my wife, of course. What do I have to do to keep your nose out of police business?"

"How about 'can't beat 'em, join 'em'?"

"What, you think it's going to be as easy as that? You working as my little nark, infiltrating the den of thieves, secreting about in whatever you and your uncle are keeping under wraps, and suddenly Bob's your uncle, and we have the killer trapped and convicted?"

"Yes. Just like that, actually."

"You've been reading too many mysteries, haven't you? You've gone barmy over, let me guess, Agatha Christie?"

"And BBC murder mystery shows."

DCI Wentworth mumbled a phrase that sounded suspiciously like "bloody bollocks," but Eliza wasn't too sure and didn't want to ask for clarification.

"Miss Darcy, for the last time, leave well enough alone."

"But I helped just now. Doesn't that count for something?"

"A blind squirrel gets a nut every now and then. Stay out of it."

Eliza stuck her tongue out at Wentworth's retreating back. Besides, she had more important things to deal with, like a transatlantic phone call. She didn't even bother doing the math. If she woke her father, he deserved it. The phone rang and rang and rang only to be picked up by his voice recording.

"Dad. Must be at a luau or something? Anyway, got some news today from Great-Aunt Iris. Apparently, there's a secret you've been meaning to tell me. Something about Pemberley. Yeah, so if you could give me a call back, anytime, that'd be great. Oh, and still waiting for extra info on Nancy. Tell Mom I said hi. Love you. Bye."

Eliza stuck her phone in her pocket and traipsed to the house. *My house?* A mixture of fear, dread, and bliss churned in her belly. Aunt Iris had either truly gone around the bend, or it would all be hers one day. The sun seemed to take its cue and darted rays of brilliant light at the hundreds of windows. She could never keep them all clean. Oh, right. She would have groundskeepers. That brought up the image of Piers, the groundsman, who had cleaned those windows and presently lay on a cold slab in some mortuary. If Pemberley were truly her future, she would protect it. And to do that, she needed to get to the bottom of her first mystery: the reason her father had left it all behind. She had a sneaking suspicion it involved the current mistress of Pemberley, who was acting like she had wielded the murder weapon herself.

A stooped figure exited one of the side entrances and limped across the expansive lawn. "Hiya," he hailed Eliza in a gravelly voice.

"Hello."

"Name's Giles. Giles Winfield." He cracked a smile, revealing slightly yellowed but perfectly straight teeth. That slipped out of place. "Oops. Always do this after tea with Mrs. Bankcroft." He readjusted them with his tongue, and they clicked back in.

"Eliza Darcy." She shook his outstretched hand and gestured toward the rose garden. "You do beautiful work on the property. I've never seen such roses in my life."

"Ah, go on." He took his cap off and scratched the bill over the bald spot on the tippy top of his head. "They are my pride and joy, though. Would you like the grand tour?"

She looped her arm through his offered one and matched her step to his hobble. In the distance, two groundsmen mowed the lawn, and two more weeded a flower patch.

"It's nice you have such good help."

He spat on the ground. "These muppets are worthless. All got university degrees and come to work here? I can work circles around them."

Eliza doubted that, as a snail could beat them at that pace. "That's too bad. Why do you keep them on?"

"Humph! I don't do any of the hiring. Lady Darcy does all that. And the firing." He glared at the two men weeding. "Felix, where's your hoe?" he yelled.

Felix hollered back, "Broken."

"Use mine."

"Can't find it."

Giles clicked his tongue against his fake teeth. "I'd have given them the boot their first day. Do nothing but gossip like old biddies. Caught them sneaking food from Mrs. Bankcroft's cupboards, too, one day." The crevices in his cheeks softened. "Ah, my beauties. Meet Miss Darcy. She's a beauty too." He pulled a set of shears from a large leather tool belt slung around his waist and clipped a stem. "I call the pink ones my princesses and the red ones my queens."

Eliza smiled and tucked her nose in the yellow rose Giles offered her. "What are the yellow ones?" She fingered the silky petals.

"My friends." He cleared his throat and looked away.

"Thank you." Eliza touched the back of his weathered hand.

He shooed her gently. "Oh, go on now with you."

They continued strolling. "How long have you been gardener here?"

"More years than I have fingers and toes to count." He chuckled. "I've been working on the estate since I was a lad. I turn sixty this September."

"You must know this place better than anyone. Been here since the estate went to my uncle."

"Your uncle is the best man I've ever known. I had my doubts, as his father was a great man, but Lord Darcy, now there's a man you can trust."

"It's a good thing he has Nancy by his side to make sure things are run well."

A coughing fit had Giles stooped over, gasping for breath. He waved away her back-slapping attempts. "I'm well, girl. Can't an old man cough without people fearing he'll keel over?"

From his purple skin tone to his wheezing, Eliza was tempted to say no, but he recovered and returned to a normal shade of peach. "I just got something in my throat, that's all."

"Does Greta like working here?"

"That lass. I don't know what's got into her lately, but if she keeps carrying on like she is, she's going to get fired. Fool girl."

"How so?"

"Boys. What with all the guests here, she's living below stairs now, but I've caught her sneaking out the past couple of nights. Nothing but trouble coming from that, I tell her, but she don't listen to me."

"She must be upset about Piers's death."

Giles stopped and tottered. "Good riddance to bad rubbish, I say. I told Lady Darcy, the day after she hired him, he was no good. But she sent me away with an earful and a warning. So I keep my mouth shut. Odd, that. Never seen that man get his hands dirty. Some groundsman." Red blotches mottled his face. "He dared touch my Greta without her say-so. I never wanted to ki—Felix, you twit, that's not a weed." Giles tipped his cap to Eliza. "See what I mean? Now, be off with you. Mrs. Bankcroft made biscuits. Go and have some."

She chuckled when he brandished his hat and swatted the two groundsmen with it. On the way to the house, she rolled the fresh information through her mind.

A hand clasped her upper arm, and she jumped. "You scared me half to death."

Joy waved off Eliza's comment. "You and me. Date night tonight. What do you have to wear that's pub worthy?"

"A date? With whom?"

"Why, a fresh young copper who would like nothing better than to chat up a couple of pretty girls at the pub in Lambton." She leaned in for a conspiratorial whisper. "Oh, and I sort of nabbed the list of names connected to Piers. I snogged one of them. Arranged a meeting at the pub."

"That's so very wrong. I like it."

"Thought you would. Can't have Great-Aunt Iris the only one pulling her weight around here."

Joy pulled Eliza along, hurdling minuscule hedges and animal topiary. One poor tree squirrel lost its tail. "Our mission is to get the men both legless. Floored. Away with the faeries." She rolled her eyes at Eliza's blank stare. "Drunk."

"Why?" Eliza wheezed as Joy tugged her along the length of the foyer. "Oh, hello, Tash."

"Good evening, ladies. May I be of assistance?" His serious eyes held a smidgen of a twinkle. Eliza felt like an odd little pet kept around for amusement.

"Just a date." Joy continued up the steps.

"More like an investigation," Eliza clarified.

"The best of British to you, Eliza." Tash seemed to clear something from his eye, or maybe it was a wink.

Joy snatched Eliza's hand and hauled her up the staircase and into Joy's room.

"Why would Tash wish me the best of British?"

"What? Oh, he was simply saying good luck."

"I see." Although she didn't. Her father's English slang had faded years ago, an attempt to fit in with Midwest society, she guessed. Only when he was under stress did the heavy accent and colloquialisms appear.

She could have consulted the book she had brought, but she had no idea where it had ended up. She would ask Heath. Her heart flipped. But that wouldn't be anytime soon, as Charlie had commandeered Heath after the morning billiard game, announcing the gentlemen had better things to do than prattle about with the ladies. *Stupid Charlie.*

"Have anything to add to your excellent plan?"

"Why do I sense sarcasm? It's not my fault he fancied a chat up at the pub. It would have been stupid of me to pass up the opportunity."

Joy brandished a short skirt the color of a purple leopard. "*Charlie's Angels* vibe?"

"More like the Spice Girls with that outfit." Eliza dodged the flying purple skirt. "I'll meet you in five."

"Wear something that doesn't scream 'American.'"

"Don't worry. I left my American-flag-toting-eagle shirt at home." Eliza dashed to her room and dug through the closet, careful not to knock off the tiny tags stuck to each one with Belle's curvy script labeling each outfit. Finally, she came to one labeled "Date Night or Hot Guy Outfit."

She pulled the skinny jeans and diamond-encrusted cold-shoulder top off the hanger and dug in her toiletry kit for the matching jewelry stashed in a plastic baggie Sharpied with "Jewelry for Hot Guy Night." A few strokes with her hairbrush, a swipe of mascara, a titch of blush, and she was done. She peered at herself and huffed. After digging through her kit, she nabbed the eyeliner and applied that as well.

Her phone chirped at her. *Met Benny yet? And what food did you text me a picture of? It still had its head on.*

That is or was a kipper. It tastes better when seasoned with mystery, which I've fallen into. Wish you were here. You will die when I reveal my holiday flirtation.

Even though Belle's text made her smile, the only text she wanted was one from her father. But first things first. After the pub, she and her uncle would have to have a little chat.

Joy popped her head into the room. "Stop fannying around, Eliza! We're going to be late. Don't want that now, do you?"

What Eliza wanted was a quiet moment with Heath. A moment where the brave Eliza would kiss him. The universe knew that all a lonely girl wanted was a hot guy to call her own and kiss whenever she damn well wanted. *Stupid universe. This espionage spy date better be worth it.*

Chapter Eight
Pubs and Hideouts

I have some news, and I admit I know not what to do or who to confide in. Betty, as dear as she is, will surely tell all the servants. I do so wish Jane were not so far away from me. She would know how to tell a husband that one is expecting his child.
—Lizzy Bennet Darcy
Pemberley 1811

"Detective Chief Inspector Wentworth would not like me speaking with you."

Eliza cringed. Maybe she wasn't as adept at innocent questioning as she'd hoped. But it was difficult to get annoyed at Constable Rory Davies, who looked even more boy-like in his civilian clothes.

"Why would he get upset? We just happened to get a drink at the same pub at the same time. We could chalk it up to coincidence."

Rory's ears turned bright red. "Detective Chief Inspector doesn't put any stock in coincidence."

"Tell me, Constable Davies"—honey dripped from Joy's voice—"how long have you been with the department?"

"Just a few months."

"I bet you've seen some ghastly things." Joy's eyes gleamed with excitement.

He turned his body toward Joy. "A fortnight ago, we received a call about a woman's missing pussy—"

Eliza spewed beer through her nose. Rory turned and tilted his head. Joy peered over Rory's shoulder and mouthed "cat" and rolled her eyes. Eliza mopped at her face with a bar napkin and waved it in the air. "Sorry. Thought I overhead something funny."

He gave her an indulgent smile. "Anyway, this old lady's pussy goes missing, and she can't find it anywhere. She's in a tizzy over this and calls the police. We came in expecting to find it up a tree or something and thought we would have to call the fire brigade. Turns out her next-door neighbor's boy had stolen it and was in the middle of experimenting on it. Little wanker."

Joy placed a hand on his shoulder. "You were so brave."

Eliza caught Joy's gaze. She was feeling very much like Watson instead of Sherlock Holmes.

"Yes." He preened. "Some days are more adventuresome than others."

"I bet there's some sordid things about the Pemberley estate murder, yeah?" Joy ordered Constable Davies another beer.

"Quite. It is bloody annoying we can't find the murder weapon."

"What do you think it could be?" Eliza joined the conversation.

"Not sure, but it's metal and narrow in nature. And sharp enough to nearly cleave a man's skull in two. His mobile's missing as well. Can't find that anywhere."

Eliza held on to the bangers and mash she'd eaten earlier. Apparently, it was not a play on a bad porn movie name but was simply sausages and mashed potatoes. Tasty. Until then. The vision of poor Piers's head, blood spiraling through the water... The restroom seemed to move away from her as she stumbled through the pub and into Heath. Maybe the universe didn't suck after all.

"I say! You look a little green, Eliza. You all right?" His arms came about her and steadied her.

She took several deep breaths and concentrated on the checkered pattern of Heath's dress shirt. Unfortunately, those colors seemed to melt into each other. She was going to faint. But she never fainted. *What will Mrs. Bankcroft say?*

His strong arms caught her as she slipped to the floor. Voices swam in her ears, all muted, all merging into one vast cacophony of noise. She felt like Jell-O and wished the world would quit spinning.

"Don't go all wonky on me, love. There are some rather nasty bits and bobs on the floor." He patted her cheek. "Eliza?"

Heath's face cleared, and she concentrated on counting his freckles, reddish-brown splatters on his tanned skin. "Your freckles are so cute."

He wrinkled his nose as her finger traced an animal pattern. "Tell me, what have your adventures got you into? Besides legless?" Heath curled a piece of her hair around his finger.

"I'm not drunk." She swatted at his chest and jerked her head in the direction of the bar. "Really. Just ask Joy."

Joy apparently had lost Constable Davies but had collected another gentleman. That time, he was an oversized oafish-looking man with overly gelled hair.

Heath captured Eliza's hand as she made to trace another animal shape. "Joy keeps odd company."

"She kept you."

"Touché." His eyes crinkled.

Eliza, Heath at her side, hand warm against her back, sauntered to the bar. "Where'd our brave constable go?"

"Apparently, he has an elderly aunt who's a touch barmy." Joy introduced the looming giant. "Eliza, meet Harris Crawford, cheeky devil and one of my many exes. I was just talking about him. Remember?"

Eliza smiled a welcome. So that was the name Joy stole from an unsuspecting constable.

"Was on the pull tonight. Glad you gave me a bell." He winked at Joy and then Eliza. Eliza's smile dipped into the barest of grins. Heath's nostrils flared. "I heard about your problems at Pemberley. Making your reunion exciting, yeah?"

"You could say that," Eliza mumbled into the beer she'd abandoned earlier.

"I knew Piers."

Eliza's ears perked. "Really?"

"We were flatmates once. Then he knocked off my stuff. Kicked him out on his arse." Harris chuckled and sipped the dark beer in his glass. "Bugger had the bollocks to come to me just last week."

Heath raised an eyebrow when Eliza asked another question. "What'd he want?"

"Said he wanted security done for him. I do security, see? Figured I'd do him a favor. Poor bugger. Terrified, he was. No doubt about that. Said he'd got in over his head on some scheme. Wanted out. Some woman had him running scared."

"I take it you turned him down."

"Quite right." Harris saluted her with his beer glass.

"Did he say who was after him?"

"Nope, never said a name. All I got from him was a 'she.'"

Joy leaned behind Harris and hissed in Eliza's ear. "Blimey! It's Nancy."

"We don't know for sure," Eliza whispered back. Her thoughts wouldn't stay still. Like bees, they swarmed, a mad, painful attack. "It doesn't make sense. Why would Piers be afraid of Nancy? She's the one who hired him." To be a groundskeeper who never did any groundskeeping. Just like a laundromat could look like a laundromat, smell like a laundromat, and wash like a laundromat but hide a money-laundering scheme, a groundsman could look the part but play a different role. "I don't think Piers was a groundsman," Eliza whispered before stepping back and downing her beer. Nancy had hired the fake groundsman. And one would only do that for one reason. *Damn, it feels good to be right.*

"Be right back." Joy waved and jetted to the bathroom. Five minutes and one pint for Harris later, Eliza and Heath endured a narrative of how Harris had once gone on a "bender" for weeks and came out not remembering his name and had apparently gotten his "goolies" stuck in a car door. Eliza wasn't sure what those were or how they got in a car door. Eliza's toes curled in her black ankle boots as he expounded on the story.

Eliza wiggled her eyebrows at Heath, who echoed the action. She swiveled on her barstool and studied the door to the women's "loo," where Joy had gone to "spend a penny." *Probably hiding.*

"I'm back." Minutes later, Joy breezed into her chair.

"Look, ladies, you've just made a Harris sandwich. I hear it's the dog's bollocks." Harris flashed a greasy smile.

For a second, Eliza studied the bottles of alcohol backlit by the bar light and calculated how much it would take to make her forget the twit next to her. One bottle. Probably two.

"They're allergic to sandwiches." Heath towered over Harris. "And if you want to keep your own bollocks intact, I suggest you sod off."

Sweat beaded on Harris's forehead. Even though the man had at least three inches on Heath, he backed off and, with vibrating bravery, quipped, "Ladies, hate to run, but I've got other lassies to make fall in love with me. Joy, always a pleasure. Ring me."

"I'll be back." Heath stalked after Harris, wooden pub door closing after them with a jingle.

Curious, Eliza followed them into the cool evening air. No Harris and Heath, but out of the corner of her eye, she noticed two figures sharing a cigarette. The acrid scent burned her nose, and she moved farther away but halted when she recognized the voices. Poppy, the maid, and Theodore, the footman. Pretty cozy for a girl who had seemed terrified of him the night of Piers's murder. Eliza moved closer only to be stopped by a buzzing in her pocket.

Did you meet a new man? Do tell. Can I be bridesmaid? Best of luck! Miss you.

Eliza answered Belle's text. *It's the guy from the airport!*

The door behind her opened, belching out music and her cousin. Joy wrapped an arm around her. "Sorry about Harris. He's a lazy sod. Not one of my best in the long line of exes."

Eliza shivered and put her phone in her pocket. "It's not just that. It's the whole night. I'm just stupid is all. I mean, who am I to think I can solve a crime? I thought I could milk information out of a constable." A humorless laugh ripped out of her. "I need to come back to reality and do as Wentworth says—keep my nose out of it."

"Rubbish. Don't let one bad night turn you into a wimp." Joy's eyes gleamed with a challenge. "Besides, I'm having too much fun. I've never had a more cracking time at a reunion."

"A man is dead, and one is missing," Eliza pointed out.

"True. And sad, but tell me, have you missed Garrison?"

Sadly, she didn't miss Garrison. No one seemed to. "Where could he have gone? Are there many places to hide on the estate?"

"Where are we hiding?" Heath sauntered around the corner of the brick pub.

Eliza glanced at his knuckles.

Heath chuckled and held out his hands for inspection. "A man does not need to resort to violence to get his point across."

"So, how did you—"

"A gentleman never reveals his secrets, but I can tell you this"—he grinned at Joy—"this particular ex of yours won't ring you again."

Joy pouted. "He had an amazing telly. And really, he was good at—"

Not wanting to hear the rest of Harris's qualities, Eliza latched on to Joy's arm. "So about this hiding business?"

Heath mouthed "thank you" over the top of Joy's head.

"The old boathouse. No one uses it anymore. Not even for storage. I know Fitzwilliam was going to have it torn down, but it might still be there." Joy grabbed Eliza's and Heath's hands. "The hunt is on."

Heath didn't budge. "Hunt for what?"

He's going to think I'm an idiot. Eliza chewed on her bottom lip then glanced at Joy, who rolled her eyes. "A murderer."

His eyes widened with mischievous delight. "Really? Can I come?"

"You're not part of the gang. You've got to stay behind, Tilney. Oh, don't stand there all gutted. It's a girls-only sleuthing group." Joy spoke slowly as if speaking to a two-year-old. "Boys are not allowed."

Heath beamed a smile at Eliza. "Come on. Let's give it a go. I promise not to throw a spanner in the works."

Eliza grabbed a twig from the ground and knighted him on the spot. "To the next adventure." She glanced at where Poppy and Theodore had been, but they were gone, leaving her with nothing. *Or danger.* Eliza flicked the poo-pooing thought aside and led the expedition back to Pemberley.

SOMEWHERE, AN OWL HOOTED in the moonless night. Eliza held her phone in front of her, splaying the tiny beam of light on the ground.

"Let's crack on," Joy urged.

"Feel free to zip on by and sprain your ankle in a hole."

"Don't get your knickers in a twist. The boathouse is just over here." Joy swung her beam of light, and the ends barely touched the remains of a boathouse. Rotted wooden beams leaned on each other for support, and the roof beams looked like snarled teeth chomping at the drooping branches of an overhead tree.

"Ah, let's come back when the sun is shining and birds are singing." Eliza jittered her phone against her palm.

"Scared of the dark?"

Eliza glanced at Heath. He smiled and touched the back of her hand with his fingers. She trudged along, tiptoeing to the building. "No one could hide here. There's no intact roof."

"Let's just take a gander." Joy pulled on the door, which had fallen off its hinges long ago. It wouldn't budge.

"Here, let me." Heath grabbed ahold of the wooden handle, and together, they heaved. The door splintered and ripped off, sending them both to the ground.

"Oof, my bum!" Joy groaned and rubbed her backside.

"So much for our stealthy entrance." Eliza stepped over them, shone her light into the building, and crept in. Nothing. Wait... "Look!"

"Well, I'll be..." Joy crouched next to her and added her light to Eliza's. A sleeping bag, several bags of potato chips, and bottles of pop littered the floor. "We caught our rat. And one who likes salt-and-vinegar crisps and minging Cherry Vimto. Yuck."

"A rather messy rat." Heath toed at a used tissue next to a pile of cigarette butts. "How's he getting in? There's water on the other side."

For several minutes, they inspected the sidewalls. "Oi! I found it," Joy squealed. Sure enough, a piece of wood hid a hole large enough for a man to skivvy through. "I never would have taken Garrison for being clever." She eyed the white filters scattered around the floor. "Or a smoker. Do you think he's the one holed up here? Looks like this place has been used for some time. Maybe it's his version of a tree house. An escape from his posh digs at the estate."

"A creepy tree house." Eliza wrinkled her nose at the stench. "He might not have started this hideout, but maybe he's using it for now. If he's on the run and afraid, he'd hide anywhere."

"Something tells me he won't be back." Joy kicked an empty pop can.

"What makes you say that?" Eliza bit back a yelp at the dead rat. "We actually did catch a rat."

"Garrison hates rats. He won't be back."

Eliza scrounged around, looking for more clues, but only gained a few slivers and found another rat. Alive. "That's it. I'm out of here."

Joy and Heath didn't argue, and they were soon nearing the house. Most windows were dark by then, but a few emitted a warm glow.

"Joy, what do you know about the staff?"

"Nothing, really. Most are hired in for special occasions. The cook, housekeeper, Tash, of course, and the main house staff stay on all year but live off the estate. Why?"

"How does Theodore strike you?"

"Which one's Theodore?"

"He's the one who could be an extra in a hobbit movie."

Joy gritted her teeth. "He plays the silent hovering footman well. Maybe a little too well."

"I think the rest of the staff are terrified of him. We need to find out why."

"I saw Poppy sharing a fag with him outside the pub." Heath scratched at the day-old stubble on his face. "Seems a bit dodgy that a woman terrified of him one night would take a smoke break with him the next."

"Maybe she's simply off her trolley. Or she has no choice." Joy hid a yawn behind her hand. "Well, I'm knackered, and I fancy my bed. Good night, you two lovebirds," she trilled as she walked away, leaving Eliza and Heath alone in the moonlight.

"Want to know what I fancy?" Heath murmured in her ear as he encased her in his arms.

Eliza's heart fluttered, and a warmth spread through her middle. She flitted her fingers up the buttons of his shirt and rested her palm against his scratchy stubble. "Ice cream?"

"I do have this repeated dream about an American woman covered in chocolate cake, but ice cream is never part of the equation." His fingers danced along her spine.

"Pity," she hummed. *This is it.* The universe was finally smiling upon her. His lips, parted and full, descended slowly, deliciously—

"Belt up, Theodore." Poppy's voice sliced through the quiet.

Eliza and Heath hit the grass and military-crawled into the darkest shadows of the rosebushes. His stubble scratched her cheek. She didn't think herself capable of hating someone as much as she hated Poppy in that moment.

"I'm not a muppet. But what about Jonas? I don't see you badgering him none," Theodore whined.

"He knows what side his bread is buttered on. A fact you can't seem to accept."

"Look here, you—"

"I'd be careful. You heard what Nancy said and what to do when we find Garrison."

A grunt came and then nothing but silence.

Heath held up a staying hand and peeked over the hedge. He hauled Eliza to her feet. "That was interesting."

"Come on. Let's follow them."

Heath's white teeth flashed in the moonlight. "Lead the way."

Ducking between rosebushes and using the occasional squirrel topiary as cover, Eliza and Heath followed Theodore and Poppy to one of the servants' entrances. Before they could reach it, it locked behind the two servants.

"Bloody hell." Heath scraped his hand through his hair.

"Let's split up."

"No."

"Yes."

"Blimey," he hissed, "do you ever listen to reason?"

"Not usually. You know we have a better chance of spying on them if we split up. Now go. We're losing our chance."

With a growl, he launched from his squat and sprinted around back. Eliza chose the road most traveled and glided into the front entrance as if coming home at midnight were an everyday occurrence. The foyer was empty and dimly lit, and Eliza tiptoed to each room on the main floor before pressing her ear against closed doors or peeking into doors that were ajar. Nothing. Nobody.

Wondering what Heath had found out, if anything, she crept up the stairs and launched into phase two of her snooping. Most of the doors hid sleeping relations, but one could never be too sure, especially if the killer were still in the house. *Probably Margery.* Eliza pictured the nasty woman, chin hairs and all. *Yeah, most definitely Margery.* She rounded the corner and stuttered to a stop. Her door, shut when she left it hours ago, swung open. She plastered herself against the wall, praying for sudden invisibility or that the person or thing exiting her room was an incompetent boob.

Wish granted. Theodore slunk from her room, clicked the door shut, and instead of heading in the opposite direction, turned toward her. *Fight or flight. Fight or flight.* That man had been in her room doing who knew what to her things. And Caesar, poor baby. The cat mama in her sharpened her claws.

Eliza unpressed herself from the wall and stepped into Theodore's path. "Find anything interesting?"

The footman squeaked. Eliza never thought a grown man—she peered down at him and scratched that thought.

"Well?"

"I was told you, uh, needed new bed linens."

Eliza made a show of checking the watch she didn't own. "At midnight?"

"Can't question my orders."

No "miss," no "ma'am," no politeness. *Well, well, someone doesn't want to play the doting footman. Well, I don't have to play nice house-guest either.*

"I saw you tonight."

His ferrety face narrowed even further, his sallow skin pinking in blotches. His tongue darted out and licked his chapped lips. "It's not a crime to be off the estate. I had a night off."

"Do you often provide extra bedsheets on your nights off? Or is it customary after a date to snoop around?"

"I wasn't snooping. I told you, I was—date? What date?"

"Poppy."

A laugh ripped from him. "Date Poppy?" Another laugh came, a painful-sounding hack. "You're daft. She ain't my cup of tea. We was just having a friendly smoke at the pub."

Eliza didn't bother stopping him as he sprinted away. Shivering, she checked over her shoulder. Darkness yawned behind her. If her gut instincts were right, a killer was still on the loose.

Her phone gave a kissy chirp. Heath. *Mission aborted. Poppy escaped to the bowels of below stairs. Want me to follow her?*

She replied: *Abort mission. Reconvene tomorrow morning. Will regroup the troops. Had a run-in with Theodore.*

He answered: *Need me to rescue you?*

Eliza wanted to type yes in all caps, bold, and size forty-six font, but ended up texting, *I'm a big girl. And I have Caesar.* She added a terrified-looking emoji face.

You made a dog's dinner out of that lie.

She crammed her phone in her back pocket and locked herself in her room. A small meow squeaked out from under the bed.

"Hey, Caesar," Eliza purred and got down on her hands and knees. His green-slitted gaze met hers when she peeked under the bed. "It's okay. The bad man is gone. Come on out of there."

He bumped his head against her outstretched hand.

"I missed you too. What have you been up to, besides not being an attack cat?"

Caesar sawed his body back and forth between her legs as she readied herself for bed.

"It's been a pretty interesting evening for me too." After he perched on her hip, she flopped into bed and scratched between his ears, kneading away his stress.

She caught her bottom lip between her teeth. *Very interesting evening.* The staff and Nancy were in cahoots, but in what, Eliza had no clue. But she would find out. Closing her eyes to the hypnotic purring of Caesar, she wished that it wasn't her cat's paw on her hip. Her English heartthrob was probably tucked up in bed, his hand nowhere near her, but she had learned after her disastrous relationship with Seth that slow and steady really did win the race. *And also doesn't lead to a broken heart.* She punched her pillow and willed the morning to come quickly.

Chapter Nine
Blood and Dresses

Drat! Wickham happened upon me on my morning exercise. I find walking calms my nerves, which are rather high. Darcy questioned my obvious sickness over the goose liver pâté during supper last night. I shall have to tell him. He shall be happy, but I know he will worry, as he lost his mother in childbearing with Georgiana. And how shall I tell him Wickham forced a kiss upon me?
—*Lizzy Bennet Darcy*
Pemberley 1811

And quickly the morning came. All too soon, Eliza rolled away from the Friday sunshine filtering through the window and groaned into her pillow. Her phone chirped at her. After wrangling it from the bedside table, she pressed the voicemail icon and put it on Speaker.

Hey, Eliza. It's Dad. Got your message. Sorry I haven't been able to call you back. Never seems to line up quite right. I assume Aunt Iris let the secret slip? I didn't know how to tell you. Your uncle can fill you in on the details. Look, sweetie, I've got to run, but I'll talk to you later. Stay out of trouble. Oh, and leave Aunt Nancy alone. Keep the past in the past. Love you.

Her father's voice, an odd mix of Midwestern and English, sent a wave of homesickness through her. But she couldn't go home. Not until she'd solved the mystery keeping her family separated by more than just an ocean. Add to that the other mysteries piling up at her feet—a murder and naughty Pemberley staff—and she had work to do.

Caesar pawed at her head.

"I know. I'm up." She placed her feet on a tulip rug and froze. The same scuffling sound that she'd heard the morning before whispered outside her door. Channeling her courage, she stomped to the door and yanked it open. "Heath?"

He whirled around, pillow and blanket snuggled to his white-undershirt-clad chest. A blush worked its way up from the collar and spread over his chiseled features. "Hiya. Sleep well?" He readjusted the slipping linens. His bare feet toed at the slippers on the floor. A pair of dancing-taco pajama pants encased his long legs.

"Is this your alter ego costume?"

"Missing the cape, actually."

"Seriously, what are you doing?" Eliza leaned against the wall, sticking her thumbs into the waistband of her pajama shorts.

Heath plunged his hand through his hair, leaving little tufts and waves. "I didn't like the idea of you being unprotected. So I camped out."

Her heart yo-yoed between her toes and chest. "You didn't have to. I can take care of—"

"I know. I wanted to. Needed to." Heath dropped his bedding bundle and took a step, then another, until his slipper toes brushed up to her bare ones. "Besides, when else would I get the chance to see your cat pajamas?" He pointed at one of the felines on the design. "Is he drinking tea?" He tipped her chin up and met her gaze. "I think I fancy them."

And her heart stayed in her toes. Which was just as well, for if she could have reached it, she would have handed it over to him that very second. "You know, if this were not so long ago, and someone saw us together in our pajamas, I'd be ruined. You'd have to marry me."

"Pity." His top lip pulled up in the corner.

"You're incorrigible."

"One of my many talents, believe me." His fingers traced the lobe of her ear. "Care for breakfast? There's a little café in Lambton that's good."

"Full English?"

"My treat. I'll meet you in the foyer."

Eliza floated back into her room, her toes full of heart and her heart full of Heath. She rummaged through her closet, cursing the overlooked "breakfast-with-hot-guy-that-you'd-like-to-kiss" outfit.

"Caesar?" Eliza's right hand displayed a sleeveless teal top and khaki capris, her left a cream swoop-neck top with sage-green leggings. "You pick."

Caesar pawed at the cat on her pajamas.

"Useless."

Choosing the cream and green, Eliza readied herself to conquer the world. Or breakfast and Heath's heart, at least.

"WHAT EXACTLY IS BLACK pudding?" With her fork, Eliza poked at the round black disc on her plate.

Heath chuckled and speared a roasted tomato. "Try it first, then I'll tell you."

She eyed him, clipped off a piece, and stuck it in her mouth. "Um," she mumbled around the chewy, gelatinous mixture in her mouth. "Is it supposed to taste like this?"

"Like what?" Heath hid a smile behind his coffee cup.

"Like I'm chewing on a scab?"

He managed to swallow his coffee without making a scene. "And you have firsthand experience?"

"Don't tell me you didn't try one as a child."

"I had refined tastes even then." He speared another tomato and plopped it in his mouth. "Glue was my pièce de résistance."

She choked on a laugh. The man's starched and ironed shirts hid a comedic soul. And muscles, as showcased by his T-shirt that morning. "What did I just swallow?"

"Oh, a little bit of pork meat, some oatmeal..."

Eliza held her napkin to her face. "And?"

"Pig's blood."

"You let me eat that?" she whispered across the table.

He leaned over, his nose dangerously close to hers. "I thought you liked adventures." He sat back in his chair. "I know how to give my lady what she needs."

My lady? Eliza snorted and shoved the pucks into her napkin. "There is adventure, and then there is torture."

"Please accept my apologies." He gave a little bow, his hand curlicuing from his forehead to his lap.

She pardoned him with a regal nod. "Done. Although I think I still need to come up with a punishment for scaring me in the garden the other night."

"I can't wait." His gaze dipped to her lips then met her eyes again with intensity. "You might not believe me, but the happiest surprise of my life was when you dropped into the plane seat next to mine."

Eliza's pulse thundered through her veins.

Heath swallowed, his Adam's apple taking a dip. "The second happiest surprise was stealing you away from Willoughby's croquet team."

"For which you have my eternal gratitude." She saluted him with her orange juice glass. "Do you have a third happiest surprise?"

A smile spread over his lips. "I predict I'm going to taste it very soon."

Oh. My. Giddy. Aunt. Eliza had never experienced a whirlpool in her tummy and decided she quite liked the feeling.

"I look forward to it." She cooled her parched throat with orange juice.

He flashed her a smile that had the whirlpool draining into her very core. "Me too." Sitting back in his chair, he steepled his fingers under his chin. "So, how do I become an official member of your sleuthing gang?"

"It's a tough initiation process. Not sure you're up to it."

"Do I have to take a secret oath and kneel on corn kernels in the middle of a full-moon-lit meadow?"

"Nope. You have to ride a donkey backward and speak in tongues."

"I can swear in German. Does that count?"

"You bring the donkey, and you're in." Eliza slathered marmalade on her toast and waved it at him. "I'm giving this orange stuff another try. Mrs. Bankcroft swears by it. Anyway..." She took a bite, shook her head, and set it on her plate. "I have all the clues on my phone. Here." After wiping her hands, she slid her open memos across the table.

"Blimey, you have a collection of clues, yeah?"

"And none of them make sense."

Heath signaled the waiter and asked for a pen and paper. Within seconds, the table was cleared, and they sat thigh to thigh, heads together, as Heath scratched out her notes in neat, small letters.

He tapped the end of the pen on each name as he said it. "Piers, the victim, groundsman, terrified for his life, said 'she' was out to get him. Greta, indoor staff, a victim of his physical violence. Giles, Greta's father and head groundskeeper. He hated Piers. You overheard him saying Piers had it coming. Also, he can't find his hoe? Odd, that. Theodore, according to you, a 'creepy footman with too much creep for his own good.'" Heath nudged her knee with his and grinned. His grin turned into a frown. "I have to agree. I don't like him, especially knowing he was in your room. You think he has some influence over the staff?"

"You should've seen him with Greta when I caught them in my bedroom. I thought she was going to ask for permission to blink next. And that girl, Poppy, she seemed terrified of him."

"But she was smoking with him outside the pub and seemed to be driving the crazy train in the garden last night."

Eliza stretched her neck in both directions. "It doesn't make sense. But she made it clear on the night Piers died that I shouldn't tell Theodore." Heath's strong fingers stroked her neck and worked their magic, massaging her tense muscles. "I just can't figure her out. She's quiet, and no one seems to notice her. But that's the job of staff in a grand estate like Pemberley. Why would she be fiddling with Garrison's door the night someone was murdered and he went missing?" She grabbed Heath's hand. "Oh! Do you think... no... that's too easy."

"Eliza, I'm not a mind reader. What are you thinking?"

"It's Theodore. He's the killer. And Poppy saw it."

"She shares a fag with a murderer the next night?"

"Maybe she has no choice, like Joy said. If he is Nancy's watchdog, Poppy wouldn't have a choice but to play by his rules. Maybe he's blackmailing her. I kind of feel sorry for her." Eliza rubbed her temples. "My brain is going to explode."

"What about your notes on Nancy and Garrison?"

She growled. "I just can't." Her phone vibrated. "Besides, I have a dress date with Joy."

"You sound like you're going before a firing squad."

Eliza sighed and leaned in. "Save me. Please," she whispered.

His face closed in on hers. *This is it. This is the third happiest surprise—*

"Would you like your bill, sir?" a nasally voice interrupted.

Eliza huffed, pressed her lips into a prim smile, and moved away, nabbing the piece of paper off the table and shoving it into her pocket. Heath looked as if he could throttle the waiter.

Heath's hand warmed the small of her back as he followed her out of the restaurant and onto the bustling sidewalk. All too soon, he removed it. "It's been a pleasure. I'll see you later back at the estate."

"Eliza!" Hallooing from across the street, Joy looked both ways and darted across to the tune and two-fingered salute of an angry motorist. "Shite drivers." Joy latched on to Eliza's arm. "We're off, Tilney. Shopping."

"Quite right." Heath stood, looking slightly stupefied. "See you soon, Eliza?"

Eliza nodded and was whisked away by her cousin, who was convinced she was the fairy godmother to Eliza's Cinderella.

"...dress so fantastic every guy will think you are absobloodylutely peng."

Eliza finally tuned in to Joy's chatter when they entered the first shop. The scent of expensive perfume wafted from secret places, enticing customers to spend, spend, spend. Joy slung dress after dress over Eliza's shoulder.

"This one will look tidy on you." Joy flung a hot-pink sequined dress the size of a handkerchief at Eliza. "Ooh, and this one? This one's for me." Joy all but drooled over a black dress with a slit higher than any panty line. "This will make Willoughby go barmy."

"Didn't Charlie punch him for making a move on you?"

Joy continued making selections. "Whose idea do you think it was to snog?"

"Poor Willoughby."

"He took it on the chin like a proper gentleman." Joy pursed her lips. "I might marry him someday."

"He might want to know about your plans."

"Chaps never do. They just want to show up and enjoy the wedding night bonk." Joy scoffed. "Speaking of, has Heath kissed you yet?"

Eliza situated the slipping clothes. "No."

Joy planted her hands on her hips. "Oi, just because English boy doesn't know when to kiss a girl—"

A throat cleared, and they both whirled about. "Heath," Eliza squeaked.

The glint in his eye proved he'd heard every single word. "Thought you might want this." He proffered her wallet. "You left it on the table. It took some time to find you. Looks like my timing is impeccable."

"Get lost, Tilney." Joy snatched Eliza's wallet from his hands.

With a smile, he whispered in Eliza's ear, "We have business later."

He left, leaving Eliza with an outbreak of goose bumps and a hive of bees in her tummy.

"Insufferable man. Glad I gave him the boot." Joy gushed with glee and ushered Eliza into an empty dressing room. "Now, let's start this fashion show. In no time, we'll have the most splendid dress for you."

Two hours later, Eliza's hair and nerves stood on ends.

"Let's find somewhere for tea, shall we?" Joy looped an arm through Eliza's.

"You've never had a better idea." Eliza tucked the bag containing her new garment over her free arm and hoped Heath would drop dead when he saw her in it. Joy had promised he would, but she'd also promised no more dresses before throwing fifty more at Eliza.

When she was just about to cross the street with Joy, Eliza caught sight of Greta slinking into the local bank, a large black purse tucked closely to her hip.

"Joy." She pulled her cousin to a stop. "We have business at the bank."

"We do?" Joy looked wistfully at the tea shop just a few brick storefronts down.

"Yup." Eliza dug around in her purse for American dollars. It was time to exchange them. Keeping one eye on Greta and choosing a different teller's line, Eliza moved up, occasionally tugging at Joy's arm. "What do you think she's got in that bag?"

Joy cocked her head and pursed her lips. "Rubies, emeralds, and diamonds. Maybe the Crown Jewels."

"Don't be dumb."

"Well, how am I supposed to bloody know what's in there? Could be body parts for all I know. Left my X-ray glasses at home."

"You're pissy."

"I need tea. And you are keeping me from it. You shall suffer the beastly consequences."

Eliza shushed her as Greta approached the teller. Even though several feet and a few heads got in Eliza's way, she could make out the stack of bills Greta placed on the counter.

"That's an awful lot of money," Joy whispered in Eliza's ear.

"What's a maid like her doing with a crap load of cash like that?"

Greta swiveled her head and locked eyes with Eliza. Eliza waved and fanned out her money, mouthing "exchange."

With barely an acknowledgment, Greta grabbed the receipt from the teller and left.

"What are the odds of her keeping her receipt?" Joy asked as she and Eliza entered the sunlit sidewalk.

"Depends on whether that stack was legit or not."

"I'm going with not."

"Then we better find it before she tosses it in the bin." Eliza tried herding her cousin into following Greta, but Joy refused to continue sleuthing until her predicted death by starvation was alleviated.

Cousins could really be a pain in the arse.

A BUNCH OF CACKLING crows was considered a "murder." Eliza wondered what a group of giggling cousins would be as she slipped behind a topiary, avoiding the herd of relatives whose names she still hadn't figured out. According to muttered complaints, Callum and Jasper would use their karaoke skills to provide background music for an upcoming bridge tournament. Poor boys. They just wanted a rematch after the fight fiasco between Garrison and the now-dead Piers three days ago. Despite the jumble of clues surrounding that horrid event, there was one mystery she was going to solve. *Now.*

"Knock, knock." Eliza poked her head around her uncle's half-opened study door.

"Ah, Eliza dear. Do come in. I was about to look for you."

"Am I in trouble?"

"On the contrary. Although that wouldn't be too far from the tree, if that were the case." Uncle Fitzwilliam smiled and gestured to a large leather chair next to an unlit fireplace.

"I bet this place is pretty cozy in the winter."

"You should stay and find out for yourself." A wistful look flitted through his eyes. "Right, then. It appears Aunt Iris has let the cat out of the bag."

"She's right?" Eliza curled her feet under her and slouched against the side of the chair.

He knelt before her and took her hand. "I know this must come as a shock to you. I can't tell you how pleased I was when I heard you were coming. I've been waiting for this day for a long time, my dear Eliza." He paused and looked off toward the large picture window. "When your father left England, left us, I knew I had lost part of myself." He turned his attention back to her, his warm gaze seeming to drink in her features. "You are so much like him, you see."

He got to his feet and moved to the bookshelf that covered an entire wall. He grabbed two books from the shelves and returned to her side. "Aunt Iris is correct. When I die, the estate goes to your father, as I have no heirs." He breathed deeply. "After your father passes away, Pemberley and the entirety of the estate will go to you."

The bottom fell out of Eliza's world, and her stomach plunged as if she'd fallen from a cliff. But instead of a hard landing and certain death, an uncertain future awaited her. She opened her mouth to speak, to question, but no words formed. Question after question collided. The only one she could verbalize was "What if I can't handle the responsibility?"

"I believe there is more to you than meets the eye. Much like your namesake." He offered her the leather-bound journals in his hands. "After reading these, you will find out how much."

She opened one of them. "Goodness' sakes," she whispered and traced her finger along the name on the first yellowed, aged page—Elizabeth Bennett Darcy. Age had faded the ink but hadn't destroyed the elegant script.

"Quite the treasure, I'd say."

"Uncle Fitzwilliam, this is better than treasure." She reverently placed one of the journals in her lap. "Can I read them?"

He tucked her hand in his. "You can have them."

She gaped. "Are you sure?"

His muttonchops all but quivered in laughter. "I've been waiting to give them to you for some time. Your mother kept in contact with Sara, and she would pass on information to me. You share many of Elizabeth Darcy's traits. I believe she'd want you to have them."

She pecked his cheek. "Thank you. You have no idea what this means to me."

"You're welcome, but let's keep this our little secret for now." He ran a finger under his shirt collar. "Some don't even know of their existence."

"Can I keep them in here for safekeeping?" Eliza shivered at the idea of Greta or Theodore or Poppy spying them. She didn't want any of those fingers touching Elizabeth Darcy's journals.

"You are welcome in my study at any time. And provided you go about it stealthily, you can use the tunnel." Her uncle winked at her and pulled her to her feet. "I believe we are invited to an afternoon tea in the garden. Wouldn't want to keep your cousins waiting. Especially Margery."

"Why is she here if she hates it?"

He patted her hand, which was woven through his arm. "She's a typical Wickham, sad to say. Hates me for not welcoming back Garrison's father. That'd be much like having the cat watch the pigeons. But she likes the action and the gossip so comes as often as not."

"What about Garrison? I wish we knew where he was."

Her uncle opened a door leading to the gardens. "He's always been a bit barmy." He stopped and turned to her. "Eliza, please be careful. I don't... this whole situation feels off." He bent and kissed her forehead. "Promise me?"

"Yes." The lie burned in her throat, but the scent was back, and like a bloodhound, she was going to follow it wherever it led.

"Fitz." Aunt Nancy sashayed to his side and planted a kiss on his cheek. She slid Eliza a look. "Can we speak away from the guests?"

"Nancy, Eliza is family." Uncle Fitzwilliam placed a hand on Eliza's shoulder.

"Of course, my dear. Slip of the tongue is all."

Eliza ignored her aunt. "That's okay. I'll leave you to it. The food looks too good to resist."

Uncle Fitzwilliam bowed over her hand. "Make sure you taste Cook's cucumber sandwiches. They were a favorite of mine as a boy," he whispered, "and as I remember, quite smashingly good."

Eliza chuckled and did as ordered. Mrs. Bankcroft and her army of cooks and kitchen elves had outdone themselves. Towers of tiny cakes, platters of sandwiches, including cucumber ones prettily cut into tulips, trays of hors d'oeuvres, and pitchers of cool lemonade called to her. She filled her plate and wandered around looking for Joy, who had wandered off in the hunt for Willoughby. Great-Aunt Iris was putting her husband down for a nap, leaving nameless faces swarming the lawn. And Heath had been kidnapped by some of those nameless relatives.

"Getting your fill?"

"Heath!" Eliza's heart fluttered in her chest. "Where have you been?"

"Sorry. Your relatives are talkative. I finally escaped a theological discussion on global warming. Do I have any scars?"

"Did the claws come out?" She caressed his cheek, enjoying the sensation of his stubble against her fingers.

He stole a cake from her plate and plopped it into his mouth. "Nothing I couldn't handle."

"I've punched people for less." She slid her plate behind her back, protecting her goodies from his roving hand.

"Really?"

"Once I stabbed a boy's hand with a plastic fork when he reached for my brownie. First and only time I was ever sent to the principal's office."

"You were the model of perfection after that?"

"I never said that. I just didn't get caught." Eliza took pity on him and handed over another bite-sized cake. "Here. Consider this a sign of my affection."

"Any other signs of affection you're willing to share?" He bent his head lower, his lips a breath away.

Time stopped. Eliza's lips tingled in anticipation. His kiss would taste of chocolate cake, and she wanted every morsel. Heat swirled in her belly.

A movement out of the corner of her eye diverted her attention. Heath's lips smashed on her cheek when she turned her head to follow a red-faced Poppy, Theodore hot on her heels, into the house through a side door.

"That was not what I was aiming for," Heath whispered in her ear.

"Come on, sidekick. Let's crack on as you Brits like to say." She grabbed his hand and pulled him along. "You can practice your aim later."

Silently, they slipped through the same door into an ordinary hallway, devoid of fancy embellishments and the large, man-sized flower vases Nancy seemed fond of. Angry voices echoed down the passage. Eliza and Heath crept closer and came to a stop outside a cracked door.

"Shouldn't they be helping with the tea?" Heath whispered.

Eliza held her finger to her lips.

"I told you I wouldn't tell anybody," a male voice pleaded.

"That's not Theodore's voice. Or Poppy's," Eliza mumbled. She stepped closer and peeked through the crack. Jonas.

"You know she expects absolute loyalty. If she senses you going all sixes and sevens, she'll make good on her promises." Poppy's voice wavered.

"You have a quota to fill. And you didn't fill it." Theodore's voice cut through the air like a whip. "Don't fail again. You won't get a second chance."

"Let's go before we're missed," Poppy directed, her voice closer to the door.

Heath grabbed Eliza's hand, and they sprinted down the hall and out the door, putting a safe distance between them and the house. A few people turned their heads and stared. "Sorry, bloody big rat."

"Or three." Eliza puffed next to him, eying the "rats" as, one by one, they emerged from the house.

"You follow Jonas. I'll keep an eye on the other two."

Heath dropped a kiss to her hand. "Your wish is my command." He traipsed off then shook some hands and greeted people before slipping out of sight after Jonas.

Eliza cuddled the back of her hand to her cheek, her skin tingling where his lips had branded her, and copied Heath's moves, finding people she sort of recognized, and made small talk, usually about the weather and always keeping an eye on either Poppy or Theodore. Nothing appeared out of the ordinary. Trays were being carried, and guests were being served.

Eliza excused herself from a group of Kitty's descendants and approached the table where Poppy was posted, rearranging platters of food.

"Hello, Poppy."

Poppy's gaze, perfectly subservient, met Eliza's. "Hello, miss. May I help you?"

Eliza tilted her head. "I've had some things rearranged in my room. I'm not used to such posh digs. I think I can make my own bed from now on. Would you care to spread the message, please?"

"Are you accusing—?" For a split second, Poppy's meek and mild gaze flashed with anger.

"Me? Nope." Eliza recalled the night she and Heath found Poppy in front of Garrison's door, the night they heard the metallic clink in her pocket. "Do you know who has the keys to all the rooms?"

Poppy's tongue darted out and licked at her upper lip. "Just the Darcys. Oh, and Tash and Mrs. Underhill, of course."

"Petunia, can't you see the lemonade is gone? Get back to work and stop conversing with the *guests*." Nancy stalked over, her heels spiking the grass, and slid her hard gaze to Eliza.

"Ma'am, my name's not—"

"Does it matter?" Nancy bit out the question.

Poppy's lips thinned, and her face reddened. "No, ma'am."

Nancy slid one last look at Eliza and strutted off.

"I'm sorry, Poppy." Eliza wanted to feel bad for the misused staff, but the hatred in Poppy's eyes kept Eliza's sympathy in check.

"It doesn't matter. I'm used to it. One day, I'll—" The hardness in Poppy's voice made Eliza back away. Poppy snatched the empty glass container and marched to the house, her back straight and unyielding.

Eliza blinked and looked for any sign of Heath. Not seeing him, she hunted for Joy or Great-Aunt Iris or her uncle. Intent on finding a familiar face, she almost missed the face sticking out of the shrubbery on the far side of the party. Biting back a startled cry, she hoofed it over to where the human's head had been.

"Psst!" she hissed into the greenery.

"Scram" came back an echoed hiss.

"Good grief! Is that you, Garrison?"

"No" came Garrison's voice, muffled by leaves and twigs.

"Are you always this friendly and easygoing?" Eliza tried to squeeze through the bushes. "Is there an easier way through here?"

"I'll only tell you if you bring me food."

She tossed a gingersnap over the hedge. "There."

The gingersnap came flying back. "Don't like these."

Eliza crumbled the cookie, imagining for one therapeutic moment that it was Garrison's head. "Fine. Starve." She pivoted and walked away.

"Wait! I'm sorry. I love gingersnaps. Go get me a whole tin of them." Garrison stuck his head through the shrubbery. "I'm starving."

Eliza peered at him and agreed. "You do look like death warmed over. Where have you been?"

"Can't say." When she lined up a pitch with another cookie, he ducked. "Don't. Please."

A wave of pity for the poor creature lapped at her better nature. The same creature had, only a few days ago, wanted to make babies with her cousin Joy. She shoved that to the side. As icky as he was, Garrison was still family and famished family at that. "Wait here. Oh, and don't go disappearing again." As quickly as possible, without drawing attention, she sauntered over to the tables and piled her plate again. No one seemed to notice her second trip through the buffet.

She stalked to the bushes. "Garrison?"

"Follow the sound of my voice."

She rolled her eyes and tiptoed along the border until a divot in the bushes appeared. She had just enough room to squeeze in sideways. Garrison snatched the plate and gulped everything in under a minute.

"Maybe you should have saved some for a midnight snack or something."

"I never eat after eight p.m."

Oh, for the love of... "Well, spill it. Where did you go after I found you in the rose garden?"

"You mean 'fell on.' You don't look as heavy as you feel."

"Get on with it, Garrison," she growled.

"I had to hide. He's dead. I don't want to share his fate."

"Why would you share in his fate?"

He opened his mouth and snapped it shut. "I can't tell you."

"You got to give me something. A hint, even?"

A faint flicker of cleverness lit his face. "Don't expect great things."

"What? What is that supposed to mean? How is that supposed to help me catch the killer?"

"You can't catch her—" He turned ashen. "Please, Eliza, don't tell anybody you saw me. I mean it. No one." He darted panicked little looks around him, making Eliza check for hidden assassins. When she looked at Garrison, he was already squeezing himself into another copse of trees, disappearing.

Goose bumps exploded on her arms. If Garrison, with the IQ of a pebble, was running scared, maybe she should too. Eliza traipsed back to the picnic, clutching the china plate.

"Finding the hedges interesting?"

Eliza jumped. "Aunt Nancy, you scared the living daylights out of me." When Nancy didn't offer an apology and continued to pin her with an icy stare, Eliza stuttered, "I was just... ah... feeding the squirrels."

Nancy smiled tightly. "I make it a habit not to feed vermin. Of both animal and human kind. Understood?"

Eliza's throat worked around the lump lodged there.

"Glad we understand each other." When Uncle Fitzwilliam sauntered over, Nancy's face split into a sugary smile. "Ah, dear, look who I found feeding our lovely squirrels."

Uncle Fitzwilliam slid an arm around his wife's waist and gave a cheeky grin. "Ah, good. Now we'll have fat squirrels running around." He kissed his wife's cheek. "I'm afraid you are needed, my dear. Excuse us, Eliza?"

Eliza watched her aunt and uncle join a group of extended family. Maybe her original theory of Theodore being the killer was wrong. Maybe she was related to the killer.

Chapter Ten
Battleship and Other News

The house is in an uproar. Betty, my dear lady's maid, heard it from the first footman, who heard it from the second footman, who heard it from one of the cook's assistants that my husband punched Wickham in the town square under the chestnut tree. I should have expected it, as I've never seen that look that was in my Darcy's eyes upon telling him about Wickham's unwelcome kiss. I think I was successful in changing my dear husband's mood when I gave him the news of our upcoming child. Oh, how my cheeks burn at the memory of his reaction about the baby. I only hope he repeats it often. I shall not write it in words, for it is forever written on my heart.
—Lizzy Bennet Darcy
Pemberley 1811

"In case I haven't told you, this is a stupid way to spend a Saturday morning." Joy shivered in the morning chill.

"You have told me. Like, ten times already."

"What do you expect to find?" Joy ambled along after Eliza, back to the old boathouse, in the early morning hours after the garden party.

"Think. Someone has Garrison so scared, he'd rather rough it in the wild than take cover in the mansion. He also mentioned a 'her.' Who's to say she's not the one holed up in the boathouse and not Garrison?" Eliza paused midstep and strained to listen. "Do you hear that?"

Joy cocked her head. "It's kind of a crackling sound, I'd say."

"Run." Eliza ran toward the noise, a sense of dread accelerating her.

"Why are we running to the sound? Shouldn't we leg it in the opposite direction?" Joy puffed next to her.

Eliza's response became unnecessary. Flames licked at the decayed wood of the boathouse, sending the structure to a fiery grave.

"Should we call the fire brigade?"

Eliza kicked a clump of wet grass. "To what purpose? The grass is too wet for the fire to spread. And the shed is gone. The evidence is gone. Might as well grab some graham crackers, chocolate, and marshmallows and make some s'mores." She kicked the same clump of grass again.

"Could we?" Joy clapped. "It's been ages, well, since we visited you in the States."

Eliza cracked a smile. "Sadly, I didn't pack the required ingredients."

"We can whip something up, I'm sure. We, at least, have better chocolate."

Eliza couldn't argue and instead watched the structure burn. "Maybe we should tell Uncle Fitzwilliam about this." She trudged back to the house with Joy.

Someone had set fire to the building. Someone who didn't want to be found and had left incriminating evidence behind. But what? She hadn't seen anything. Only bags of chips, empty bottles of pop, and a dead rat or two.

"Looks like we'll have an extra audience member," Joy whispered as they neared the house.

DCI Wentworth, looking as serious and stoic as ever, stalked from his car. "Ah, good day, Miss Darcy. Miss Bingley." He nodded to Eliza and Joy. "Out and about on an adventure?"

Eliza squirmed under his gaze. "Joy was showing me the grounds. We were just on our way to speak with my uncle."

"Ah, excellent. So was I. Allow me to escort you?"

She didn't trust his smile. Not one little bit. The silent trio moved past Tash, his bow reassuring to Eliza. Things hadn't outwardly changed since the fire, but something had clicked. Murder was horrid, but fire was sneaky.

"Hello, Eliza." Uncle Fitzwilliam smiled from behind his desk. His lips faltered slightly when Wentworth stepped in behind her. "Good day, Wentworth. To what do I owe this pleasure?"

"I'm afraid it's not a social call." The detective motioned to Eliza. "I'll let your niece speak with you first, though."

When DCI Wentworth showed no sign of leaving the study, Eliza forged on. "The old boathouse is on fire."

"Was," Joy corrected when both men jolted into action.

"Right. Was. Not anymore, obviously, as there was nothing we could do to save the poor old building, so we watched it burn... to the ground." Eliza stopped babbling.

Her uncle's lips twitched, and Wentworth cleared his throat. "I'm just glad to see you two are safe." Her uncle sat back in his chair and motioned for them all to have a seat. "It was an eyesore. I had planned to demolish it months ago, but it had slipped my mind. I guess Mother Nature took care of things for me."

Eliza ignored Wentworth's gaze and jumped slightly when he countered, "How could a fire start in conditions such as this? It rained cats and dogs just last night."

Fitzwilliam shrugged, a motion Eliza hadn't yet seen him perform. It looked strange. "Must be some lads looking for trouble, I suppose. I'll have some groundsmen keep a lookout, but I wouldn't worry about it."

Eliza wanted to tell her uncle everything, but with Wentworth looking too much like a bloody bloodhound, she kept her mouth shut.

"Speaking of cats and dogs," Joy whined as a spattering of rain pelted the windows. "If you don't need us, gentlemen, we are off."

Eliza kissed her uncle's cheek and nodded curtly to Wentworth. Before she closed the door, she heard Wentworth ask, "Tell me, Fitz, have you seen a missing footman? Jonas is his name, I believe."

After shutting the door with a click, Eliza leaned against it. "Not Jonas. This is not good, Joy. Not good at all."

"He's probably gone on holiday or something."

"I don't think so. He, like the rest of the staff here, was into something big. But what?" She whipped out her phone and texted Heath: *I need your brain. Meet Joy and me in the kitchen.* "We need reinforcements. And cookies."

The kitchen contained no cookies and no Mrs. Bankcroft. "There goes that idea." Eliza frowned into the empty cookie jar.

"When God closes a door, he opens a window." Joy plunked a carton of ice cream and two spoons on the center kitchen island.

"Amen." Eliza dug in and waved her spoon about. "I'm telling you now, something fishy is going on."

"Save some for me, ladies." Heath leaned against the island counter.

Eliza slid the carton out of his reach. "Only room for two in this carton."

"Hey, you should be giving me that whole thing. I have information for you."

"Make it good. This ice cream is laced with caramel. I won't surrender it easily."

"Guess who I saw having a heated discussion last night?"

"It seems everyone has heated discussions in this house. Didn't think you Brits had those." Eliza licked her spoon.

Heath ignored her comment. "Theodore and Greta."

Eliza lost interest in the ice cream. "And?"

"They were arguing about Jonas. Greta mentioned something about him screwing up, that he had come to her last night, worried. Said he wanted out. And now he's missing."

"With the threats Theodore and Poppy made to him yesterday, I think it's worse than that." Eliza pushed the carton over to Joy, who grinned and dived into the carton. "Who's the estate manager?"

Joy looked at Eliza as if her cousin had sprouted ten heads. "You don't know? Nancy."

Eliza's skin tingled. "Isn't that unusual?"

"Not anymore. It's hard to keep estates this large running, so owners try to cut costs themselves. I guess she always has been since they got married."

Snippets of conversation clicked into place. "Holy crap! Nancy's been embezzling from the estate."

Joy's spoon clattered to the counter. "Blimey."

"Think about it. The groundsmen not being groundsmen, the fact that Nancy hires whoever she wants, fires whoever she wants, the mention of quotas, the fear of the staff. I wonder what happens to the staff who don't want to play Nancy's game? There's no way she's letting her secret out." Eliza motioned slicing her finger across her throat.

"That's a pretty wild accusation." Heath jammed his fingers through his hair.

"You'll need proof," Joy piped in, chucking the empty container into the garbage.

Voices sounded.

"Let's go." Eliza entwined her fingers in Heath's and escaped the kitchen.

Something wicked had polluted the shades of Pemberley, and Eliza was going to find out what. Starting with her aunt. Evading the gaggle of extended family, Eliza, Joy, and Heath took refuge in the library.

"If I see another relative, I shall go berserk." Joy sighed and fell into a leather chair.

"Does that include me?" Great-Aunt Iris popped up from a high-backed chair facing the unlit fireplace.

"Good heavens." Eliza clutched her chest. "You scared me half to death."

"Oh dear," her great-aunt tutted, "do you have heart problems too?"

Eliza shook her head. "No, it's just a manner of sp—"

"Because your great-uncle can't get too excited anymore, if you know what I mean. Poor dear, does try. Why, just last night we attempted something new. You know, to keep things fresh, and well, the picture was a little misleading, and your poor uncle sprained his—"

"About this rain," Heath interjected, "horrid, really."

"Quite right," Aunt Iris quipped. "Makes my knees ache."

With only a slight cough, Eliza steered the conversation to more pleasant waters. She hoped. "Aunt Iris, have you learned anything new?"

"I watched a show on the telly about aliens. Did you know that aliens use proboscis to—"

Eliza choked on a laugh. "I meant with the murder case."

"Nothing. Unless you consider the disappearing footman a clue."

"How do you...? Where did you...?"

"You didn't see me when you entered the room, did you, my dear? And don't forget about the tunnel." Aunt Iris seemed to glory in gloating.

Eliza cleared her throat. "And what did you glean from eavesdropping?"

Her aunt harrumphed but didn't deny the accusation. "No one has seen the lad. He's been missing since last night. Didn't have breakfast with his mum as they had planned. Poof!" Aunt Iris flicked her fingers and danced them back to her polyester-pants-enclosed thighs.

Joy bolted in her chair. "I heard something last night."

"Don't worry, dear, I hear things all the time." Aunt Iris tutted and rummaged around in her jumbo-size bag. "Would you care for a jelly baby?" She held her hand out and proffered unwrapped candy babies with an assortment of tissue lint and fuzz clinging to them.

Eliza and Heath took a few and pretended to eat one.

Joy shook her head. "I have a dress that is just perfect for the ball, and I already have to lie on the bed to get it zipped. Anyway, I heard a noise last night. Around midnight. It was an odd sound. It was like a groan and a squeak. And a thump."

"Did you look outside to see what it was?"

Joy pinned her with a glare. "Would you have?"

"I don't know what's up with you modern girls nowadays. When I was your age, I was killing Nazis. At least thirty of them."

Eliza did some quick math. Ten more than the last time she'd heard the story. "Yes, Aunt Iris. But I'm sure if any Nazis walked in now, Joy and I would be sure to kill them good and dead." She leaned into Heath's side.

Aunt Iris tutted and pinned Heath with a stare. "Do you intend to marry my grandniece?"

"Pardon me?"

The library door opened, stemming Great-Aunt Iris's retort.

"Miss Bingley." Tash bowed. "Your mother requests your presence in the drawing room. Bridge, I believe."

Joy groaned. "Tash, can you pretend you didn't find me?"

Tash glanced about the room, his mouth open, but no sound came out.

"Oh, never bloody mind. I'll go play bridge." The last word was said with the same tone Eliza used with the word "spiders." "Would you care to join me, Aunt Iris?"

Aunt Iris waved away Joy's attempts at herding her from the room. "You go, dear. I'll act as chaperone. Wouldn't want the baby at the wedding. Take it from me, the dress just doesn't fit right."

Joy gave Eliza a toothy grin and slipped from the room. Aunt Iris chirped, "Anyone for whist? No? Well, there's a cupboard of games over there against the wall."

Eliza and Heath rummaged around the game cupboard before finding Battleship.

He grinned with boyish charm. "Care for a battle?"

"I am a Battleship aficionado. Be prepared to be annihilated," Eliza quipped.

Ten minutes later, Eliza slumped farther in her chair, scrunching her knees up to protect her classified information. There must be a spy somewhere. She glanced over her shoulder at her aunt knitting placidly behind her.

"B4."

Eliza growled. "Hit."

His eyes gleamed. She rolled hers in response.

"B5."

"Sunk it."

"Yes!"

"You know this is just a game." She scowled at the white pegs dotting the blue "water." She had yet to hit one of his ships.

"Why is your warrior face on?"

"I don't have a warrior face." She bit out the comment and questioned whether his ships were even on his board or if he had secreted them in his pockets.

"That's too bad. I like your warrior face."

She managed not to choke on her spit, scowled at the empty spots, and made her informed, practical, militarized... *Oh, who am I kidding?* She made a shot in the dark. "G9."

His jaw dropped. "No way. No one ever guesses my pattern."

She cracked her fingers. "Like I said, aficionado."

He spared her a glance, and after five more minutes, they were neck and neck, aircraft carrier to aircraft carrier, five shots to five shots, end match.

"A9," she gritted out between clenched teeth.

"Bugger."

She pumped her fists in victory, almost upsetting the tiny sea, sunken ships, and remaining bombs on the paisley carpet. "Uh-huh, uh-huh, uh-huh."

"You Americans have weird ways of showing your superiority."

She held out her hand. "In a show of good sportsmanship?"

He took hers but didn't shake it. Instead, he held it gently in his and absently stroked the top of her hand with his thumb. "I've never enjoyed losing more." He released her hand and put the game away. "Care for a walk?"

Eliza glanced out the window. Rain trickled down the glass.

"I hear taking a turn about a room is refreshing." Aunt Iris piped up from her chair, her knitting needles never ceasing. With an almost imperceptible wink, she pursed her wrinkled pink lips and wiggled her eyebrows. "I know young lovers need some space."

Lovers? Not looking at Heath, who seemed to be struggling with a sudden malady of the throat, Eliza turned on her heel. "Are you coming?" She left the room and walked briskly down the hall toward the picture gallery.

He trotted to catch up with her. "I love little old ladies. They're the same everywhere."

"Sooo." She extended the word for as long as possible. "Have you had time to consider my crazy idea that Nancy could be behind it all?"

"Would your aunt kill to keep her embezzlement a secret?"

"Look around you. This is her domain. She sees it as hers. I think she'd kill for it. And the rest of the staff wants out but is too terrified to say anything. I get the impression that Theodore is the watchdog." Eliza pulled him along down the gallery, toward the back steps. "After we dress shopped yesterday, Joy and I saw Greta deposit quite the load of cash in the bank."

"Do you know how much?"

"Nope, but at this time, the staff should be busy with work and not in their quarters. Hopefully."

They headed for the back staircase, pausing occasionally to listen. After three flights of stairs, Heath pushed open the door, and they crept into the beige staff quarters separated into different sections for male and female staff. Once housing a small army of servants, the below-stairs arrangements succumbed to the modern need for economy and technology, turning most of the rooms into yawning, empty caverns.

Eliza shivered at the echoing quiet. Secrets would not last long down there. Thin walls and horrible acoustics made even the slightest of whispers dangerously loud. And secrets did not make friends. She stored that tidbit of information in her basket of clues and opened one of the bedroom doors. *Jackpot.* Eliza sifted through the odds and ends on top of the simple dresser while Heath checked under the bed.

"Nothing." Heath dusted off his pants and stood by her side. "Got anything?"

Eliza grunted and rifled through Greta's socks. Any guilt she felt dissolved at the thought that the very people who were supposed to help Pemberley run were possibly stealing from it, burying it in an early grave. They deserved no reprieve from her nosiness.

She touched flimsy paper. It was the bank receipt.

"Ten thousand pounds," Heath read over her shoulder and whistled.

"Tell me"—Eliza snapped a picture of the receipt—"where would she get a stash of cash like that? And why on earth would she keep it? If I were her, I would have tossed it in the first garbage can I came across in town."

"Not from her Pemberley-estate paycheck." Heath ran his finger over the money amount on the receipt. "She's obviously keeping it for a reason. Blackmail?"

"Just when I think I have something figured out, loose clues like this get tossed in the mix." She slipped the paper under the socks and put everything back in its place. "Let's blow this popsicle stand."

Five minutes later, they entered the library, hand in hand.

"Did you enjoy your walk?" Aunt Iris asked, her needles still knitting.

"Very refreshing." Heath sauntered over to the bookshelves, and his fingers skimmed the spines.

Something niggled at the back of Eliza's mind. Something about books, something Garrison had said.

"I don't know about you two, but I'm ready for some tea." Aunt Iris eyed them. "Behave?"

"On my honor." Heath walked Iris to the library door and bent over the old woman's hand. His fingers were crossed behind his back.

The door shut after her aunt, then Heath sauntered over to Eliza. Her heart hammered in her chest. He leaned against a row of bookshelves.

"There's something I've been wanting to do for quite a while." His finger traveled down her neck and loop-de-looped along her collarbone.

Eliza wanted to speak, to say something witty and sassy, but with his finger swirling over her skin, she had lost the ability to speak. Or think.

"Got any guesses?"

"I'm more of a visual learner." Eliza held her breath as Heath leaned closer, his lips only a kiss away.

Finally. His lips intertwined with hers. Her insides melted, and her heart fluttered. His hands caressed her hair, his fingertips dancing along the nape of her neck. He seemed to taste her, to explore every part of her lips, her tongue. She forgot how to breathe.

Breaking the kiss, he rested his forehead against hers, his hand cupping the back of her neck. His lips curved into a smile as he descended again. That time, his lips just brushed hers, skimming the surface. "My dear Eliza, that was the third happiest surprise," he murmured against her lips and kissed her once more. "And to keep the record straight, this English boy bloody does know when and, might I add, how to kiss a girl."

Eliza licked her lips, wanting more. "Well, it did match my expectations, but a girl needs to be sure, so why don't you—?" Like a gear locking into place, Garrison's earlier odd statement of expectations, while he hid in the bushes, clicked.

No. It can't be. Eliza spun out of Heath's embrace and hunted for a specific book, her least favorite book: *Great Expectations.* She shuddered at the thought of having to teach it again the coming school year. All things English were inherently awesome, except for Charles Dickens. Feeling blasphemous, she apologized to the long-dead author and snatched the slim red book beside it. When she opened it, her heart skipped a beat. Staring at the numbers marching neatly along columns and rows, Eliza hissed, "Heath." She nudged his shoulder. "Look."

"Is this what I think it is?"

"We won't know until we access the actual estate accounts. Could be the cooked books."

"You are magnificent."

"Sadly, I can't take the credit for this one. Garrison gave me the clue."

"Garrison? When did you see him?"

Eliza filled Heath in on the impromptu picnic and vanishing trick.

"We should probably give this information to Wentworth." His fingers caressed a piece of hair behind her ear.

"Probably." Still clutching the account book to her chest, she leaned into his caress. "Perhaps we could—"

When Heath's phone rang, Eliza groaned. He glanced at the screen. "I've got to take this. This might take a while. I'll find you." He kissed the tip of her nose.

As soon as he left the library, she tucked the book under her arm, whipped out her phone, and dashed off a quick text to Belle: *Oh. My. Gosh! Guess who just kissed me? Like bloody awesomely kissed me!* After inserting a crazy-faced emoji and a few exclamation marks, Eliza ran her finger down the leather ledger. If that was where Garrison had hidden it, and Nancy hadn't found it yet, the book was safe in its hiding spot, at least for the time being, until she could tell Wentworth all about it. The leather-bound books reminded her of Elizabeth Darcy's journals her uncle had given her days ago.

Alone for the first time since then and feeling romantic following her kiss with Heath, she yearned to dive into Elizabeth Darcy's journals, to connect with a woman who, by family lore, experienced a little romance herself. Eliza hightailed it to her uncle's study and grabbed Elizabeth Darcy's journals.

"What are you doing in here?" Nancy's voice cut through Eliza's plans and happiness. "Fitz's study is off limits to"—she gave Eliza the once-over—"guests."

"I was just... Uncle Fitzwilliam told me I could come in here whenever I wanted." She shoved the journals behind her back.

"Really? Well." Nancy tilted her head. Eliza hugged the journals closer to her back. "Dinner is served, Eliza. Won't you join me?"

"Yeah. I'll be right there. I just need to go to my room for a sec. I won't be long."

Nancy's lips failed to smile, taking on the shape of a pained grimace. "Yes, we wouldn't want to miss your presence, would we? Everyone is just keen to know all about you. Tell me, does your father talk much about us?"

Us? "No. Something about bad memories. Or was it a certain horrible person? Didn't pay attention. In one ear, out the other, and all that. I did text him, though, about why he fled the country. I'm sure I'll get an answer soon. Should I find you and let you know what he says? Better yet, would you like his phone number, and you can ask him yourself?"

Nancy's smile communicated not the fear Eliza had expected but a slyness that sent shivers down Eliza's spine. "Remember, my *dear* niece, the old saying 'curiosity killed the cat'? You would be wise to remember that you are not in charge here. Not ever." She spun on her stiletto heels and clicked out of the room.

"Well"—she pressed her namesake's journals to her chest—"that went well."

Nancy wasn't as stupid as Eliza hoped, and Eliza's gut told her the journals were no longer safe in her uncle's study. She would have to hide them. *But where?* She had no knowledge of any awesome hidey-holes except for the tunnel. Besides, she wanted them close at hand.

She took mental measurements of the journals. They weren't that large and were smaller than most books. *Holy... Eliza Jane Darcy, you are flippin' brilliant.* She grabbed a penknife off her uncle's desk, and making sure the coast was clear, she took the steps two at a time and then locked herself in her room. She wrestled the book on English colloquialisms and slang out of her carry-on, and praying to the book gods not to zap her with a bolt of lightning, she took the knife to the book's innards and gutted it. Finished with the job, she stared at the limp book drooping in her hands. *Great, just great. I'm a book murderer.* Stuffing that realization to the back of her mind—*I'll probably dream of books coming back from the dead and sucking me alive into their pages*—Eliza nestled her predecessor's precious journals into the carcass of the other book.

"Don't worry. Your service was not in vain, I promise. No one will think to look in you for anything important." She patted the book's front cover and placed it on a shelf, the spine pointing outward, next to a book on native English birds.

After secreting away Elizabeth's journals in her room, Eliza endured an entire evening of tedious card playing, broken up occasionally by Great-Aunt Iris accusing Margery of cheating at backgammon and offering to fight her in a duel in the rose garden. After the third challenge, Uncle Fitzwilliam escorted Great-Aunt Iris to her bedroom. After that, Eliza and Heath evaded the horde of relations by hiding in the rose garden and stealing a kiss or two or ten.

It was eleven before Eliza stumbled to her room, exhausted. After retrieving the hidden journals, she tucked herself on the chaise in her room, opened one of the books, and lost herself in a world different from her own. Bickering sisters, social visits, and yearnings to be free from the stays of society filled the first few pages in flowing cursive. Eliza jerked to attention at the first mention of Fitzwilliam Darcy: *I cannot fathom the depths of Mr. Darcy's pride and his obvious contempt of others. I overheard him, not that I was eavesdropping, mind you, say that I was only tolerable and that he would not dance with me. Insufferable man. I shall never speak to him again. 'Tis a pity, however, that one so handsome must be so prideful.*

Eliza's skin tingled. That was where it all began, at a simple ball. And just like Cinderella, it would all end in a palace like that. Knowing that someone threatened that legacy, her legacy, Eliza hid the journals once again and prepared for a night of snooping.

Chapter Eleven
Things Go Bump in the Night

*I do not know how I can write without trembling. A little while ago, a
terrible noise roused Darcy and me from our bed, only to find poor
Higgins bloodied and bruised. Darcy sent me upstairs under protection
from two of our footmen. I am not sure what to think, but I do know
this, I shall cling to Darcy for the rest of the night.*
—Lizzy Bennet Darcy
Pemberley 1811

Eliza waited for silence to descend upon Pemberley. Her only
partner in crime, Caesar, sat by her head, occasionally licking
her forehead.

"Knock it off. I have no idea where your tongue has been." But
Caesar's warm breath gave evidence of a fish dinner earlier. Tuna.
"Yeesh." She nudged the cat away and rolled out of bed. "Time for
some real sleuthing," she whispered to Caesar.

In the darkness, she kicked around for her flip-flops but decided
against them. Barefooted and clad in black yoga pants and a black
turtleneck she'd stolen from Joy, she snuck out of her room. No
Heath. Refusing to feel abandoned, she continued down the hallway,
her bare feet whispering against the carpet. The darkness and silence
surrounding her heightened her senses. Something furry touched her
foot. Squelching a yelp, she twisted around and met Caesar's slitted
green gaze.

"That's it. You're on the next plane home," she hissed.

He blinked and licked himself.

Growling, she ventured on, sans cat, and tiptoed down the steps. Creak. She held her breath, her ears straining to hear the slightest sound. When no alarms or gongs or shouts awakened the house, she scurried down the rest of the stairs and came to a halt at the bottom. Risking some light, she flicked the flashlight icon on her phone and shined the beam of light around the deserted foyer.

Eliza swallowed a scream. Tash slumped against the far wall, blood trickling from his temple and pooling on his white undershirt. "Oh my gosh." She knelt beside the butler, his eyes flicking open at her touch. "Tash, can you hear me?"

"Ah, Miss Eliza to the rescue," he rasped in a weak voice.

Finding nothing else, she whipped off one of Tash's socks and pressed it to the gaping cut.

"I am sorry you must see me in such a state."

"Shh. I've seen an undershirt and boxers before."

The old Tash might have quirked an eyebrow, but the Tash on the floor didn't flinch.

"I need to find help. Stay here." She pressed his bloodied hand over the sock and took the steps two at a time.

"Uncle?" She tapped lightly on his and Nancy's bedroom door. "Uncle?" She rapped a little louder.

A creak and a squeak and the door opened a crack. "Eliza?" Uncle Fitzwilliam's hair looked as if he'd slept with ducks.

"It's Tash. He's hurt. Come quick. The foyer."

"Give me a moment. I'll call the ambulance."

Eliza sprinted to Tash. His pale skin had grown porcelain. "Tash, Uncle is coming."

Only his eyelashes fluttered in response. His hand still held the bloody sock but had fallen to the floor, palm open. She stole the sock and pressed it against the wound.

A hand touched her shoulder. "Ambulance is on its way."

For a second, she rested against her uncle, his strength seeping into her. "Will he be okay?"

He peeked under the sock. "The wound appears to have stopped bleeding. I'm sure he's in shock. There should be some blankets in the drawing room. Grab one."

After retrieving a blanket, she laid it over Tash. "How could this happen? Did he fall down the stairs?"

Her uncle didn't respond, his gaze resting on an object several feet away. She crawled to it and poked it with her finger. It rolled awkwardly and clanged against a large bronze floral container, leaving a dotted trail of blood in its wake.

"I don't believe he fell." Her uncle's voice hummed with rage.

A flicker of fear sparked inside her. She didn't want to be a sleuth anymore. She wanted to be home, and frankly, she wanted her mother. Tash groaned.

She laid her hand upon his stubbled cheek. "It's going to be okay." Sirens wailed in the distance. "See, the cavalry is coming." She tucked the blanket closely around his shoulders and held his hand.

After what seemed like hours but took only seconds, the paramedics and police arrived. Uncle Fitzwilliam answered their questions, all the while tucking Eliza's hand through his arm. Question after question buzzed in her head, none of them making sense, none of them more important than the man strapped to the gurney. Wheels squeaked as they rolled Tash out the door and into the back of the ambulance.

On the front portico step, Eliza leaned on her uncle as they watched the lights fade into the black of night.

"I'm scared," she whispered.

He said nothing, just brought her closer to his side and kissed the top of her head.

"I'm surprised the commotion didn't wake anybody."

A slight chuckle rumbled through his chest. "This old house has the talent for hiding secrets." His arm tightened around her. "Eliza, I want you to go home."

She drew away from him, narrowing her gaze. "What? Why?"

"I don't want anything to happen to you."

At the thought of abandoning everyone she had come to care for, to love, she erased the idea of running home to her mother. "No." She latched on to his arm. "Please, I don't want to go home."

He cupped her cheek in his burly hand. "I would never forgive myself if something happened to you."

"But nothing will." She forced a smile. "I promise. And besides, I can be stubborn, and I'd make a scene at the train station, and someone would think you were kidnapping me, and terminal securi—"

"Enough." Her uncle chuckled. "You are your father's daughter."

"Uncle"—she eased away—"did my father ever write you after he, well, you know?"

"No, I always thought he would. We had been close growing up, best of friends, worst of enemies. He was the one to always apologize first." He puffed out his cheeks, his muttonchop whiskers quivering. "But I suspect some things aren't meant to be forgiven."

"Don't say that. What could you have possibly done to deserve such—"

"I told him I hated him and I never wanted to see him again." He pile-drove his hands into his thighs. "I just never expected him to take them to heart. I didn't mean them, hadn't meant them. The heat of the moment. What he said about my wife." He dug the heels of his hands into his eyes and rubbed. "If I'd known they'd make him disappear... but it's too late now." He blinked. "Sorry about that. You don't need me rambling on. Especially with Tash." He fisted her fingers. "If I ever find the person who did this to him, I'll—I can't lose someone else I care about. And I certainly don't want to lose you. Are you sure you won't go home?"

Eliza pressed a kiss to his forehead. "I'm sure."

The front door yawned open, the foyer's illumination backlighting Nancy, who managed to look regal even at such an ungodly hour. "Fitz, dear, I'm afraid you are needed." She barely spared Eliza a look.

She hadn't flown across the Atlantic Ocean for that moment of truth to pass. Eliza grasped his hand. "Did you never write to my dad?"

"Several times."

"And no response?"

"None."

"But that doesn't make sense. That doesn't sound like my father." Eliza shook her head and followed her uncle into the house, still buzzing with police.

Nancy stopped her just short of the door, and said, her voice as sharp as a blade, "Please do not mention your father in this house again. It brings up too many painful memories."

Eliza whirled and met Nancy's gaze. "Painful? For whom?"

"Your uncle."

"He seemed pretty willing to talk about my dad." Eliza bent closer, her voice a hiss. "And I'm sorry, but I *will* talk about my father. And I will get to the bottom of their estrangement whether you like it or not."

Eliza brushed past Nancy and into the foyer, where an audience had gathered. Heath, Joy, and several other relatives huddled on the steps. Eliza curled into Heath's waiting arms.

"What did Nancy have to say? Looks like she's been sucking on lemons."

Joy yawned. "That's her normal look. Too much Botox."

Eliza hid a laugh in Heath's chest.

"Ah, Fitzwilliam, are you trying to give us more business?" Wentworth stormed through the door, his voice booming above the hubbub of police work and gossiping relations.

Fitzwilliam slid a glance at the detective chief inspector. "I thought promptness was part of the job, Finn."

"Ladies and gentlemen, please go back to your beds," Wentworth directed.

No one argued. Eliza took a step.

"Except for you, Miss Darcy. Stay."

She bristled under the command. Joy whispered, "Want me to stay? I can hide out behind one of Nancy's hideous flower arrangements."

"Leave, Miss Bingley. And you, too, Mr. Tilney, if you please!" barked Wentworth.

Joy squeezed Eliza's hand. "I'm good at hiding. I could rescue you from you-know-who."

Heath kissed the top of Eliza's head. "I'll make sure Joy stays hidden and doesn't out herself with a misplaced squeak."

"I'll be fine. He looks as if he's in a fine mood."

"I will not repeat myself again." Police boots clicked on the tile.

"Tell me everything in the morning," Joy whispered before scurrying after Heath.

Eliza descended to the landing. "Yes, Detec—"

"Wentworth, remember? And how is it every time we meet, death and destruction surround you?"

She clenched her teeth, and her heart knocked against her ribs. "I could say the same about—"

Uncle Fitzwilliam stayed her with a hand. "Wentworth, you can't possibly be accusing my niece of all of this?"

"Of course not. How preposterous. I just find it curious that since her arrival, you've had one murder, two missing people, and now a banged-up butler."

"Finish up, Wentworth. I'm taking Eliza back to her room."

"I still have questions for her."

Fitzwilliam pinned him with a gaze. "Your questions can wait until morning." He put an arm around Eliza. "Now, if you'll excuse us."

Eliza shivered. "I can answer his questions. It's the least I can do."

"I'll meet you in the drawing room, Miss Darcy." Wentworth dismissed her.

"Do you need me?" Uncle Fitzwilliam asked.

"He won't eat me alive. He seems more bark than bite."

A small smile came from her uncle's lips. "I'll check on Tash." He bowed over her hand and squeezed it. "Don't be afraid to bite back."

Bolstered by his words, she bypassed constables in the foyer and settled onto a chaise lounge in the drawing room. A single lamp glowed with light. *Weird.* She hadn't noticed it when she'd nabbed the blanket, but it had been on. *Who turned it on?* The staff, when they did stay through the night, kept below stairs, in the servants' quarters.

Wentworth's appearance stilled her thoughts. "Tell me, Miss Darcy, why were you out and about at one in the morning?" He eyed her black yoga pants and turtleneck.

He probably wouldn't believe her need for ice cream. His keen gaze kept her lie in check. "I couldn't sleep."

"You got out of bed and dressed to what? Wander the halls?"

"How do you know I don't sleep in these? These old bedrooms are drafty."

He cocked his head. "Do you know how long I've been on the force?"

Judging by his weathered face and salt-and-pepper hair, she assumed one hundred years. "No more than five years, I'd say."

"No, but long enough to know when I'm being lied to."

"Could Tash's attack be related to Piers's murder and the two missing men, Garrison and Jonas?"

He blinked, his eyebrows quirking. "You never answered my question."

"You didn't answer mine."

His lips twitched. "Fair enough. I think it's all related. Your turn."

"I was on a mission to snoop."

That time, he smiled. "Care to elaborate on said snooping?"

"Not really." She flicked a look at the lit lamp. "Just some wild theories that are pretty stupid."

"Might I remind you not to—"

"Get involved in police procedure. Yes, you've told me that. There's nothing wrong with a little poking around."

"I'm thinking a little poking didn't go so well for Jonas."

"What? Did you find out what happened to him?"

"No, and unless you want me to call your parents and tell them the exact same things I've had to tell Jonas's, keep your nose out of it." He snapped his book shut. And reopened it. "Did you see anyone when you came down the stairs?"

"No. Well, except for Tash, but he was already on the floor. The wound was bleeding a lot. It must have been recent."

"Did you notice anything else? Anything odd or out of place? Was the door shut or open?"

"I only noticed Tash, to be honest. It was only after my uncle noticed the candlestick that I saw it. I'm afraid I nicked it with my finger. It rolled."

"Thank you. Knowing that, I'll delay putting your face on the most-wanted posters after we dust for prints." His pencil paused. "And the door? Was it open or shut, locked or unlocked?"

She closed her eyes. She saw Tash lying there, the blood, the sock, her uncle, and the paramedics and police. "Neither my uncle nor I had to unlock the door to let the emergency people in. It must have been unlocked. Does that mean Tash let—"

"Does any of the staff live in-house?"

"Um, I'm not sure. That would be a question for Tash..." She swallowed and continued. "My aunt could answer those questions. Should I go get her?"

"Sit." He motioned with his notebook. "I can double-check these later. Just answer the question."

"I don't think so. I mean, sometimes they do, mostly when a lot of people are here. Like now. Tash does live in the house, though." She pictured Tash in his state of undress. The poor man would never look her in the face again. "He's an immaculate dresser. He looks more regal than my uncle sometimes. He'd never walk around the house in just his underwear. Unless—"

"Thank you, Miss Darcy. That will be all for now."

The lamp. The slight clue nagged at the back of her mind.

"Are you okay? You look pale." His brusque voice softened.

"The lamp."

His gaze flitted to the lamp. "What about the lamp?"

"It was on when I came and got a blanket, but I didn't realize it because I was worried about Tash, but how could I have found a blanket in a strange room in the dark without a light? But it must have been on before. Tash would never go into the drawing room in his boxers to turn on a random lamp to investigate the foyer."

"You think he came to investigate. What if he was snooping, like you?"

"He must have heard something, come to see what was going on—"

"In his pants?"

"He was wearing boxers—never mind." She scrubbed her hand over her face before digging her palms into her eyes. "You can ask him, though. He'll be okay?"

"I'll ask him." He stood and offered his hand. "I believe you need to be off to Bedfordshire."

"To where?"

"Bed. You look all in."

Eliza moved to click the lamp off.

"Leave it. I'll have my men dust for prints."

Eliza climbed the steps to the tune of muted police efficiency. Her bed did beckon her, but she wouldn't be able to sleep, anyway. Exhaustion haunted her steps on her way to her room, but she had one more job to complete before hitting the hay. She voiced a text into her phone: *Hey, Dad, hope Hawaii is still treating you well. Quick question. Did you ever write Uncle? If not, I think you should. Tell Mom hi from me. Things are going well here.* She blushed at the lie and dictated another text to Belle: *So, England isn't as peaceful as I thought. I wish you were here. How's my apartment? Does it miss me?*

On her way to her room, she took a detour and ended up at Heath's door. Her hand fisted and unfisted then made the decision for her.

Within seconds, Heath answered the door, his hair mussed, evidence of his fingers playing through it. It was ridiculous, of course, to be jealous of his fingers, but there it was. He leaned his boxers-and-white-T-shirt-clad body against the doorframe.

"How'd it go?" He tucked a stray stand of her hair behind her ear.

"You'll bail me out of jail when DCI Stick-Up-His-Butt arrests me for being a thorn in his side?" She snuggled into his chest.

"For a price."

She swatted him. "I thought you'd do pro bono work." A sigh escaped. "I, uh, can I stay here for a while?"

"Thought you'd never ask." He led her to the chaise lounge in his room. "Here." He settled her on his lap and wrapped a blanket around them, his arms holding her tight.

She rested her head over his heart, her own relaxing to the beat of his. "I don't think I can do this," she whispered.

"Do what?"

She hissed a pained laugh. "Be a sleuth. Make a difference. I don't know. I came over to solve the mystery of my dad's estrangement from the rest of the Darcy family. I never thought I'd get caught up in murder. And now Tash." She fiddled with the collar on Heath's undershirt.

He nuzzled her hair with his cheek. "Then let's solve the original mystery first. You and me."

"Can't forget Joy and Aunt Iris."

"Even if we wanted to." He chuckled.

She popped up and smooshed his cheeks in her palms. "You're serious? You'll help me?"

His gaze heated. "I'm afraid, Eliza Darcy, that I've come to the fourth happiest surprise."

"And what's that?"

"You could ask me to do anything"—his gaze followed her tongue as she licked her lips—"and I'd have no choice but to say yes. You quite intoxicate me."

Eliza didn't wait for permission but greedily stole a kiss. Blindly tracing his freckles with her fingertips, she dove in with wild abandon. His day-old stubble, rough on her skin, only drove her closer to the brink of insanity. He tasted of spearmint and freedom and—

He broke the kiss and rested his forehead to hers. "Bloody hell, woman." His heart thundered under her hand. "Come here." Snuggling her into his lap, he rested his cheek on the top of her head and regaled her with stories of his adventures of digs and rare archaeological finds. She could never remember a time when she'd felt more at home, more safe. Even with death and violence clinging to the walls of Pemberley, she fell asleep knowing Heath would keep her safe.

Chapter Twelve
Secrets Don't Make Friends or Sense

I have had pains all day. The doctor claims it is the stress of recent events and has punished me with bed rest. I find this prison sentence tedious. I want to walk amongst the flowers and along the stream. I cannot even see them from my bed. I think I'll have this bed ordered to the window.
—*Lizzy Bennet Darcy*
Pemberley 1811

Eliza woke in Heath's arms. No doubt they would both be sore, but she'd never slept better, even curled up on a chaise lounge. Sunlight crawled across Heath's face, illuminating each freckle, each facial hair. His long eyelashes twitched in sleep. Careful not to wake him, she sidled out of his arms and tiptoed from his room. After a much-needed shower, she threw on baggy sweatpants and a sweatshirt she'd snuck in her suitcase behind the back of a watchful Belle. As if on cue, her phone dinged. Two messages. Eliza smiled at Belle's text: *Apartment weeps for you daily. You're not trying to find trouble, are you? I knew those mystery novels would go straight to your head. How's airplane guy? Miss you!*

Her father's return text killed her smile. She ran outside and found a secluded spot in the rose garden and called her father, not caring if she woke him.

"Explain your text," Eliza blurted as soon as she heard her father's greeting.

"Hello to you, too, Eliza."

"Dad. Please. You wrote letters to Uncle Fitzwilliam?"

Her father cursed.

Eliza started. Her father never swore.

"I thought I told you to stay out of this. You are only dredging up skeletons." Her father's voice was laced with anger.

"But understanding the past can fix the futu—"

"No! For God's sake, leave this all alone. Please."

"But if you wrote letters, why didn't Uncle get back to you? He wants to reconnect. Just call him. It can't be that bad."

"Eliza, I don't need a sermon from you." His voice stung through the phone. "Sorry. Look, after Nancy..."

"What?" Eliza's knuckles whitened around her phone. "What about Nancy?"

"No. I said too much. Leave it."

"But—"

"Eliza Jane Darcy."

Eliza held the phone away from her ear. Words like "airplane ticket" and "England" were muttered through the connection.

Her name came through loud and clear, though, and she slammed the phone to her ear and winced. "Yes?"

"Did you hear anything I just said?"

"Yeah. You love me and trust me and want nothing more than for me to enjoy myself."

"Eliza?" Her father's desperate voice made even her breathing still. "Please, you have no idea what you will uncover if you keep digging. Just leave Nancy alone."

Eliza's persistence faltered, and after saying goodbye to her father, without promising anything, she played her fingers over a soft rose petal. Her father seemed truly upset about something, and it all hinged on Nancy. She had to find out what the mistress of Pemberley knew then squash it or burn it or whatever it so her father and uncle could reunite.

Eliza's mind hummed with plans. All of which came to a halt when she saw none other than Nancy snipping roses just yards away from her hiding spot.

"I like to spend time with my roses on Sunday morning." Nancy waved the garden shears back and forth like a clock pendulum. "I find deadheading the flowers a religious experience. Don't you think?" She snipped off a dead rosebud, her eyes never leaving Eliza's. "One must rid their life of useless things."

Eliza couldn't take her eyes off the shears and couldn't move, staying rooted to her spot as Nancy approached, the shears pointing at Eliza's heart.

"I've always believed that about humans too. When someone stops being useful, well..." She snipped the shears, slicing through thin air and Eliza's bravery and wit. "Nothing to say? You disappoint me." Another step closer and the point of the shears would press against Eliza's left breast. "Your usefulness will end the moment I sense you have breathed a word of this to your uncle. Are we clear?"

Eliza clung to her last frayed strand of bravery. "My father knows—"

"Exactly why you should stop snooping around. It would be such a pity to ruin your father's perfect life. And with what I have?" Nancy's hands, one still clutching the garden shears, mimicked an exploding bomb.

"What—"

A car door slammed, and Eliza peeked over the rosebushes, squinting against the rising sun. Her uncle's shoulders stooped as he trudged to the house. She didn't think he'd ever stooped or trudged in his entire life.

Nancy grabbed her arm. "Remember. Not. A. Word."

Eliza tore from her aunt's grasp and sprinted from the rose garden. She shuttered the new fear from her eyes. *Pretend everything is normal. Like your bat-crap crazy aunt didn't just admit to having dirt on your dad.*

"Uncle," she panted, latching on to his arm. "How's Tash?"

"He's doing well. Weak but stable."

"When will they release him?"

"I'm not sure. He took a nasty thump."

"Did he say anything?"

"No. As industrious as Tash is, even he has complications talking while resting." He peered at her. "Should I assume you are not taking Wentworth's advice?"

"What advice?"

"Eliza." His tone so matched her father's that, in a rush of affection, she hugged her uncle and dashed off into the house.

She had some snooping to do. And that time, her conscience didn't even blink. When someone as nasty as Nancy threatened her dad, Eliza gleefully ripped off the proverbial boxing gloves. She wanted Nancy to feel every one of her knuckles.

She scampered down a flight of steps, took a sharp right, and skidded to a halt in front of Aunt Nancy's office. According to Joy, she hardly used it, preferring the conservatory, but Nancy conducted all the estate manager's business from that room. Eliza turned the knob. Locked. *Dammit!* She jiggled the knob again and hissed another swear word. If she were in a movie, she would whip out a bobby pin and pick the stupid lock, but—

"I told you I'd take care of it." Poppy's voice echoed from the stairs.

Eliza twisted around, spotted a curtained alcove, and slipped behind it just as Poppy rounded the corner. With a glance to her left and right, Poppy pulled out a set of keys and unlocked Nancy's lair.

Eliza's mouth watered at the new development. Poppy shouldn't have a set of keys to Nancy's office. Her aunt didn't even know the maid well enough to remember her name, much less give her the keys to the kingdom. But it seemed Poppy had a key to all the rooms, including Garrison's. And Eliza's.

When Theodore rounded the corner and stopped at the open door, Eliza stuck her head behind the curtain.

"Hurry up. If Nancy finds you in here, we'll both be doing porridge. Are you dim?"

"I need to find that bloody ledger, you bloomin' prat. Now don't bottle it."

"Shut your—" Theodore steepled his fingers and pressed them against his lips. "Never you mind. Nancy's asking for you. Well, she asked for Penny." His lips curved back in a cruel smile. "I assume she meant you."

Poppy stalked out of the room and down the hall. He left the door open and followed. Eliza pumped her fist in victory, scampered into the room, and softly closed the door behind her before locking it from the inside.

She slid out drawers and scurried her fingers among the contents, most of them innocuous and boring. Scissors, Post-it notes, mints. She moved to a filing cabinet. The drawers whispered open. Some files were tabbed with names of both indoor and outdoor staff. In them were normal employee information, but each folder contained a slip of paper with dates and abbreviations that made no sense. Others contained a slip of paper with *D.N.C.* written on it. She snapped a picture of each employee file with the *D.N.C.* abbreviation and sent the photos to Heath.

My room. Five minutes.

Heath met her at her door within four minutes and used the extra time to kiss her. "Good morning. How'd you sleep?"

She licked her lips. "It wasn't the worst night I've ever had." Ducking away from his revenge kiss, she pressed her finger into his sternum. "No more funny business. We have work to do."

"Yes, ma'am."

"I sent you pictures of employee files with odd letters and stuff on them. Can you look into those?"

"I'll get the full lowdown on all of them." He ran his finger along the outside of her ear. "And just for the record, it was one of my best nights. Full stop."

Instead of kissing him senseless and probably never coming up for air, Eliza pecked him on the lips and scampered down the hallway. While Heath hunted long-buried clues, Eliza knew exactly where to go for firsthand information. She whipped out a text to Joy. *Quick. Get the car. We're headed to town. Grab the secret weapon.*

A return text had her swearing. *DCI W. is here. Please advise.*

Park near the back. Act natural.

Eliza crept from the house and slinked into the passenger seat of the waiting car.

"What took you so long?" Joy hissed from the driver's seat.

"We were about to leave without you," the secret weapon scolded from the back seat, her knitting needles clicking and clacking.

"Go, go, go." Eliza ignored her great-aunt and buckled up.

Joy peered over her head. "Too late. They saw us."

Sure enough, her uncle and DCI Wentworth stood several feet away, arms crossed, a smile twitching at the corners of Uncle Fitzwilliam's mouth. Eliza wasn't sure Wentworth knew how to smile.

"Good afternoon, ladies. Off on an adventure?" Wentworth leaned an arm against the top of the car.

Great-Aunt Iris popped her head out of the back window, inciting a muffled curse from the stoic man. "If you don't mind, Detective Chief Inspector, these lovely ladies were taking me shopping. See, I've run all out of this color"—she brandished the wool and shook it in his face—"and if I don't get this blanket knitted before little..." She poked Joy on the back of the head. "What's Esmie going to name her little one again? Sasquabar? Sasquatch? Sasamo? Well, some silly name like that. And with a name like that, the little one deserves a nice blanket. Don't you think?"

Eliza gave Wentworth credit for wisely staying silent. Uncle Fitzwilliam, on the other hand, had a sudden coughing fit. Joy tooted the horn, and Eliza gave a little wave out her window as the car pulled away from the house.

"I'm afraid you have all lost the plot," Aunt Iris piped from the back seat. "What am I doing, anyway, in the back of this car?"

"Don't you want to go on an adventure?" Eliza reminded her.

"Oh dear, I do love an adventure. Had I known, I would have come willingly."

Joy slanted Eliza a look. "Apparently, grabbing someone's hand and tugging them along is now kidnapping."

Aunt Iris harrumphed from the back seat. "You two wouldn't properly know how to kidnap someone. In fact, when I was your age during the war, I—"

"I'm sure you were the best Nazi kidnapper around, Aunt." Eliza swiveled in her seat and patted her great-aunt's knee.

They rode in silence except for the knitting needles clacking all the way to the hospital's parking lot. Successfully getting Great-Aunt Iris through the revolving hospital doors, they descended upon the registration desk and, having the information they needed, entered Tash's room. A bandage swirled about his forehead, giving him a swarthy look.

"You could join a band of pirates." Eliza pulled up a chair.

"Who's to say he didn't?" Aunt Iris whisked to a chair by the window.

When Tash chuckled, Eliza pierced him with a stare. "Were you?"

"Define pirate, miss."

"Don't 'miss' me. It's Eliza."

His brow furrowed, and he winced. "Sorry, still a bit sore is all. I'll be back on my feet soon."

"No. You will take the rest you need. We can answer the door ourselves for a while."

Aunt Iris sniffed.

Eliza ignored her and continued on. "Has Wentworth been by?"

"Just this morning."

"And?"

He looked at Aunt Iris and at Joy, who had yet to say a word. "I... um... well."

"Could you give me a moment with Tash, please?" Eliza grinned in gratitude when Joy herded Aunt Iris from the room.

When the door slid shut, Tash's face reddened. "Miss Eliza, I don't think this at all proper."

"I saw you in your underwear. We're beyond embarrassment. Only the best of friends see each other in their underwear."

He raised a regal brow, but his lips twitched in a grin. "I never did understand you Americans."

"Speaking of underwear, why were you in yours?"

His face turned crimson, and he tugged his blanket under his neck. "Really, Miss Eliza, I must protest. Sorry."

"What happened?"

"After making sure all the lights were off, I headed to bed around eleven, I believe." He squirmed. "A noise woke me. I ignored it at first, as old houses make noises. But I heard it again. I decided to investigate but couldn't find my robe. The noise came again but louder. I rushed out to the foyer. The noise was coming from the drawing room. They must have heard me, as the bigger of the two charged toward me. I grabbed the nearest thing, the candlestick, but he wrenched it from me, whacked me a good one, and ran off."

"What about the other person?"

"I never got a good look at either of them. Pitch-black, it was. But I'd say much slighter of build, which isn't saying much, as they were both short."

Eliza's heart pounded. She knew of only two short people in the house—Theodore and Poppy. She patted his hand. "It's okay. Maybe more will come back to you later."

"That's what Wentworth said. He doesn't know what to make of the case."

"Well, I do." She scooted her chair closer and whispered, "Your attack and the murder are related."

"But how? What did I do?"

"You were just in the wrong place at the wrong time is all." A hospital robe draped over the end of the bed grabbed her attention. "You said you couldn't find your robe?"

"That's correct. I've had that thing for nigh on a decade and always hang it over my chair. It's gone. Took legs and walked off."

"Has anything else gone missing?"

"Come to think of it, I've had a few items go missing. Mrs. Underhill, too, was complaining the other day about some household items growing legs."

Eliza played her index finger over her thumb. "Speaking of thefts—"

"Ah, still at it?" Great-Aunt Iris waddled into the room, Joy in her wake. "We refuse to be ousted from this adventure any longer. Besides, there is a man wandering the hallway with his hospital gown not tied correctly." She shivered and plopped into the chair next to Eliza. Joy rolled her eyes and leaned against the wall.

Eliza directed her question again to Tash. "You were around when my uncle married Nancy?"

"I have proudly served them for over two decades." His chin snapped up.

"They couldn't have found a better man, I'm sure." Eliza flicked to the pictures she'd taken of the files and gave her phone to Tash. "Do you remember any of these people?"

His eyes darted over the pictures as his finger swiped the screen. His face tightened. "Irene Talbot. A slip of a girl. She was axed for stealing right after they married."

"Did you know her well?"

He sniffed. "The housekeeper at the time dealt with the maids. But when I did interact with Irene, she was skittish as a church mouse. Cried when I had to scold her for dusting the drawing room when Lord Darcy was present. Imagine."

Aunt Iris tutted from her seat, and Eliza jumped in before her aunt could comment. "What had been taken?"

"A few trinkets. A couple of pieces of silver. Nothing big or overly expensive. Things people wouldn't normally notice."

"How were the thefts detected?"

"No one knows. No one came forward as the whistleblower."

"That's odd," Eliza murmured. "Who said she'd stolen the items?"

"Lady Darcy found out about it. The maid's room was searched, and when the items were found, she was fired on the spot." Tash's skin took on a translucent color.

"We've bothered you long enough, Tash. Thank you." Eliza squeezed his hand. "I hope to see you on your feet soon."

He tutted her away, but a ghost of a smile haunted his lips. "Oh, go on with you, Miss Eliza."

As she headed to Pemberley, Eliza's mind ached with questions, but at the sight of Heath sitting on an ornamental lion statue, her mind sighed in enjoyment. Finally, something she loved to think about.

He rested his forearms along Eliza's open window. "I see your journey must have been arduous."

Eliza followed his gaze to the back seat, where Great-Aunt Iris napped, her head against the backrest, mouth open.

"Poor dear," Joy cooed, "I'll help her in. You"—she winked at Eliza—"have much better things to do."

Eliza ignored the wink and hopped out. "Like what?"

Heath captured her hand in his. "Like getting lost with me in the rose garden." His voice dropped. "I have some interesting news to share."

Hand in hand, they wandered across the lawn and entered the garden through a trellis covered with purple wisteria. He let go of her hand and ushered her through the opening first, his hand on the small of her back. Once through, he slowed her step with a gentle tug and placed his hands on her shoulders. "I managed to ring several of the people on those files, or at least their family members. It seems they were all fired."

"Just like Irene."

"And just like Irene, they were fired for knocking off items. They all swore they never stole as much as a biscuit."

"But why?"

"They refused to be part of Nancy's embezzling scheme."

Eliza's brain buzzed. "So she set them up, threatened that if they told anyone, she'd turn them in to the police. Could *D.N.C.* mean did not cooperate or something like that?"

"One point for the lady." Heath blew out a breath. "They were young and dim, didn't know any better, and let her run roughshod over them. I bet Piers wanted out. Talked to the wrong person. And—"

Eliza hugged her middle and stooped in misery, remembering Nancy's open threat, the garden shears aiming for Eliza's heart.

"Eliza." Heath palmed her cheek. "What's wrong? Please, what is it?"

Before she could control them, tears burned her eyes, breaking for an escape. One succeeded. He thumbed it away, pulled her into his chest, and nestled her head under his chin.

"Tell me what's wrong."

She sniffled, an unladylike snort. "Nancy knows I know. Know about her involvement with keeping my father and uncle apart. She threatened me and said that if I squealed on her, she'd reveal something damaging about my father. At least, that's what she alluded to, and... I can only assume that pointing garden shears at my heart is an open promise of violence."

A growl rumbled in his chest, and his arms tightened around her.

Eliza bit her lip. Hard. "What am I going to do? I can't just let her win. It seems she has no problem doing whatever is necessary to keep secrets. But..." Her unfinished what-ifs floated in the air between them. With Heath near her, her aunt—not that she deserved the title—didn't seem so scary. With him, she could defeat the dragon lurking in the shadow of secrets and manipulations. She would. Eliza straightened her shoulders. "I came here to solve a mystery. I can't leave with this knowledge. I can't get back the past twenty-six years without my uncle and family, but I can guarantee that I'll have them for the next twenty-six. Nancy be damned." She pawed at the wet spot her tears had left on his crisply ironed shirt. "I'm sorry."

He clasped her hands against his beating heart. "Leave the apologizing to us Brits, who do it from the womb, I believe. You have nothing to be sorry for. Besides, I've already sworn my undying fealty to you, remember?"

The look in his eyes made her stomach twirl. "Thank you," she whispered, her emotions too loud, too boisterous for anything else. She ran her fingers over his shirt. "Your shirt has wrinkles now."

"Bloody shirt doesn't matter." His eyes narrowed as a giggle snuck out of her. "You cheeky thing, you."

"I like bringing out the inner Brit in you. You're too starched." She fingered his collar, her skin coming in contact with his warm skin.

A hedgerow over, a twig snapped. Eliza froze. When the apparition of Nancy didn't appear, blood dripping from the business end of the shears, she relaxed into Heath's chest.

A low rumble in his chest preempted The Kiss. And indeed it deserved capital letters, Eliza thought, once thinking was again possible with his lips on hers, his hands in her hair, his body backing her toward a prickly rosebush. And into it. She grunted against his lips.

"Sorry," he murmured, his head coming up for air.

"Don't apologize."

"Sorry."

She kissed his cheeky grin, then gravity took over, and she toppled fully into the bushes, thorns tearing at her skin and ripping her favorite pair of leggings. "Ouch." She struggled away from the bush, rubbing her backside.

"Are you all right?"

"Who knew kissing you would be dangerous?"

"The danger hasn't even started yet."

Eliza rolled her eyes. "Time to assemble the team for some tunnel time."

"What for?"

"Think about it." Eliza pulled him along, out of the rose maze and into the green expanse of Pemberley lawn. "The murder weapon has not been found. If we assume that someone in the house is the killer, which really is affecting my beauty sleep—"

"I haven't noticed."

"Then we can also assume that the murder weapon is on the property."

"Wentworth's 'boys' have combed the estate, though, and haven't found it yet."

"Exactly." Eliza tapped the side of her nose. "But they don't know about the secret tunnel."

"There's a secret tunnel?" Heath's eyes glimmered like a five-year-old's on Christmas Day.

Eliza hoped that the tunnel would give them the best present ever: the murder weapon.

A car's tires crunched to a stop in the rounded driveway of the estate, and Nancy's voice cut through the rosebushes. "I'll be back in an hour."

Eliza poked her head over the bushes.

Nancy bussed Uncle Fitzwilliam on the cheek. "Please make sure the guests are happy, dear."

As soon as the car pulled from the drive, Eliza tugged on Heath's hand. "Let's go."

"Go where?"

"I think it's time I found out *Aunt* Nancy's secrets, don't you?"

"I thought we were going to look for the murder weapon."

"All in due time. First, Nancy."

Heath kissed her. Her stomach plummeted to her toes, and her heartbeat forgot how to thump properly. He pulled back with a tiny nibble on her lower lip.

Remembering how to breathe again, she whispered, "What was that all about?"

"I always wanted to know how a Cheshire cat grin tasted. Now I know." He kissed the tip of her nose. "Delicious."

"How am I supposed to think now?"

"Not my problem." He traversed the rose maze, Eliza hot on his heels. It was time to shine some light on Nancy's dark, dark secrets.

Chapter Thirteen
Cookies and Tears

There is no need to move the bed. The hole in my heart shall never heal. Oh, my heart, my babe! Darcy clung to me last night, his tears mingling with mine.
—Lizzy Bennet Darcy
Pemberley 1811

Nancy's office had been a bust, and so had the humid conservatory with enough plants to make a jungle jealous. "We have an hour." Eliza pushed open the door to her uncle and Nancy's bedroom. "So let's plan on forty-five minutes. Tops." She kept the door unlocked.

Unlike her aunt's other haunts, a homeyness, a masculinity reigned in the room. From the information she'd gathered, that was the original bedchamber and bed of Elizabeth and Fitzwilliam. Eliza traced the solid mahogany bedposts, her fingertips dipping and curving along the intricate designs etched into the surface. Even though she was looking for Nancy's secrets, Eliza couldn't help feeling guilty for snooping on such sacred family ground, but Nancy's deceptions were tearing apart Eliza's family and future. Snooping be damned.

"I'll start with the dressers." She pointed at the bed. "You can start there."

"Aye, aye, Captain."

Eliza rolled her eyes at Heath's mock salute and searched the dressers. She removed each drawer and felt along the bottom of each for secret panels. Fruitless.

"Nothing but dust." Heath grunted from a prone position, his phone's flashlight beam aimed under the bed.

Eliza eyed the curtains, a heavy blue paisley brocade, and gave them a good shake. Not even a speck of dust appeared.

Heath moved from the floor and stood on the mattress, reaching for the canopy that matched the curtains. "I'll give you one bloody good guess at what I found."

"Nothing?"

"Exactly."

Clamping her teeth on a growl of frustration, she moved on to the mementos stashed on top of her aunt's dresser. Various bottles of perfume, probably more expensive than Eliza's rent, littered the surface. Necklaces were draped across a large, ornate jewelry box instead of hanging organized inside it. She opened the box's double glass doors. More necklaces. She plucked them out and laid them in a pile. She opened the little drawers and emptied them of their baubles. She tipped the jewelry box to check for a secret compartment. Her hands stilled at a rattle. Bringing the box close to her ear, she jiggled it again. Something rattled. "Heath."

He quit fiddling with the fireplace, came to her side, and laid his hand on the nape of her neck. "Did you find something?"

She shook the jewelry box again. "I think so."

Blood pumped through her veins. Her palms beaded with sweat. Her fingers shook as she pressed and prodded at the box. *This is it.* She could sense it. She opened the glass doors again, jammed her fingers inside the empty necklace compartment, and tapped and scraped and—*click.*

She hooked her fingernail under the exposed crack and lifted the fake bottom out of the jewelry box. A folded piece of paper along with a picture lay at the bottom of a secret niche. She plucked them out. Heath took the letter and unfolded it. Yellowed with age, it bore smudges and creases from repeated openings and readings.

"Well, I'll be..."

Eliza tore her gaze from the picture quivering in her hand. "What?"

"It's a letter to Nancy." His gaze locked with hers. "From old Digory Wickham."

Eliza circled her temples with her index fingers, conjuring the visual of the Wickham family tree. The Digory branch gave fruit to four leaves: Samuel, the naughty embezzling former estate manager and father of Garrison; Margery, the nasty lobster canapés aficionado; and Gertrude and Lucy, nodding yes-women who might as well be tied at the hip.

"Why would he write a letter to Nancy?"

Heath pointed at a word smudged as if it had been stroked over and over again. "Because he's her father."

Eliza stared at the word "daughter" and scanned the letter. "Revenge," "comeuppance," and "duty to the Wickham bloodline" jumped out at her. The picture she'd been holding fluttered to the floor. She grabbed it and studied the image. A young woman who looked remarkably like Nancy stood an arm's length away from an older man, both staring unsmiling into the camera. The dreary graffiti-tattooed cement wall behind them did nothing for the ambience.

"I assume that's Nancy and Digory." Heath pointed at their faces.

"It looks like Nancy, but I have no idea what Digory looked like. We can assume it's him. And they either hated each other, or the ability to smile got lost along with the ability to show love or affection."

Heath snorted. "Probably a messed-up stew of both." He peered closer at the picture and shook his head. "This means Nancy is a bastard."

"I'd go with the other *b* word."

"We can add that to the ever-growing list of insults."

She tapped her lip and pictured the Wickham family tree again. "There's no record of her ever existing as a Wickham." Eliza paced the room, her hands clutched behind her back, her face screwed up in thought. She double-timed it back to Heath and tapped out a fast tattoo on his chest. "Oh my giddy aunt! She's Digory's secret daughter, probably through an affair. He must have groomed her for just this purpose. And when Samuel got caught, that's when Nancy's mission started. Infiltrate the castle from the inside. Digory must have known Lucy, Gertrude, and Margery were too nasty to be taken seriously." Eliza shooed away his cocked eyebrow. "It makes sense. No one knows about Nancy's and Garrison's relationship. She must have seen the butt-kissing suck-up he was and oozed her way into his psyche."

The clicking of heels echoed down the hall and permeated the door. Eliza and Heath stared at each other before rearranging the necklaces and jewelry back into some semblance of their original state. Upon closer inspection, Nancy would surely know her precious gems had been messed with, but with the picture and letter secreted away in Heath's pocket, Eliza was willing to risk her wrath. Nancy couldn't very well out them, as she would out herself and a lifetime of lies.

The doorknob twisted, and so did Eliza's stomach. Heath grabbed her hand and squeezed it as Pemberley's mistress sashayed through the door.

"What in the bloody hell are you two doing in my bedroom?" Nancy's face reddened.

Eliza attempted a sheepish look. "Uncle asked me to look for something for him."

"What exactly are you looking for?" Nancy's gaze flitted to her dresser, back to Eliza, and again to the dresser.

"His pipe."

"Pipe? He never smokes it in here." Nancy took a step closer, her heel driving into the paisley carpet. Eliza imagined that heel wanting very much to dig into the soft flesh of her neck. She swallowed.

Nancy eyed Eliza with a tilt of her head, like a dog hearing a high-pitched whistle. It should have looked ridiculous. It didn't. It was a challenge. "I trust you will give your uncle his pipe. When you find it, of course." With one last glance at the jewelry box on the dresser, Nancy pointed at the door. "Leave."

Eliza sailed through a wake of Nancy's expensive perfume, nausea churning in her gut, Heath hot on her heels.

"Oh, and Wentworth would like to see you. It would be a pity if he left knowing more than he should." Nancy played her fingers down a strand of pearls, her gaze locking on Eliza's.

Eliza maintained the stare and knew she couldn't be the first one to blink. Nancy broke first and turned her back to Eliza. "Leave."

Eliza didn't have to be asked twice. She grabbed Heath's hand and, after the bedroom door safely shut behind them, asked, "Care to join me in facing Wentworth?"

"Now what kind of sidekick would I be if I left you at your darkest hour?"

She wanted to laugh, but her joy was stifled by the sneaking suspicion that this would not be her darkest hour.

"DETECTIVE CHIEF INSPECTOR Wentworth is talking with Lord Darcy and not to be disturbed." A stout-looking constable, probably picked because he resembled a bulldog, all but put his arms out to protect the study door.

"Can you tell him Eliza Darcy wishes to speak to him?"

The bulldog-ish man remained standing at attention.

Not wanting to waste any more time with a scowling constable, Eliza huffed and turned away and gave Heath a task. "Can you go and gather Great-Aunt Iris and Joy?"

"Where are you going?"

"Securing our newfound evidence." She dashed up the steps and into her room. After emptying a plastic bag of jewelry and nabbing a safety pin, she zipped the letter and photo in the baggie and pinned it to the inside of her shirt. If Nancy wanted the evidence back, she would have to get it over Eliza's cold, dead body. Her mind blanked in panic. *Well, crap... No, Eliza Jane Darcy, suck it up. You figured out Nancy's dirty little secret. You are a rock star!*

Eliza lost count of how many times she'd repeated the rock star mantra, but eventually, she believed it enough to salivate for another mystery to be solved: finding the murder weapon. And she had a pretty good idea of where it might be. Eliza and Heath scrounged up the rest of the team and found Aunt Iris and Joy in a quiet drawing room, a tray of tea things in front of them.

Eliza plucked a teacup from her great-aunt's grip. "Aunt, we have a special mission."

"I say." Aunt Iris brushed her polyester pantsuit jacket.

Eliza rolled her eyes. "It's time for some tunnel time."

"Why didn't you say that in the first place?" Great-Aunt Iris snatched a cookie from Joy. "To the library."

"But I could use a spot of tea," Joy whined. "With maybe a nip of brandy."

"That will have to wait. Unless you don't want to be part of the official unofficial sleuthing gang." Eliza waved away Joy's protests.

"We need a snappier name than that, my dear," Aunt Iris chirped, nabbing two cookies before being towed away.

Heath chuckled but said nothing as they traversed the hallway and entered the library.

Eliza flicked her finger against the hidden switch of the bookcase, and the secret door to the tunnel sprang open. "Let's sleuth."

"This is bloody awesome." Heath's grin slipped. "Sorry, Mrs. Darcy. I mean bloomin'."

Great-Aunt Iris tutted and waved off his apology. Everyone grabbed a flashlight and crept into the tunnel. Eliza took the lead. Four beams of light swaggered in the dark as they shuffled along. Male voices seeped through the walls. Eliza paused and pressed her ear to the cold wall. "This should be the study." Eliza opened the peephole.

"What are they saying?" Joy whispered.

"Lift me up," Aunt Iris demanded.

Eliza remembered the last time her great-aunt had asked to be hoisted in midair. "Why don't I take over this time?"

With a grand harrumph, Aunt Iris moved aside. Eliza stood on tiptoe and still couldn't see clearly. "Just a second." She jogged through the tunnel, dashed through the secret door and grabbed a footstool, and lugged it back down the tunnel. "There. Easy peasy."

She stepped up and peered through the peephole. All she could see was the back of Wentworth's head. And in spite of the opened peephole, their voices, quiet and intense, were kept to a low hum. *Drat!*

Eliza jerked at the warm breath tickling her cheek. She came nose to nose with her great-aunt.

"What are they saying?" Great-Aunt Iris hissed.

"What on earth are you doing, Aunt Iris?" Eliza whispered back.

"The young man you tote around was obliging to an old lady. Unlike some people I know." This was followed by a finger to Eliza's ribs.

Eliza speared Heath with a glare. In the soft light of only one flashlight, his grin spoke volumes, as did the bulging veins in his neck and his body, shaking from the sustained squat.

"How many stone did you say you weigh again, Mrs. Darcy?"

She walloped him on the head. "A lady never tells."

"Yes, ma'am," Heath ground out between his teeth. "Do you see anything, or do you want to come down now?"

"I'll let you know when I'm good and ready to get down."

"Aunt Iris, please take pity on Heath. Besides, you can't hear anything." Eliza stepped off the chair, and Heath eased Aunt Iris to the floor and stretched out his back.

"Let's split up." Eliza pointed at Joy and Great-Aunt Iris. "You two go that way"—she pointed her beam of light behind them—"and Heath and I will forge ahead. Then, we'll all meet in the drawing room for tea and Cook's cookies."

"Biscuits" came the trio of Brits.

"But Cook's cookies has a better ring to it." Eliza took her posse's silence for agreement and grabbed Heath's hand. "Let's march."

Five minutes later, and at the tunnel's and her wits' end, she was ready to fly the white flag, pack her bags, and head back to the States, her sleuthing tail tucked firmly between her legs. They were to the end and would spill out into Elizabeth Darcy's favorite room.

"Does this tunnel have any outlets, other passages?"

Eliza flicked her beam of light around the walls. "Uncle never said, but we could look for something. A crack, some kind of irregularity in the wall."

In wide sweeping motions, they plied the wall with swaths of light.

"Blimey! Look here." Heath jiggled the light beam over a circular indent six inches in diameter in the wall, a finger-sized hole in its center.

Eliza's heart skipped. She worked her index finger into the hole and pushed. Nothing. All the moments of fear, of looking over her shoulder for an unnamed killer, converged, and with a strength she didn't know she possessed, she gave one final shove. The wall slid open, and she tumbled in and landed on something sharp.

She hissed in pain and cuddled her hand to her chest.

"You all right?" Heath knelt beside her, his flashlight illuminating a darker, danker passageway. He swore. "It appears, my dear Eliza, that you have the uncanny knack of finding trouble even when you are not looking for it."

"What now?"

He aimed his flashlight on the blood-encrusted hoe she'd landed on. "You'd make your precious Hercule Poirot proud, I'd say."

She clamped her hand over her mouth and stifled a squeak. "No, mon ami. I don't believe he ever fell on a murder weapon."

"YOU WHAT?"

Eliza veered her face away from the spraying spittle of DCI Wentworth. Flicking a drop off her eyelid, she inched backward. "I sort of fell on it."

"How do you 'sort of' fall on something?" He cut off her reply with an air karate chop and directed his team. "I want every inch of that tunnel searched and everybody gathered in the ballroom. Now!" He paced the foyer, his boots clicking on the tile. Occasionally, he eyed Eliza, but she ignored him and clung to Heath's hand.

"What put his knickers in a twist?" Heath whispered in her ear.

"Maybe it's the fact he hasn't solved this case yet."

"Excuse me, Miss Darcy? Did you say something?"

Apparently, she'd forgotten to whisper. "Nothing."

"A moment of your time, please."

Eliza eased her hand out of Heath's and followed Wentworth's clipped steps into the drawing room. The sunlight pouring through the open curtains did nothing to dispel the gloominess surrounding her.

"I told you to stay out of this case." He had yet to turn around, but she could see his shoulders quivering.

"I was staying out of it…" Her voice faltered when he spun around and speared her with a look. "Well, I had every intention of it. And then I fell on the hoe."

"You went and visited Tash on kindness only? No curiosity in the mix? No questions were asked except for the 'how are you' variety?"

She sensed the trap and felt the teeth close in on her conscience. Her mouth opened, but only a squeak emerged.

"I knew it." He blew out a breath and plopped on a settee. "Have a seat, Miss Darcy."

She sat. Silence filled the air. The awkwardness consumed her. Maybe a joke would clear the air.

Wentworth saved her from herself. "I have a strange feeling you will be a thorn in my side for the duration of your stay." He silenced her with a hand motion. "As much as it pains me to say, I think you have insider information that would prove vital to this case."

She blinked. "You mean?"

He smiled tightly. "As you Americans say, 'Can't beat 'em, join 'em.'"

Eliza snorted at his attempt at an American accent, an odd mixture of Bostonian and Southern. "Do I get a badge?"

He quirked an eyebrow. "No. You get the honor of being my eyes and ears around this estate. You are not to breathe a word of this to anyone. Especially your great-aunt."

"But she's *my* eyes and ears. My secret weapon."

He growled in reply. Eliza took it as permission to share with her spy group.

He flipped open his notebook and tapped his pen against the paper. "Catch me up."

"Be right back, actually." She scampered to the library, snatched the ledger still housed between Dickens's books, and ran back to the study. Panting, she plopped the book into his lap. "Here."

While he skimmed the pages, she regaled him with her knowledge of the hidden Garrison Wickham and the staff who were fired when they wouldn't play Nancy's little game.

He grunted and flipped through the pages some more before taking out his notebook and scratching his pen across the pages.

"Oh, and this." Eliza dug inside her shirt for the safety-pinned evidence. *Belle will be so proud to know her safety pins and little baggies were so useful.*

His eyes widened, and he tilted the letter then the picture in different directions. "Where did you get this? No—never mind. I don't want to know." He paced the room, his feet plowing into the floor.

As he wouldn't stop pacing, Eliza joined him, folding her hands behind her back. "She was bred, like an orc, to destroy from within."

Wentworth quirked an eyebrow. "I'm sure she wasn't spawned."

"Prove it."

He blew out a frustrated breath and continued pacing. "The ledger book and her dodgy connection to the Wickhams is intriguing, but—"

"But what?"

"It doesn't have anything to do with the murder."

Eliza's body flushed with heat. "Really? Listen, I might be crazy, and I really can't pinpoint one thing. It's like a puzzle, and all I have are the couple pieces that fell off the table, got shoved under the couch, and collected dust bunnies."

Wentworth settled on a brocade chaise lounge. "Brush 'em off. What do you have?"

Eliza ticked off items on her fingers. "One, she does all the hiring and firing. Two, according to Giles, the groundsmen she hires are all incompetent. Three, she is behind all the firings of maids for stealing, even though they swear they never stole anything. Four, she was hunting for something in Garrison's room the day he ran off. These"—she jabbed her finger at the photo and letter—"along with the ledger book don't paint a pretty picture."

"Those aren't motives for murder."

"Told you they were fuzzy." Eliza scrubbed at her forehead. "But think, if you were her, and you'd been sitting there for twenty-plus years, filling your evil little nest egg slowly, methodically, you wouldn't want that to go bye-bye, would you?"

"You think she'd kill to hide her embezzling? That's a stonking accusation."

"It has to be someone on the inside." Eliza chewed her bottom lip. "Someone who knows of the secret tunnel."

"Who all knows about it?"

Eliza ticked off on her fingers the people she knew who were aware of the tunnel: Uncle Fitzwilliam, Great-Aunt Iris, Joy, Heath, and herself. The idea of someone tiptoeing through the dark in secret sent a shudder skittering up her spine.

"That narrows my list."

She glared at him. "Really? You think it was one of us?"

The corner of his mouth twitched. "Your great-aunt is rather full of beans."

"It's a good thing she uses her powers for good."

"Someone else knows about the tunnel." He drilled his gaze at her. "We'll dust for prints, but with decades of prints and DNA, whatever we get will be a bunch of codswallop, really." After straightening his jacket, he asked, "Does your uncle know about Nancy?"

"I don't think so." She scrubbed her hands over her face. The odds of Nancy narcing on Eliza and Heath being in her room were slim. For once, Eliza held all the cards. All except the ace of spades, which she suspected Nancy had. Eliza just had to connect the ledger books to Nancy before Nancy got overly nasty and revealed the juicy secret she claimed to have. "Love is blind?"

"I'll give your little theory twenty-four hours. If we give Nancy enough rope, maybe she'll hang herself with it. If we can get her on embezzlement at least, she'll be doing porridge for several years."

Eliza blinked. "Porridge?"

"Jail time." He stood. "Use your charming ways and see if you can extract information from any of the staff."

"You think I'm charming?"

Another growl. "Am I going to regret my decision, Miss Darcy?"

She snapped to attention. "Yes. I mean no. Maybe?"

"Let me know what you find out as soon as you find it out." He fiddled with the tie loosened around his gray dress-shirt collar. "It's time to get to work. To the ballroom."

Seconds later, she followed him out into an empty foyer and to the ballroom, where the family—from the Darcy trunk to the farthest-reaching leaves—and servants milled around in muted curiosity. She found Heath slouched against a wall next to Joy and Great-Aunt Iris.

"Did you get a good tongue-lashing?"

"You sound a little too happy about it, Aunt Iris." Eliza kissed the woman's leathery cheeks. "No, but I did get permission to assemble a spy ring."

Joy and Heath both raised an eyebrow. Aunt Iris grinned. "Finally. In fact, since I was a little girl—"

DCI Wentworth's voice boomed across the ballroom. "A break in the case occurred this afternoon. From now until you receive further notice, no one will be allowed to leave the estate or enter it. You will be questioned separately and throughout the day. Be sure to make time for my men."

A rumble flittered through the room. "But what about the ball? It's in two days." Nancy's voice permeated the din. "We still have to get supplies, and some of us need to leave to shop."

"I am sorry for the inconvenience, Lady Darcy, but you will remember one of your staff is dead and one is missing. I believe this supplants any ball. You do agree, do you not?"

Eliza couldn't see her aunt but heard the disdain dripping from her reply. "Of course, Detective Chief Inspector."

He seemed to pin each person in the room with a gaze then stalked out, Eliza's uncle and aunt in tow. The whole room seemed to exhale when the large door clunked shut.

Mrs. Underhill, the housekeeper, clapped. "Chop-chop, everyone. You heard the detective chief inspector. Housekeeping, you will continue your duties until retrieved for interview."

"All this stress makes me hungry. Come on. Let's get something to eat." Joy grabbed Eliza's hand and dragged her from the ballroom, Heath and Aunt Iris bringing up the rear.

"Nancy seemed put out. I bet Wentworth has a few scratch marks," Aunt Iris tittered. "Well, I'm in need of a rest. If anything happens, I want to know everything." She gave the three of them a stern look, swung her bag over her shoulder, and squeaked down the hall.

"Aunt Nancy might have found the one person who won't roll over and play dead on her command." Eliza swallowed the fear clawing up her throat.

"Speak of the devil," Joy hissed in Eliza's ear.

Nancy, Theodore slumping after her like a disciplined puppy, dipped down the hallway, heading toward the conservatory.

Wordlessly, the trio followed and stationed themselves in a hidden alcove kitty-corner from the open door to Nancy's domain.

A curse word belched out of the doorway. Eliza had spent enough time snooping in Nancy's lair of choice to prefer the comforting smells of her uncle's old books and pipe smoke to the cloying humidity of her aunt's perfume and gossip. But she'd never heard so much as a peep out of her aunt's inner sanctum.

"That's a word I never thought I'd hear in a classy place like this." Heath whistled.

Eliza laid a finger over his lips, and he nipped at it. "Just a second. Wait here."

"What are you doing?" Joy whispered. "You might get eaten. Alive."

Eliza wanted to roll her eyes at the idea but couldn't convince her roiling stomach not to believe such lies. She peeked inside the conservatory and took a few steps into the glass-enclosed room. The moisture of the plants clung to her skin. Big fern leaves skittered across her arms and face as she weaved her way through the indoor forest. Maybe that was why Nancy always looked dewy. Her aunt's voice pierced through the foliage from somewhere near the back of the room.

"... not put up with any more incompetence."

"Not my fault, my lady... can't find the book," Theodore whined.

Eliza grabbed her phone and clicked on the video icon, holding the phone against her thigh to mute the recording ding. She edged closer, sticking her face between two tiger lily plants, and almost passed out from the overwhelming aroma.

"What do you mean you can't find it? Garrison was a sniveling prat." Her aunt's voice weaved in and out of the greenery. If only Eliza could get closer. As cover, she used a large garish Chinese vase overflowing with wild grasses and a stuffed pheasant. She touched the cold feathers and eyed the beady black left eye. Maybe she should have listened to Joy's advice. That poor pheasant obviously hadn't.

"Are you not in control?" Nancy's voice sliced through the pheasant's feathers. "You promised me you'd find him. Find them. I don't like people who renege on promises, Theodore."

"I do, my lady. I mean, I will. It's just that—"

"Your incompetence bothers me. If Fitz finds out, it's the end of both of us. I didn't hire you for your footman skills, you bloody idiot. Eliza knows everything. End this. End her."

Eliza gulped.

"What about Greta?" Theodore whined. "And Poppy, she's—"

"Stop that insufferable whinging. Deal with it. I pay you well enough. Move. Now."

The scuffling of feet propelled Eliza down the aisle she'd come, moving as silently as possible through the jungle, the ferns whipping at her face. She didn't bother swishing them out of the way. She fell through the door, sprinted to where her posse waited, and took refuge in Heath's embrace.

Joy put a finger to Eliza's cheek. "You're bleeding."

Stupid fern leaves. She hated the conservatory, and she was near hating Nancy. Scratch that. She was beyond hating Nancy. Eliza dabbed at the spot where she felt a stinging sensation on her left cheek. Blood. Hers. Her mind swirled with visions of Piers's dead body, the bloody cloud of water surrounding his floating corpse. Nancy knew. Eliza wilted into Heath's side. Nancy's words had been clear. Eliza fingered her cut. That would not be the only blood spilled before good vanquished the evil that was stalking Pemberley.

Chapter Fourteen
Trouble in Paradise

Mamma is here, even though I encouraged her to stay with Pappa and Mary and Kitty. So she brought them all. A house full of guests is certainly diverting, but there are moments when I must pause for the ache in my heart. Pappa caught me crying in the library. I do not remember the last time I sat in his lap and cried.
—Lizzy Bennet Darcy
Pemberley 1811

E liza needed a shower and privacy and some time with her predecessor's journals. Her footsteps traveled the same floors, the same stairs, the same gardens as Elizabeth Darcy's had. Instead of satin slippers, Eliza's flats climbed the stairs and trekked through the portrait gallery. She frowned at Elizabeth's grin. "I promise I won't let anything happen to your Pemberley." Intent on keeping that promise, Eliza rounded the corner and stuttered to a stop. Her door opened, and Poppy exited.

What the... "May I help you?"

Poppy smacked a hand over her heart. "You gave me a fright, Miss Darcy."

Eliza met Poppy's gaze with one of her own. "Did you need something?"

"No, miss. I was told you needed new linens."

"Really? This is the second time I've apparently needed new ones. Tell me, is every family member getting the VIP treatment, or is this a special service reserved only for me?" Eliza came toe to toe with Poppy. "And if I remember correctly, I specifically asked that no one be allowed in my room."

Poppy's stare never wavered. "Just following orders. I'll be sure to inform Lady Darcy of your wishes." She gave a slight bob and scampered down the hallway.

Eliza cracked opened her door and peeked in. Sure enough, a stack of clean linens sat on her bed. If she were a betting woman, she would bet all the money in her savings account that Poppy was one of Nancy's little stooges, a thief.

Eliza checked her drawers and inventoried her jewelry, some still labeled with Belle's handwriting. Nothing had been stolen or tampered with. Maybe Poppy was telling the truth. The stack of linens proved that. Eliza knew that if she worked for the likes of Nancy and had to deal with Theodore, she might be an angry bomb ready to explode. She double-checked the placement of the British slang book. It was in the exact spot she'd put it along with a strand of her hair to alert her to anyone trifling with her stuff. It worked for BBC murder mysteries and her beloved mystery authors and—she eyed the strand of hair again, ensuring it hadn't moved—apparently for her. *Success! Take that Mr. Poirot and Miss Marple.*

Needing time away from her mystery-solving adventures to rest her fevered thoughts, she grabbed the journals and found a secluded rosy nook in the middle of the garden. She felt like an interloper, invading the privacy of her predecessor, but she yearned to learn more about the woman whose name she shared. Maybe she could become more like her.

We have a guest, a Mr. Collins, and as soon as Mamma discovered that one of her five daughters, myself included, were potential brides, she forgave him the sin of inheriting the estate upon Pappa's death. He is an odious man, and I find even my love of the odd and peculiar tested to its limits. I can sense he has made me his future bride in his mind. I shall have to dispel this soon. And if Kitty and Lydia do not silence themselves on the subject of soldiers, I shall... well, I shall have to tear off a strip of my petticoat and stuff it in their mouths. Harsh, I know, but needs must.

Eliza kept reading, her bottom lip held hostage between her teeth as she journeyed through life with Elizabeth. She laughed at the recounting of Mr. Collins's horrid, pompous proposal and did a little dance when *Pappa took my side in the whole proposal debacle by informing Mamma that he would never see me if I did accept the offer.*

She closed the journal and drummed her fingers on the leather-bound cover. Her escape into the past only bolstered her whispered promise to Elizabeth's portrait. She needed to vanquish the dragon Nancy from the castle. On returning to her room to hide the journals, she skipped through the door and screamed.

Caesar's convulsing body lay on her bed, a chain of dead rose-buds tied around his neck. Next to him lay a letter.

ELIZA CUDDLED CAESAR in her arms, stroking his fur and crooning nonsense words in his twitching ear. He meowed weakly and licked her hand with his scratchy tongue. Heath snuggled Eliza to his side, his fingers stroking her hair, his lips brushing her temple.

"How could she do this to Caesar?" she whispered, the memory of the vet's office and Caesar's close call with death still too fresh in her mind for loud words. She fluffed Caesar's furry tail, thankful to see it twitching again.

"Maybe he got into the hydrangeas in the garden."

"The dead roses? It's a clear threat." Eliza dug the letter out of her back pocket and unfolded it for the thirtieth time. "No matter how many times I read this stupid thing, I still can't make sense of this."

She knew the contents. Phrases unmistakably written in her father's hand had tattooed themselves in her mind. *Undying love. Secret. If Fitz ever finds out...*

"What did my father do?"

"He fell in love with the wrong woman."

"That woman is no woman. She's a snake. A demon sent from hell to destroy—"

"Eliza. Stop." Heath massaged her temple. "We need to think. What's our next move?"

"I have no clue." Her father's betrayal of his brother left a gaping question mark in her plans. If Nancy revealed the secret, along with the paper trail leading right to Andrew Darcy, she could destroy Eliza's parents' marriage and put the final nail in the coffin of the Darcy brothers' dying relationship.

Eliza glanced out the floor-to-ceiling windows of her uncle's study, and it was dark. The quiet of her uncle's sanctuary and the stroking of Heath's fingers calmed her. Despite Nancy's malicious nature and the ace she had up her sleeve, Eliza assured herself that her aunt would still want to keep her embezzling a secret. *Right?* If she could outlast and outsmart Nancy through the minefield of secrets, Eliza knew she could win. Not that anyone won after playing in a minefield. If she could come out of everything with her life intact, she'd be—

When the study door opened, she jumped.

"Ah, and how is our tiny"—Uncle Fitzwilliam stroked Caesar's belly—"or should I say plump patient doing?"

"He's better. He'll be up to his old tricks soon." Eliza quickly folded the letter and stuffed it back into her pants pocket.

"Much to the delight of Mrs. Bankcroft, I'd say." Uncle Fitzwilliam crouched in front of Eliza. "The vet was sure it was from ingesting hydrangea petals?"

"She couldn't say what part of the plant, but the whole thing is poisonous to cats."

"And he couldn't have got into the garden himself?"

"He's afraid of the garden. Don't you remember how he attacked poor missing Jonas for rescuing him from an angry mother robin? Since then, he's stayed inside the house, stalking Mrs. Bankcroft for food." She rubbed Caesar's belly. "Someone must have given it to him."

"But who? Who here would want to hurt Caesar?" Uncle Fitzwilliam scratched Caesar between his ears. "Is there something you're not telling me, Eliza?"

There was so much she couldn't tell him. *What will he do when he finds out my father not only loved Nancy but continued to love her after she and Uncle were married?* She didn't want to meet her uncle's eyes, but his gentle hand on hers brought her eye to eye with him. "Someone wants me to stop meddling with the murder investigation." Half-truths were not lying. *Right?*

A pregnant pause. "What do you mean by 'meddling,' exactly?"

"I sort of in a roundabout way have been snooping for clues."

Her uncle's skin bleached of color. "This could have been you."

"Humans can't be killed by hydrangeas. Cats and dogs and..." She swallowed past the lump in her throat. It could have been her. Nancy clearly meant that. Which meant that Nancy was probably not only up to her eyeballs in embezzling but also elbow deep in blood as well. Nancy might not kill to keep her embezzling a secret, but she would if her hands were stained with murder.

She hopped up, sending both her uncle and Caesar to the floor. "But this is great. Don't you see?" By the stunned faces of her uncle and Heath and the glare from her cat, they clearly didn't see. "I'm close. If I were way off, the killer would maybe even enjoy watching me fall on my fake detective face. But she... uh... or he is scared. And trying to scare me off."

"Am I supposed to rejoice in this?" Her uncle picked himself off the floor and settled in a leather chair. Caesar hopped on his lap in solidarity.

"Yes." Eliza clapped her hands together and tucked them under her chin. "I could solve this case. I'm close. I can feel it."

"You are not going to solve this case."

"But I told you, I—"

"Because you are going home," her uncle finished in a tone that would have set even the queen herself on her backside.

"No."

Heath choked. Her uncle fumed. Caesar blinked.

"I'm staying here. You said yourself Pemberley is mine someday. I can't go running away at the first sign of danger. If I'm to be the future mistress of this estate, I will stay and fight for it." *Fight for my father. Fight for you.*

"You can't fight for something if you're dead."

She rounded on Heath. "I can't fight for it if I'm thousands of miles away either." She grasped her uncle's hands. "Please. Let me do this. Don't take this away from me just when I found it." In light of everything Eliza and those she loved could lose, Nancy's dark secret could not win.

The steel in his eyes softened. "You are too much like your father for your own good."

"Probably."

"Promise me you'll be safe."

"I can't."

"I know." Uncle Fitzwilliam drew her into the security of his arms. "I trust you will take precautions and not go off half-cocked. What would I do if anything happened to you?"

His last words were little more than a rumble through his chest. The only question remaining was how she would protect him from the knowledge that his brother had betrayed him and how Nancy was a conniving little—

"Now"—he released her—"I must visit Wentworth and make sure your family is behaving themselves."

"My family?"

He grinned and left the room. Caesar, choosing sides, sashayed out the door with him.

Eliza sank into the nearest chair and scrubbed her hands over her face. "Tell me I'm doing the right thing." When Heath remained silent, she dared a peek at him. His back was to her as he looked out the window, his hands in his pockets. His shoulders, rigid and square, seemed as if they carried the weight of the world. "Heath?"

His shoulders shivered when he exhaled. "Tell me, what am *I* supposed to do if anything happens to you?"

She crossed to him and touched his shoulder. He flinched. "You don't understand," she whispered to his back.

"No, you don't." He faced her and gripped her shoulders. "Do you not know how precious you are to so many people? Can you imagine the phone call your uncle would have to make to your parents if the worst did happen? It would break them all."

"But I can solve this. I can't let Nancy win. I know who did it, or at least I'm ninety-nine point nine percent sure who did it. I can't just sit back—"

"What if this takes longer than the summer? Are you going to quit your job, or just when it's convenient for you, will you leave to go back to your old life?"

"That's not fair." She swallowed against her rising tears. "I didn't even know this place was mine until a couple of days ago. I have a life, a family, a job to go back to."

"What are we doing?" He gestured between them. "I have come to..."

"Come to what?" She took a step to him.

"Care for you. Crazy, I know." He threaded his fingers through his hair. "Look, I have to go." He didn't even make a pretense of looking at his watch.

"You can't. Police orders."

"This is a big place." The door closed on him, leaving her standing alone in the gaping room, which no longer seemed comforting.

Eliza had no time to wallow in self-pity. A scream echoed through the house. Following the animal-like cries, she sprinted to the drawing room. A constable barred her entrance.

"Let her pass," DCI Wentworth's voice rumbled from within the room.

The constable stepped aside, giving Eliza access to the room.

Greta, her normally starched uniform torn and rumpled, latched her wild gaze on Eliza. "You." She pointed. "You tell them he didn't do it."

Eliza flicked a glance at Wentworth. His stoic face seemed to have grown a few fissures. "We have made an arrest, Miss Darcy." In the corner, Giles Winfield stood flanked by two constables, his hands cuffed behind his back.

Eliza knew better than to laugh. She took a tentative step toward Greta. "I don't know who did it."

"Yes, you do. You've been snooping around the house. Everybody's talking of it. You're doing more than these stupid plodders." She jerked her head in the general vicinity of DCI Wentworth.

"We are all trying to figure out who killed Piers. He must be missed—"

"He was a wanker," Greta spat. "I'm glad he's dead." She exhaled so violently Eliza wasn't sure the girl would be able to inhale again. "I did it. I killed Piers."

"Now, Miss Winfield, calm down."

Greta ignored Wentworth. "I mean it. I killed him."

"With what?"

Eliza's gentle question stopped Greta midwail. "I... well, I used a..." Her face crumbled, and a fat tear plopped down her cheek. "I don't remember," she whispered to the floor.

DCI Wentworth motioned to the constables holding Giles, and they moved toward the door. Greta snapped out of her stupor and lunged at her father, clinging to his neck. Wentworth dragged her off of him and sat her firmly on the couch. "Stay," he ordered.

"But I confessed. You have to arrest me. He's dead because of me."

Wentworth flicked his head at one of his men. In seconds, father and daughter, handcuffed and flanked by police, left the room.

Eliza heard the ragged breathing of the terrified woman echoing in her ears. "Well, that was interesting."

Wentworth spared her a glance. "What do you make of it all?"

"She thinks she honestly is responsible for Piers's death. That she did it herself? No. I don't believe that for a second."

"What about the head gardener?"

"What about him? What evidence did you find?"

He puffed out his cheeks. "The hoe, which you kindly found for us, has his fingerprints all over it. It was his hoe."

"Well." That one word hung in the air.

"There's more. States he lost the key to the shed where his hoe was kept but never informed anyone. Claimed he didn't want to seem barmy to his boss." He circled his pointer finger at his temple. "And he couldn't find his hoe but didn't think anything of it. Thought one of the groundsmen had nicked it."

"All plausible. But would he know about the tunnel?"

"His were the only fingerprints on the murder weapon." He puffed out his cheeks. "Nothing he says can be proved. Anyone can claim to misplace something. Anyone can claim he didn't want to seem crazy, so he kept his mouth shut. I don't like it."

"You don't think he did it either, do you?"

"I don't bloody know. This whole case has been at sixes and sevens from the start. He has the means, certainly had opportunity, and after confessing that he knew about Piers's sexual assault on Greta, has the motive." He slumped in a chair. His modern-looking suit seemed oddly out of place against the magenta velvet brocade. He scratched at a fresh batch of facial whiskers, their whiteness stark against his dark skin. "Any father would."

"Do you have kids?"

For the first time, he smiled. Its allure made her see why there must be a Mrs. Wentworth somewhere. "Two boys, twins, and a girl. Oldest two just graduated from uni. My princess is in her last year of secondary. Me and the missus will have to come up with something other than the kids to talk about soon."

"What does your wife do?"

"Besides put up with me?"

"Besides that."

"She's a social worker. Between the both of us, we see some of the worst of society."

"It's good, though, you both understand that. You can help each other through it."

"More than you know." He cleared his throat. "Tell me, where did you find the ledger you gave me?"

"You told me not to tell you." She met his quirked eyebrow with one of her own. "In the library. It was crammed between some Dickens books. Horrible place to be."

"The book is at the lab. Can't be sure it's fake until cross-checked with the actual accounts." His face softened a smidge. "I'm sorry to hear about your cat."

"He's a trooper." Eliza swallowed hard. "I want to pack him up and send him home."

"Your uncle wanted to do the same with you." He fiddled with a button on his sleeve cuff. "I'm glad you talked him out of it."

Her jaw dropped. "I'm sorry, what?"

"Don't get all wishy-washy on me now. I just reinforced how I could use you and your sharp mind. You figured things out we hadn't. That's all."

She could hug him. Wanted to hug him. But all those buttons, and the scowl as well, had her smiling from ear to ear.

"Now, don't go getting killed or anything stupid like that."

She figured that was the closest he would ever get to "Good job, kid. You're kind of awesome." Brushing her hands on her pants legs, she made her way to the door. "I'll do my best. Oh, hey, if I do survive, could I have a badge, a billy club, and one of those cool-looking hats?"

His frown twitched.

She paused. In elementary school, she'd been forced to squeeze an entire tube of toothpaste onto a paper plate and try to stuff it all back in—a waste of good toothpaste—but she'd learned the lesson: you can't put words back in your head.

"I, ah, I'm not sure how to say this, but Nancy did it."

He blinked. Once, twice. "Come again?"

"Nancy. She's the one who poisoned Caesar. She must have overheard me tell Heath I wouldn't let her scare me into keeping her evil little secret."

"Explain."

Eliza looked over her shoulder, took a deep breath, and revealed the affair between Andrew Darcy and the newly wedded Mrs. Fitzwilliam Darcy. The retelling of the details blistered her tongue. "And that's all I could glean from the letter left for me. She has to have more of them stashed in her evil lair. She probably has enough to destroy my family from the inside out. But what I don't understand is why she didn't just go for my uncle to begin with. Why play with my father's heart, string him along, to then marry Fitzwilliam?" The disjointed information from Great-Aunt Iris days earlier snapped into place. "Holy—it all makes sense now."

"What makes sense?"

"Nancy, my dad, Uncle Fitzwilliam. She went after my father first because no one thought Fitz would survive into adulthood. As soon as Uncle Fitzwilliam recovered, Nancy changed her allegiance, dragged my father's heart through the dust, probably seduced him after she became Lady Darcy, and then blackmailed him into leaving England. I just want to smack her in the—"

"Do not under any circumstances take this on yourself. Do you understand? If Nancy is capable of the attack on Caesar, you've been playing with fire already. I don't like my boys crispy."

"How about slightly grilled?" She didn't wait for his response and fled from the room and straight into Heath.

"Oof." She pushed away from him, the memory of their argument still stinging. He reached for her hand, but she whipped away. "You said this was a big house."

"It is. And trust me, I've found every nook and cranny in this old thing." He halted her with a hand to her upper arm. His grasp was strong but gentle, allowing her to escape if she chose to. "But I found none of them had you hiding in them."

She refused to be wooed by such words. Well, maybe just a little wooing. "Inconvenient, I'd say. Mission failed."

"My mission was never to evade you. I just needed time to get my head straight. A place to beat myself up for being a complete sod."

"I think that's a dirty word."

"Very."

A thrill went through her as his voice deepened and turned gravelly. "I don't forgive easily."

"Wouldn't be worth the effort of achieving it."

Her skin prickled under his touch as his hand traveled from her upper arm to rest at the nape of her neck. She swallowed. "I don't think that's the foundation of a good relationship."

"We'll make up for it in different ways." His finger traced the outline of her jaw.

"What if I'm not here to find out?"

"I'll forsake my English roots and live in America." The playful gleam in his eyes deepened. Something else took its place.

"What if I want to stay here and find out who the killer is?"

His Adam's apple lurched, but he never broke their gaze. "I promised to be the best sidekick a woman could ask for. I keep my promises." He pulled her to him and burrowed her head under his chin. "I'm sorry, Eliza. I should never have said what I did earlier. I just, for a moment, thought about my life without you in it, and I didn't know quite what to make of it. Crazy because a week ago, you weren't in my life." He tilted her chin and planted a kiss in the center of it. "But now that you are in my life, I don't want to lose you."

"No need to worry." When his eyes remained too serious for her liking, she attempted a joke. "Wentworth said if I survive this, I get a badge." She tried for a smile but feared it probably resembled a deflated whoopee cushion.

He kissed her. There in the foyer. But she didn't care. Even if the queen herself tapped her on the shoulder and wanted to talk about parliamentary procedure, she would shoo her away.

"Eliza?" Tap, tap, tap on her shoulder.

She growled against Heath's lips. "Go away."

Something thin and metallic whacked the back of her head. "Ow." She broke away from Heath and spun around.

Brandishing her knitting needle, Aunt Iris looked like a warrior.

Eliza rubbed the back of her head. "Was that necessary, Aunt?"

"Do I need to whack you, too, young man?" The little old warrior woman pinned Heath with "the look."

"No, ma'am. In fact, I heard the men are having an evening of billiards. I might join them." He pecked Eliza's cheek and jetted out the door.

"Please don't scare him off, Aunt Iris. I kind of like him."

She harrumphed. "You more than kind of like him, my dear. Besides, if he scares off so easily, he doesn't deserve you." She latched on to Eliza's arm. "Let's go for a walk."

The full moon provided ample light, and after they'd reached the relative seclusion of the garden, her aunt announced, "Someone has been through my room. In fact, your uncle William almost had a stroke at the notion of someone pawing through my knicker drawer. Can you imagine? Can I order new ones online? Joy talks about ordering all her unmentionables online. Do you know how that works?"

"What do you mean?" Eliza stamped out the tiny flicker of panic.

"I mean someone ransacked our room. Obviously looking for something. But what?"

Heath's earlier scolding about how pained her family would be if Eliza's recklessness ended... badly... echoed in her mind. Knowing her great-aunt could be in danger, Eliza felt her stomach churn. *Is this how Uncle Fitzwilliam and Heath felt at my stupid declarations of bravery?* The realization that she and her snoopy nose could harm those she loved popped the illusion of her avenging-angel alter ego. She opened her mouth to speak, but her great-aunt's bony finger to her lips stilled her words.

"Give it to me straight, my dear. Don't sugarcoat it. This is war. And I've lived it."

Eliza had the urge to pluck her aunt off the ground, smack a kiss in the center of her forehead, and set her down again, but she settled with a comforting hand on Aunt Iris's shoulder. "Whoever killed Piers is still in the house, and I'm pretty positive he—"

"Or she."

"Yes, or she, does not appreciate our snooping."

"That's rather inconvenient of them, don't you think?"

"Yes, Aunt. But we have two choices. We can relent and back off, allowing the police to do their thing, or we persist and continue on."

"Persist."

"It could be dangerous."

"Good. Old age is boring."

Eliza maneuvered her aunt to the house. "We must keep this as quiet as possible. Don't ask too many obtrusive questions, especially of the staff. I'm not sure we can trust any of them."

"Good help is hard to get nowadays." She huffed as they entered the house by the main entrance.

"Except for Tash. We can trust him."

"It's good to know my service has not gone unnoticed."

"Tash!" Eliza hugged him as he rounded the back of the door. "It's good to see you."

Tash awkwardly patted the top of her head. "Yes, well, glad to be back and of service, Miss Eliza."

"Oh no you don't." Eliza released him. "We were—"

"Eliza, dear, I'm afraid I'm feeling a bit faint." Aunt Iris clawed weakly at her arm.

Eliza waved off Tash's assistance. "I got her. You go rest and—"

"Eliza." Her great-aunt's voice wavered.

Eliza had yet to hear that tremor in her great-aunt's voice. True concern had her shuffling Aunt Iris into the drawing room. Eliza grabbed a nearby book and fanned her aunt, who surprisingly looked pink and hearty.

"Oh, stuff and nonsense. Stop bandying that dust about. You'll make me cough." Aunt Iris waved her hand as if shooing away the dust motes.

"But you said you were feeling ill." Eliza stopped the book midair. "Aren't you?"

"I haven't felt ill my whole life." She brushed an imaginary crumb from her bosom. "I was saving you from wrecking that poor man out there."

"Who? Tash?"

"Yes, Tash." She screwed up her eyes at Eliza. "At times, I think the younger generation has—"

"I know, gone barmy."

"Yes, well, at least you know. That's the first step to fixing a problem is knowing there is one."

"And?"

"Telling Tash he is not needed is the cruelest thing you could tell him."

"But we don't. We can answer our own doors, clean our own plates, fetch our own friends and family. We don't need him. Wouldn't he want to hear that? That he can rest and relax and maybe go soak some rays in the garden."

Aunt Iris shivered. At the mental picture in her own head, Eliza understood why.

"My dear, sit, please. You're making me nervous."

Eliza sat, the book perched on her lap.

"We English are an odd bunch. I often think you Americans have the right of it. But listen, your aunt and uncle don't chain Tash to the newel post or to anything else in this house. He chooses to do this. This is who he is. Just like you are a teacher. Or our Andrew a pediatrician. Tash is a butler, and he takes pride in his job. If he knew he were not needed, it would crush him."

Eliza's heart sank at her near blunder. She jumped to her feet and pushed a button secreted behind a curtain. Within seconds, Tash entered the room and stood awaiting her direction.

"Tash, I believe Aunt Iris is in need of a refreshing tea." She flicked a glance at her aunt, who weakly waved the dusty book in front of her face for effect.

"Right away, Miss Eliza." With a bow, he left the room.

With a thump, Aunt Iris dropped the book on the floor and scooted to the front of the chair. "That's my girl." Taking out her knitting needles, she continued chattering. "He will have plenty of tasks to keep him busy. Apparently, with the arrest of the head groundskeeper, that dashing Wentworth has given permission for the ball to commence." She grinned. "It's sure to be a jolly do. Can't wait to get my knees up."

Eliza said nothing. With the murder of one footman, the MIA status of another, the aftermath of learning the depravity of Nancy's secrets, and the impending doom she held over Eliza's head, she found no joy in the upcoming event. She had the dress and had the date but didn't have the heart.

"You can't let it get to you." Great-Aunt Iris laid a papery hand on Eliza's.

Eliza blinked at her great-aunt. "What?"

"The evil. If you let it get to you, destroy even the tiniest bit of happiness, it has won." Great-Aunt Iris continued knitting, her eyes on the colorful wool. "Learned it during the war. We all did." She made no mention of Nazi killing and had no glint in her eyes.

Eliza swallowed past a lump in her throat and rapidly blinked. Nancy had already destroyed so much, had erased years of family connections and happiness, and had undermined the foundations of Pemberley itself. If getting her knees up, as Great-Aunt Iris put it, spit in the face of everything Nancy had manipulated and corrupted, Eliza would squeeze herself into her dress and dance until her toes fell off.

Chapter Fifteen
The Cook's Dog Takes the Shirt

Darcy has threatened to unearth his dueling pistols. I had to get my information from Betty, as Darcy will not tell me the matter. I am tired of being treated as if I shall crumble and break at the slightest ill news. And the ill news? Kitty has embroiled herself in scandal. And the scandal? I cringe to even write this, as I'll have to see these words inked into permanency... she eloped. Apparently, Lydia's influence can transcend distance.

—Lizzy Bennet Darcy
Pemberley 1811

"No amount of makeup is going to cover these scratches." Joy huffed and tipped Eliza's face away from the pages of Elizabeth's journal to dab concealer on her cheeks. "Although I kind of hate you right now."

"Why?" Eliza pouted at her reflection and fingered a nasty scratch just below her eye.

"You're still gorgeous."

Eliza snorted on a laugh and continued reading from Elizabeth's journal as Joy moved from fiddling with her face to fiddling with her hair. *I do love a good ball. According to Mamma, I am not as pretty or important as Jane, but as she is my dearest sister and an even dearer friend, I hope—no, pray, that Mr. Bingley falls madly in love with her. What can keep him from doing so? She is but a perfect angel, all sweetness and gentleness. I am a veritable east wind to her and shall die an old maid. Perhaps I can teach her ten children to embroider. Alas, as I*

206

often sew my dress to the design, that shall not do at all. I must go and write later. Mamma is bringing the walls down with her pleas to hurry. I hope to write with news of some import soon.

Joy flicked her on the ear. "Did you hear me?"

Eliza blinked. "Sorry?"

"Have you ever had a bad hair day?" Joy curled a swath of Eliza's hair around a wide-diameter curling iron.

"I'd trade my crow-black hair for yours any day."

"You'd get tired of hearing blonde jokes," Joy warned and snagged another ribbon of hair then wound it around the hot iron.

"Hmph. Anyway, I just got caught up in Elizabeth's story. Jane is in here too. I'm just getting to a good part. Want to hear it?" She took Joy's smile as permission. She cleared her throat. "Now, where was I? Oh yeah. *I'm afraid I do have something of import but not the good news I had hoped. It is apparent my family is out to destroy Jane's and my future by making themselves ridiculous in every way possible. Lydia and Kitty are unpardonable flirts, and my mother does not know how her voice carries, or maybe she does, which makes it all the more worrisome, for I fear Mr. Bingley overheard her discussing her happiness over an anticipated wedding. Oh, how my eyes sting at the humiliation. What's worse is Mary's need for public gratification with no talent to welcome it. And my vow to never speak with or dance with Mr. Darcy was broken. I could not think of an excuse and had to dance with him. Insufferable man. I do have to say, however, despite his haughty looks and prideful disposition, he cuts a fine figure in evening clothes and led me down the dance very well indeed."*

Joy attempted to tame one of Eliza's curls. "That is the ball where my great, great—well, a ton of greats ago—grandparents fell in love. How thrilling to hear it firsthand. I don't believe any of Jane's journals survived. If only I had her celebrated beauty, I'd take that as a consolation prize."

Eliza bent toward the mirror and smudged eyeliner along her upper lid, giving herself a satisfactory smoky-eye look. A swipe of mascara left even her appreciating her blue eyes. "You get along well enough with your looks."

On anyone else, Joy's self-assured preening would have seemed arrogant and vain, but on her, it came off like agreeing that the weather was indeed quite nice. "I've seen how Heath looks at you, and I'll tell you this." Joy released a springy curl. "He never looked at me like that."

Eliza's insides twirled. They might as well have been wearing a tu-tu for all that spinning. "Really?"

"As if you didn't know."

"Sometimes, I just think it's wishful thinking."

Joy pulled Eliza from the chair upholstered in tulips and spun her around in circles. "I bet you five of Cook's biscuits that Heath will melt into a puddle at your feet tonight when he sees you." She turned Eliza around until she faced the full-length mirror snugged into the corner of her bedroom. Her breath caught, and she couldn't help caressing the cherry-red material sheathing her body. The plunging neckline dipped in between the swells of her breasts, and the off-the-shoulder sleeves stopped midway up her biceps. Her raven-black hair hung in heavy curls, cascading over her shoulders. A ribbon of hair swooped up the side and was held securely with a diamond hair comb.

"You turned me into Cinderella." Eliza spun in a circle.

"Not just yet." Joy grinned and rummaged around in her bag of tricks. "When you picked out that dress, I just knew I had the jewelry for you. I've been in so many weddings, I could open a jewelry store." She pulled out a black pouch and handed it to her. "Merry first ball day."

Eliza eased open the velvet bag and whispered the diamond necklace over her palm, each diamond tentacle tickling her skin. "It's exquisite."

"It's fake."

Eliza clasped the necklace around her neck and situated the longest strand in between her cleavage, leaving the rest of the strands to fan out along her chest. She slid the diamond earrings, each with five dangling strands, into her ears.

"Now, you are Cinderella." Joy clasped her hands. "Prince Charming is going to faint. I can't wait."

Eliza couldn't stop giggling and didn't want to. "How will we revive him?"

"A bucket of ice-cold water?" But Joy's exaggerated kissy fish face belied her words.

Eliza hugged her middle. Kissing Heath had proven an invigorating experience, and she looked forward to doing so again. Soon. But the dark cloud that was the unsolved murder of a hated footman kept the silver lining to a dull gray. *Dammit.* Her aunt's—no—*Nancy's* open threat and attack on Caesar made her stomach churn with more than nerves over a grand ball. That woman had sucked all the joy from Eliza's world, her father's world, and maybe even the world at large.

"Hey, are you okay?" Joy laid a hand on Eliza's shoulder.

Great-Aunt Iris's words flittered through her mind. Eliza would spit in Nancy's face. *Not literally. Although...* Eliza imagined actually doing it. She grinned at the certain look of shock that would shatter her aunt's fake, smiling face. Slinging her arm through Joy's, Eliza waltzed from her bedroom. "Perfect. Now it's your turn to get all Cinderella-y."

Joy hid a yawn behind her hand. "More like Sleeping Beauty-y. If I keep this up, you'll find me passed out behind some huge palm frond somewhere."

"Maybe I'll scrounge up Wickham to bring you back to life."

Joy shuddered. "Or something exciting had better happen." She wrinkled her nose. "You have a better chance of scaring up Mr. Creepy from his hidey-hole."

"OH, MY DEARS, YOU ARE perfection personified." Great-Aunt Iris spread her arms and engulfed Eliza and Joy in a bath of pink taffeta and lily of the valley perfume.

Eliza bussed her aunt's withered cheek. "You look... scrumptious." If her aunt were a cupcake, she would be the best dressed or frosted, as it were, in a baker's dozen. Her dress was a concoction of baby-pink frills, lace, ribbons, and pearls, all baked to perfection. All she was missing was an equally perfect pink fascinator.

"Ah, my dear, you forgot this in our room." Great-Uncle William, who seemed to finally emerge from an everlasting nap, limped to them, clutching a pink feather. Aunt Iris adjusted the various textures of pink and plopped it on her head.

"There." She eyed Eliza and Joy from under a wayward piece of lace. "Where are your fascinators?"

Eliza glanced at Joy, her rose-gold blond hair tumbled back into a messy chignon, stray wisps curling behind her ears. The elegant hairstyle mirrored the elegant simplicity of her short vintage gown of teal lace. "We forgot."

A grand tsk came. "I do say that even without them, you shall make a grand entrance." Great-Aunt Iris flicked her wrist at her husband. "My dear, shall we go and sample all of Cook's delicacies? I heard she made lemon drizzle." Aunt Iris tugged her husband from the room, leaving a waft of scent and a few pink feathers floating through the air.

Eliza dragged Joy down the staircase. "Come on. Let's go make our grand entrance."

And a grand entrance it was, although not due to the nonexistent applause or the lack of fainting men. But if Eliza were honest with herself, the only man she wanted fainting at her feet was late. She was captured by her grand entrance into the ballroom where, just two days ago, a pissy DCI had captured the attention of a horde of angry family members. Not even her imagination had the chandeliers dripping with thousands of drops of light, fresh flowers flowing from antique urns—not a palm frond in sight, for which her face was thankful—and waiters and waitresses milling around in crisp black-and-white uniforms, handing out flutes of champagne and offering delicacies the size of a silver dollar. Even the menagerie that was her extended family turned out well. Dresses twirled around legs, sliding over the pressed pants of the gentlemen as a ten-piece orchestra waltzed out a melody.

"I've never seen anything like it." Eliza pressed a hand to her throat, feeling like a fairy-tale princess. If only her Prince Charming would show.

"Oh," Joy hissed in Eliza's ear, "look who showed up." She pawed at Eliza's forearm as Willoughby, in a crisp black tuxedo, sauntered over to them, a lazy grin on his lips. "Remember, I cannot under any circumstances be trusted with him."

He winked at Joy then pressed the back of Eliza's hand to his lips. "May I ask for a dance?"

Joy poked her in the hip with her finger.

"Yeah. Sure."

His eyes twinkled at Joy. "You're next, my fair friend." Willoughby rested his hand on the small of Eliza's back. "Shall we?"

For the next several minutes, Eliza twirled and swirled, nearly upending a nearby waiter and his tray of champagne glasses. A quick smile seemed to forgive all, and she laughed as Willoughby circled her around the room. Her laughter came to an abrupt end when she smacked into something solid. And male. A pair of arms captured her against a wall of muscle. They released her, and she lost herself in Heath's blue gaze. A lock of dark hair escaped its hold and fell over his forehead. Eliza curled it back into place. His gaze darkened. His hands slid up her arms, his thumbs playing along the edge of her sleeves. His throat worked as he swallowed. And swallowed again.

"Hello." His roughened voice made her insides all gooey. He glared at Willoughby until he removed his hand from Eliza's back.

"Hi," she whispered. She fingered the crisp white collar folded over his tuxedo jacket. "You're late."

"You're... you're..."

Joy flittered over to them. "This is where you're supposed to drop dead at her feet," she murmured in Heath's ear.

He flicked a glance at Joy but found Eliza's gaze again. "Beautiful."

Even though that word had been uttered millions if not billions of times before in the history of humankind, from the look in his eyes, the purr in his voice, and the texture of his finger tracing one of the myriad diamond rivers, she knew no one had ever murmured *beautiful* that way before.

"Come." He slid his hand down her bare arm and captured her hand, guiding her away from her cousin and dance partner and through the crowd. He plucked two glasses of champagne and held them in one hand as he drew her out into the deserted balcony and the starlit night.

"This is how an unsuspecting woman finds herself betrothed to a man she hardly knows." She sipped from the flute, enjoying the sensation of tiny bubbles trickling down her throat. "A hundred years ago."

He studied her over the rim of his untouched glass. "Would you mind terribly?"

Oh. Well. Oh my. She drank more of the clear liquid. Tried to make light of her next words. "Not terribly. You would make a satisfactory husband."

Heath removed her champagne flute, tangled his fingers in her hair, and captured her lips with his. He must have had a glass of champagne before then, as he tasted bubbly and sweet and hungry. Hungry for her. Her head swam, her knees weakened, and her lips opened. He ended the kiss with a nibble on her bottom lip and a growl deep in his chest.

He rested his forehead against hers, his eyes closed. "Just satisfactory, huh?"

She traced a finger around the top buttonhole of his jacket. He grasped it and brought it to his lips before kissing her fingerprint. Needing to breathe, to get some clarity, she quipped, "Just."

His eyes opened, and humor glittered in their depths. "Do you need another demonstration?"

Yes! No. She'd surely lose her mind with another kiss like that, and she would have to marry the man, her uncle standing in for her father, shotgun in hand. But no one had ever accused her of being smart. "Maybe."

"Are you prepared to marry my niece, young man?" Aunt Iris tutted from behind them.

Heath simply held her, his arms not relinquishing their hold.

Eliza banged her head on Heath's shoulder and muttered, "Why me?" She could hear Heath's chuckle rumble in his chest.

"Mrs. Darcy, you have my word. I have nothing but the highest regard for your great-niece."

Great-Aunt Iris sniffed and thumped Eliza on the head with her fan. "And you, how did you learn to kiss like that?"

Eliza had no words.

Great-Aunt Iris opened her fan and spoke behind it. "If you have that book around here somewhere, I wouldn't mind accidentally coming upon it in my bedroom." She snapped her fan shut and waddled inside, a piece of her pink dress limping along.

Heath stared at the retreating figure of Eliza's aunt. "Did that just happen?"

Like the bubbles in her glass of champagne, her laugh burbled up as giggles and erupted. Before long, he joined her, flicking an errant tear off his face. His laugh dissolved to a chuckle then silence. His breathing deepened, and he trailed his thumb along her bottom lip. "Care to dance?"

Eliza finished the last of her champagne and set it on a nearby table. "I thought you'd never ask."

He swept her into the ballroom, one hand firmly on her waist, the other holding her hand in a tender embrace. His eyes twinkled. "I might have to punch Willoughby."

"Why?" She scanned the room and locked eyes with Jack. He saluted her with his drink, his lips curling in an easy smile. "He's harmless."

Heath pulled her tightly to him, his chest hard against hers. "Harmless my bloody ar—"

"Eliza, you look a picture tonight. If only your father could see you." Uncle Fitzwilliam slapped a hand on Heath's back. "Mind if I cut in?"

"Sir." Heath squeezed her hand before letting go.

Uncle Fitzwilliam twirled her about the room, guiding her expertly through the throng of other dancers, the orchestra's melody taking her for a sensory ride. His salt-and-pepper muttonchops, which somehow did not make him look ridiculous, curved down sharp cheekbones that quivered in a suppressed smile.

"What is so funny, Uncle?"

"Nothing." His whiskers quivered even more.

"Uncle."

"Oh, just that a man overwhelmed by love tends to add some humor to innocent bystanders."

She blushed. "He's not in love with—"

He swung her around a couple who had come to a standstill in the middle of the dance floor. "Does he deserve you, dear?"

"The question is do I deserve him?" Eliza scoured the room for Heath and found him, tall and strong, laughing with a few of the nuts from the Darcy-Bennet-etcetera tree. His chiseled face, made even more so by a recent shave, made her fingers want to trace the sharp lines of his cheekbones and nose, his full lips. He must have sensed her gaze as his eyes found hers and communicated across the large room filled to the brim with people and noise. *Does he love me? And why?*

"You sell yourself too short, my dear. These past few days have taught me many things. One of them being how much I regret not having you in my life from the start. If only I could go back to the day your father left, I'd do things differently, you know. I'd—"

A scream cut off her uncle's words. He clutched her to him, broad hands protecting her. Another scream pierced the air, that time from multiple voices. Her uncle broke through the crowd, scattering people in his wake, and planted her in Heath's embrace. Another scream came. And another. They rippled through the crowd. Her uncle planted a kiss on her forehead and marched toward the sounds of horror.

"What is going on?" Eliza slid her hand into the warmth of Heath's grasp.

Heath tucked her protectively to his side. They didn't have long to wait. The screams got closer, and the ebb of the crowd crushed into the walls, leaving a wide berth, a circular void in the middle of the ballroom floor. There, center stage, where couples had waltzed in dizzying turns and revolutions seconds before, sat Mrs. Bankcroft's dog, a once-crisp white shirt now caked with dried blood hanging from its jaw.

Chapter Sixteen
Stabbed through the Sole

The intruder attacked again last night. Darcy threatens to move us all to London. I hate London. The stench, the dirt, the crowded streets. I long to stay at Pemberley, my home. I feel connected to my child here. What if I go to London and lose my baby's memory? My heart breaks to write that Kitty has been located, unmarried, and brought back to live with us. Shall the ghost of Lydia's childish mistake haunt us forever?

—Lizzy Bennet Darcy
Pemberley 1811

"That's one way to keep the party going."

Eliza flicked a glance at Joy, whose skin had turned slightly green. Her mind chanted, *Keep it light, keep it light,* and her stomach agreed. "Glad to know you won't be napping behind one of the flower arrangements." Not a fern—Nancy's apparent favorite plant—in sight. Eliza smoothed her index finger over the tiny scratch on her cheek.

"No ferns as was assumed, so fewer places to hide." Joy's voice cracked as Gizmo tore at the shirt, flakes of dried blood fluttering to the polished dance floor like rusty snow.

A squeak. Eliza wasn't sure how Margery ended up next to her but attempted to stabilize the teetering woman only to be rewarded with a sniff.

"I do not need—"

A bloody button flew off the shirt and pinged the woman in the forehead. Margery's skin faded to a virgin white, and she crumpled to the floor in a pile of lime-green silk.

"Oh dear." Joy prodded the prone woman's body with the toe of her high heels. "Oh dear," Joy whispered again, "do you think we're next?"

Whether the dog's new chew toy or her fainting relative or the wails of the distressed around her had her vision going sparkly, she wasn't sure. Heath pulled her into his chest with a strong arm.

"What is all this commotion about?" Nancy's voice cut through the thick silence that had descended upon the stunned guests. Like the waters of the Red Sea, they parted in large swaths as she oozed through the room.

"My dear, you might want to stop—"

"Nonsense, Fitzwilliam." She paused and seemed to finally take in the stunned gazes. "What has happened?"

Fitzwilliam took his wife's arm and guided her through the crush to the edge of the circle, where Eliza stood in Heath's embrace. Joy, who had lost a game of rock, paper, scissors, sat on the floor, ministering to a moaning Margery. Nancy stiffened, her normally ramrod-straight back on the verge of bending in the opposite direction. She opened her mouth several times, but no words came out. Only a large exhale as if the dog in the middle of the room tearing at what used to be a pristine white men's shirt was a normal occurrence. *Who is this woman? Does she even own a heart?* Nancy's gaze flittered about the room, and when she met Eliza's eyes, an icy coldness seeped into Eliza's soul. *Nope. Woman does not own a heart.*

"Ah, Theodore," her aunt crooned, crooking a finger in summons of the footman.

He approached, and beads of sweat condensed on his forehead.

"Please take care of the dog and... and that thing in his mouth."

The footman blinked as if not sure of his order. "Ma'am?"

"Dog, Theodore. Remove it."

He approached the little canine. Gizmo bared his teeth, the sleeve dangling by its button from the sharp teeth.

"Have you called Wentworth?" Heath murmured into Eliza's ear.

Eliza gestured to her dress and croaked, "No pockets. No phone." She placed her hand to her throat as Gizmo and Theodore played tug of war. "You better call. Now."

The dog tried for purchase on the waxed dance floor, but its paws kept slipping from under it. As if seeing this as an advantage, Theodore latched on to the shirt and pulled Gizmo, still clutching the sleeve with a vicious grip, from the room, the dog growling as its back legs and hind end slid along the floor. Even when Theodore's short frame was no longer noticeable, Eliza gauged their movement though the crowded room by the gasps and retreating bodies.

Nancy brushed her hands together and gave a tight smile. "Fitzwilliam, dear, would you see to our guests?"

A frown burrowed wrinkles into his forehead as he watched his wife wade through the crowd. He turned his attention to his guests. "I sincerely apologize for the strange turn of events. Many of you have traveled long distances to be here, and I am remiss in ending the night early. If you care to leave, no insult will be given. However, if you want to stay and enjoy the festivities, you are more than welcome to. I will go and see to things and be back shortly."

Murmurs and whispers echoed through the room, but the orchestra, seemingly receiving an invisible cue, struck up a waltz, and most of the guests whirled about the room once more, much like before, but the shadow of doubt and fear darkened the corners of the room. Laughter again filled the room but stilted and unsure of its place among the grisly scene.

"Eliza"—her uncle leaned closer—"could you assist Margery back to her room? Heath, would you help her?"

"Anything else you would like us to do, Uncle?" Eliza laid a hand on his forearm.

He scrubbed a hand over his whiskers. "Not now, my dear. Not now." As if in a daze, he left the ballroom, the weight of the world seemingly on his shoulders.

"Righto. Let's get started." Heath clapped his hands together and hooked his arms under Margery's armpits. "Up we go, madam."

Margery pinned Eliza with a glare or at least the best glare she could muster when looking green about the gills. "We never had this kind of trouble at our family reunions until you came along."

Eliza smiled sweetly. "Maybe you should stop coming to them, as I plan on coming to every single one."

Margery sputtered and collapsed from the effort, sending Heath's reflexes into overdrive. He sent Eliza a look over the top of Margery's head and half assisted, half dragged the woman from the room. Eliza and Joy gathered the rest of the guests who didn't look so hot and herded them to their various rooms, one by one, until Eliza and Joy were alone in the gallery, the past faces of Pemberley peering at them.

"I wonder if Elizabeth ever had to deal with this at her parties?" The shock of Gizmo playing with a bloody shirt started to wear off. Adrenaline dissolved into tremors racking Eliza's body.

"Who does that shirt belong to?" Joy whispered as if the shirt's owner would appear at the mention of it.

"I'm afraid to find out." She was afraid it was the shirt of the missing footman, Jonas. Afraid that with two dead bodies, Pemberley housed a killer who had gained an appetite for killing.

Eliza jumped as a hand clutched her arm. Joy squealed next to her as another withered hand descended upon her as well.

"There's no need to squeal like a stuck pig, Joy," Great-Aunt Iris scolded.

"There's no need to go sneaking up on people," Joy retorted, her breath coming in short gasps.

"Where have you been?" Eliza laid her hand over her aunt's hand, still clutched to her arm. "Did you see—"

"Of course I saw. And thought I'd whisk on out of there and follow that odd-looking footman."

"Where did he go?" Eliza pressed her aunt as they moved down the grand staircase.

"I lost him when he ducked into the hallway leading to the kitchens."

"What would he want in the kitchens?"

Aunt Iris planted her hands at her waist. "He wasn't in there. Although the other maid... what's her name? Petunia? Pansy?"

"Poppy," Eliza offered.

"Yes, that's it. Rather rude, she was." She sniffed grandly. "Dared to ask what *I* was doing down there. I say, rude."

Odd. "But no Theodore?" They were nearing the end of the staircase and their privacy. Eliza lowered her voice to a whisper. "It's important to know where he went."

Aunt Iris murmured, "There is a door leading out of the kitchen to the kitchen gardens. He might have used it."

Aunt Iris's face pulled in a bright smile as they neared a group of relatives. Eliza admired her aunt's stamina. She wanted to flop to the floor in a puddle of stress and tears, but the pink frothy woman before her kept her going, stopping occasionally to make small talk, mostly about the weather and the food but not a word about the dog and its new toy. Finally, they made it back to the ballroom, still full of people, still gliding, still twirling, still faking normalcy. Not seeing Heath, Eliza excused herself from Joy and her aunt and wandered in search of him. She hiked up the skirt to her dress and trotted down the hallways, dipping her head in each room, glancing over her shoulder for hidden killers.

She had no doubt the killer was still there. Lurking. A groan gurgled from her throat at the thought of the game of Clue. In the fountain with the hoe. *By whom?* Eliza shivered. *Nancy? Theodore?* The same person responsible for Jonas's disappearance and possible death?

Eliza's ears pricked at a sound. It could have been a laugh or a sob. Ignoring her inner warning systems, she tiptoed down an uncarpeted beige passage reserved for servants. She toed off her high heels and crept through the female servants' entrance and to the bedroom door hanging ajar.

Poppy lay on a small cot, her arms behind her head, feet crossed at the foot of the cot, one foot wiggling as if to music. A floorboard squeaked, and Poppy jerked her head up, staring at the door. "Who's there?" she demanded.

Eliza pushed the door open. "It's only me, Poppy."

"You're not supposed to be here."

"Sorry. It's easy to get lost in a big place like this." Eliza sat on the edge of the cot, the entire thing sinking under her weight.

Poppy pulled away from Eliza's outstretched hand. "You shouldn't be here." She flicked a gaze at the open doorway. "Leave."

"You know what happened, don't you?" Eliza kept her voice soft.

Poppy stared at the door. "I don't know what you're talking about, miss."

"Please tell me. I can help."

A laugh ripped from the maid. "No one can help." She lunged for Eliza's arm and pushed her off the cot. "Please leave. Before—" A door banged in the distance. "Leave," she whispered harshly. She shoved Eliza from the room and pointed her in the opposite way she'd come. "Take the third door on the left, go up the steps, and that will lead into the kitchens." She gave Eliza one last push and slammed the door shut. Another door clicked closed, closer than Eliza preferred. Forgetting about her high heels, she darted down the cheerless corridor before ducking into the third door as Poppy had instructed. Pausing to listen, she heard clipped footsteps, closer and closer. Lifting her dress, she ran up the steps and burst into the kitchen.

"Warn a person before you come clomping through their kitchens, dearie," Mrs. Bankcroft scolded and melted into tears, a soggy tissue pressed to her nose.

"Oh, Mrs. Bankcroft, I'm sorry." Eliza slipped an arm around the cook's shoulders. "I didn't mean to scare you."

"It's not you. It's Gizmo. Will they have to put him down?" Another shower of tears. The all-too-familiar emergency lights filtered through the windows. "They've already taken him. They're going to kill him."

"There, there, Mrs. B. Why would they do that?"

"Can't have a killer dog on the loose, can we?"

Eliza grabbed Mrs. Bankcroft's shoulders. "You think Gizmo killed a person and then tore his shirt off?" She planted a kiss on the old woman's forehead. "You'll get Gizmo back. I'm sure they're just running tests."

Mrs. Bankcroft sank into a chair and dug the heels of her hands into her eyes. "Where would he have found such a thing?"

"That's what I plan to find out."

When she got back to her room two hours later, the clock striking midnight on her Cinderella spell, her plans changed. On her pillow sat one abandoned high heel with a knife through its sole, spearing a note that kindly told her to "bugger off."

"DOES THIS HAPPEN TO you in America?"

Eliza eyed Wentworth. "No, apparently only the English have charming ways to welcome tourists."

"Eliza, please be serious." Uncle Fitzwilliam's hand twitched on her arm.

She jerked her chin in Wentworth's direction. "Tell him that. He started it."

Her uncle squeezed the bridge of his nose. "Anyone care for tea?" He glanced at the mantel clock in his study. "Something stronger, perhaps?"

"I'll take whatever brown liquid is in one of the decanters." Eliza, not needing the paper bag thrust into her hand—yet—played with the material. The paper crinkled in the otherwise quiet room.

Uncle Fitzwilliam's eyebrow quirked, but he poured her a finger's worth of brandy and pressed the cut crystal into her hand. She set the bag on the floor, took a sip, and coughed. "That's going to put some hair on my chest."

Wentworth fixed her with a gaze, opened his mouth, then snapped it shut. After Uncle Fitzwilliam settled back in his chair, a glass of amber liquid in his hand, Wentworth opened his notebook. "A few hours ago, Mrs. Bankcroft's dog, Gizmo, disrupted the ball with a new toy." He ignored Eliza's squeak. "You"—he flapped his notebook at Eliza—"disrupted the bee's nest a little too much and got rewarded with this." He brandished the impaled shoe encased in a large evidence bag.

It didn't look as intimidating locked in a baggie, but Eliza's heart still leapt into her throat. "The only ones who knew about my shoes were Poppy and whoever was coming down the hallway." She poked at the bag, sending the shoe swinging. *Poppy.* "What have you learned about Poppy?"

Wentworth flipped through his notebook. "Age thirty-one." His brow furrowed. "Blimey." He growled and read on, "Parents deceased, no siblings, piss poor until she started working here." Wentworth glanced at Fitzwilliam. "You pay a pretty penny, I see."

"Nancy sees to all that." He exhaled, his eyes clouding. "What does this all mean?"

Wentworth flicked a gaze at Eliza. She swallowed, knowing what was to come. She just hoped it wouldn't kill her uncle, a man she'd come to love and respect.

"I'm not sure of anywhere else in England a house staff member can make a hundred thousand pounds a year."

Fitzwilliam's face whitened. "A hundred thousand?"

Wentworth rasped a swear word. "I don't know how to break this to you, Fitz. Bollocks." He snapped his fingers, and a constable hovering in a corner jumped to attention. "The records, please." Within seconds, Wentworth brandished a file folder and held it out to Uncle Fitzwilliam. "These are the estate accounts." He handed over another batch of papers. "These are the accounts from books found by"—he slid a glance at Eliza—"your niece."

"I don't understand." Uncle Fitzwilliam seemed to shrink within his chair. Realization dawned on his face. Eliza felt his pain and hated Nancy for putting it there. "No. No, there's been a mistake."

Wentworth bent his head then raised it again, a look of friendship instead of authority on his face. "Your wife has been embezzling from the estate. For years. And with the amount of money you pull in a year from your investments, she could have been sitting there sucking off the estate for years, and unless you knew to look, you would never have noticed." He nodded to Eliza. "Why don't you tell your uncle what else you discovered?"

"I—" Once she let the words out, no amount of force would put them back in. Maybe it would help if she said them quickly, like tearing off a Band-Aid. "Nancy is Garrison's aunt."

"Pardon?"

"Your wife is Garrison's aunt."

"That's not possible." The skin under his muttonchops reddened, and his eyes widened.

"I overheard Garrison call her that one of my first days here, and I couldn't let things rest, so I snooped around a bit."

Wentworth handed Uncle Fitzwilliam the letter and photo.

Eliza folded her hands together. "I found these in Nancy's jewelry case."

Uncle Fitzwilliam's knuckles whitened as he clutched the picture. He blinked and read the letter. Then he read it again. "How could someone hate so much? Dear God, to think I loved her, gave her everything." He scrubbed his hands over his face. "I am a fool."

"Don't say that."

"And why not? She played me like a fiddle. I honestly believed I'd finally met a woman who didn't care about the estate, the family, the money. I trusted her. With everything. Said she could handle the accounts, make sure she hired the right people, wanted to help out, ease my burden so I could concentrate on business. I thought she had. The whole time, she's been bleeding me drop by drop."

Eliza dropped to her knees and took her uncle's trembling hands in hers. "No. She is the fool. Look at what she could have had. But she threw it all away out of greed and entitlement."

His eyes met hers. "Doesn't make me any less of a fool. My blindness could have ruined Pemberley. Ruined your future too." He skimmed over the letter again. "But it wouldn't be the first time someone from that family wanted to destroy this estate."

Eliza flicked back into her memory. Beyond Garrison's father's embezzlement, hundreds of years ago, another Wickham had tried to destroy what a Darcy had held dear. The flowing references about George Wickham in Elizabeth's journal made Eliza roll her eyes. All too soon, Elizabeth would find out what a cad he truly was, but until then, Eliza had to deal with tales of long walks and overly long stares at card parties. Eliza shook herself. It was not the time for dillydallying in the past.

Eliza squeezed his hand in return. "No, Uncle, she has not. We have figured it out. We can fix this. Together."

Wentworth clapped Eliza on the back. "If it weren't for your niece here, Fitz, we would never have thought to look at the estate finances. Never would have figured this all out." The man's bravado wilted from his face, and the tips of his shiny shoes seemed to intrigue him. "Ah, Fitz, here's the rub, you see. I need to arrest your wife. Do you, ah, know where she is? Sorry, old mate."

Fitzwilliam's face sagged, and his huge hands shook as they scraped along his cheeks. "Bloody hell."

Eliza blinked. She hadn't heard her uncle swear before. Now was as good a time as any, she decided and rested her hands on his quivering shoulders.

"Bloody, bloody freezing hell." Uncle Fitzwilliam cleared his throat and stood, a quiet strength and a rooted anger making him seem taller than his six-foot frame. "She's probably still in bed."

DCI Wentworth snapped his fingers, and a constable who had been stationed by the door jumped at the silent command and left. For several minutes, the only sound echoing through the room was the mantel clock ticking and tocking. The sound of high heels and boot clicks soon joined in. Dread slipped down Eliza's throat and, much like a chunk of poorly chewed food, stalled behind her sternum and refused to move farther.

Nancy, resplendent in a soft-pink silk robe with matching slippered heels, sailed into the study. "Fitz, dear, what is the meaning of this"—she gestured to the constable blushing at her side—"person disturbing my sleep." Her gaze flittered from her husband to the other police officers in the room, to Wentworth, and finally to Eliza. "What, pray tell, is going on?" She speared Eliza with a glare and jutted her chin out in Eliza's direction. "What has she done now?"

"Lady Darcy"—DCI Wentworth stepped between Eliza and Nancy, effectively killing the death glare—"you are under arrest on suspicion of embezzlement. You do not have to say anything, but it may harm your defense if..."

Eliza tuned the rest out, concentrating on her uncle's face. He never once looked away from his wife. The only crack in his stoic expression was the occasional tic winking at the corner of his right eye. Eliza's heart broke for her uncle. She wished with all her heart she could—

"You bloody bitch, I warned you." Nancy dived for Eliza, the constable behind her pulling on her handcuffs like a pair of reins. Spittle flew from Nancy's mouth, her teeth gnashing. "You... you... slag, you twat, you—"

"Enough!" Uncle Fitzwilliam's voice cracked like a shot. The entire room fell silent, and Nancy's mouth gaped open. Uncle Fitzwilliam's thunderous chest deflated, and his voice softened. "Nancy, enough. Just stop."

DCI Wentworth jerked his head toward the door, and the constables holding Nancy shuffled her to it. She cut Eliza a final look before the door shut. A stream of obscenities filtered through the door and finally echoed to nothingness.

For several seconds, silence thrummed like a racing heart through the room. Eliza wilted into her uncle's arms. "I'm sorry, Uncle."

"Don't ever apologize for doing what you did." He held her at arm's length. "Can you imagine the damage she would have done? I'm a bloody idiot for not seeing it before." He let go of her arms and ambled to the fireplace, a stoop in his broad shoulders.

A knock echoed through the room.

"Come in!" Wentworth barked.

A constable poked his head around the door. "We found it. By the old boathouse."

"It" meaning the body that was missing a shirt. DCI Wentworth excused himself, then the door snicked closed behind him.

Uncle Fitzwilliam leaned against the fireplace, one hand clutching the mantelpiece, the other stuffed in the back pocket of his khakis.

"Uncle?"

"How could I have been such a fool?"

"There's something else."

A laugh ripped from his chest, but he said nothing, his eyes downcast and staring at the stone flooring.

"Here." She couldn't bring herself to verbalize her father's text confirming Nancy's intrusion in their lives. She swiped her phone screen, opening her father's text. "Read."

His face leached of color. His knuckles whitened as he gripped her phone and brought the screen closer to his face. "He wrote to me? He called?"

"I'm sorry," she whispered.

"Why didn't I get the letter? Why didn't he try contacting me again?" He eyed her phone as if it were poisonous.

She slid her phone from his open palm then stuck it back into her pocket. The answer wasn't hers to give. *Or is it?* It needed to come from her father. For the moment, her uncle would stay in the dark.

Uncle Fitzwilliam sank into a nearby chair. "All I missed... oh Lord, I—I would have forgiven him. I was angry, yes, but I would have forgiven him."

She kneeled before him and grasped his hands resting on his knees. Wordless, she simply held his hand, praying that part of her could absorb his pain.

But she could barely control her own and longed for Heath's arms around her, his strength seeping through her, but she hadn't texted him. He was snuggled in bed somewhere. Without her. Part of her rebelled at always being the damsel in distress. She hated her stupid pseudo bravado.

Another knock came. Heath, in boxers and a white T-shirt, charged through the door. His face, imprinted with pillowcase lines, crumpled when he saw her. Before she could squeak his name, he swooped her into his arms, squeezing her tight.

"Heath."

"Eliza." He whispered a kiss over her hair. "What happened? Tash woke me. Said there'd been an emergency."

She burrowed her face into his chest. "Someone had a present waiting for me on my pillow last night. A knife stabbed into my shoe with a note telling me to do something rude to myself. At least, I think that's what 'bugger off' means, in a knife-through-a-shoe sort of way."

He tightened his hold on her, his arms crushing her ribs.

"If you kill me first, you'll take away all the fun for our bad guy."

"Sorry." He released her.

"They found the body. It was buried by the burned-down boathouse. I'd bet the farm it's Jonas." Eliza sat and swirled the amber liquid she didn't want.

"That's it. You're staying in my room." Heath latched on to her hand.

"No."

He cursed. "Why not? You did the other night."

"By accident. Besides, it would give Great-Aunt Iris a heart attack, or she'd make us marry."

Heath beseeched Fitzwilliam with a look.

"Don't look at me. I wash my hands of this." Uncle Fitzwilliam pushed himself from the chair. "I'll leave you two to figure this out. I should see to my, ah, wife." He paused by Eliza. "Thank you. For everything." He planted a kiss on the top of her head and left the room.

Heath poured a glass of brandy, swirled it, then sipped. "Still a no to staying in my room? I thought you'd love the idea of seeing me twenty-four seven."

"Moderation is best." She folded her hands primly and angled her chin higher.

"Someone's a sore loser."

"Am not."

"Are too."

She huffed and turned her body away, only to be dragged back around and swallowed against his chest. "You're not wearing any pants."

Heath released his hold on her, and his hands dove to cover himself. "Wait, what? I—"

Eliza giggled.

Heath shushed her with his lips. "You like changing the subject, don't you?"

"Maybe."

Wentworth, a scowl etching fissures on his face, stepped through the door. "It's Jonas."

Eliza slipped from Heath's arms, her heart sliding to her toes. "How? Where?"

"Not sure. The coroner will confirm, but it looks to have been blunt force trauma to the head. Death would have been quick by the looks of it." Wentworth blew out a breath, his cheeks inflating and deflating like a puffer fish. "Someone buried him near where the boathouse used to sit. Not deep enough, though. The recent deluge of rain must have washed it back up, I'd say."

"That's how Gizmo got the shirt." Eliza slumped back into her chair, struggling to breathe normally.

"If I were a betting man, I'd say yes." Wentworth laid a hand on her shoulder. "I'm posting a constable outside your room. No harm will come to you." He flicked his gaze to Heath. "I'm also posting constables around the house until this whole mess is figured out."

"I don't feel so good." Eliza wobbled to her feet. "Am I free to go?"

"Mr. Tilney, please take Miss Darcy to her room."

Heath wrapped an arm around Eliza and led her from the study. The hallway yawned before her. A scream steamed inside her. She killed it with a bite to her bottom lip.

"I don't need a babysitter." She knew she was being unfair to Heath, but fear gnawed at her good manners with vicious little teeth.

"Have we come to the crux of the matter?" Heath halted her steps as they neared her room. He tipped her chin, his gaze delving into hers. "I promised to be your sidekick, and I keep my promises. I'm not babysitting. I'm alongside you. For you. There's a difference." He kissed her long and deep, full of that promise. Eliza clung to it and almost asked him in. Tonight, she didn't want to feel the fear clawing her skin, didn't want to dwell on damage done by Nancy's manipulations, and didn't want to imagine what future strings Nancy would pull from jail to destroy Eliza's family. She wanted to touch Heath's skin and feel his heartbeat thumping with hers.

A throat cleared behind them. Davies, the stoic fresh-faced constable from the pub, blushed in his crisp uniform. "Sorry, miss. But I'm to be posted outside your door."

Heath whispered in her ear, "I'm here for you. Don't forget that."

Eliza watched Heath round the corner and drew in a shuddering breath.

"Don't worry, miss. I won't leave my post."

She smiled weakly at Constable Davies and locked herself in. Her bed enticed her, taunted her. She flopped spread-eagle on the bed, too tired to change from her dress or peel the makeup from her face. Caesar meowed a greeting and licked her forehead. She would look like death in the morning. The hairs on the back of her neck twitched. She prayed she would only look like death and not... well, be dead in the morning.

Chapter Seventeen
Another One Bites the Dust

I had a stern conversation with Kitty, which ended in tears for us both.
It appears she loved him deeply and had thought he loved her as well,
but she has promised to mend her ways, as she hates disappointing
Darcy and me. Darcy has changed his mind about London. His eyes
give him away. I think he knows the attacker's identity. I only wish he'd
share it with me. I am not weak. I miss our closeness, our confidence in
each other.
—Lizzy Bennet Darcy
Pemberley 1811

Eliza woke up alive and with a raging headache clanging demented cymbals within her head and a blinking light on her cell. With a heavy heart, she cooked herself in a steaming shower and tugged on a pair of skinny jeans, which seemed a bit skinnier than before.

Eliza opened her door and stepped out, tripping over the prone body of a sleeping Heath. He grunted and rolled to his side, the blanket falling from his torso, his white T-shirt exposing a dusting of hair on his stomach. Eliza swallowed.

"You don't need to keep sleeping in front of my door." She wanted him in her room, in her arms, in her soul.

"Good morning to you too." Heath grinned sleepily at her and glanced at Constable Davies, upright and wide awake in a folding chair. "Davies and I spent the night telling ghost stories. First one to get scared got the floor."

Eliza glanced at Constable Davies, his face as red as a beet. "Did he screech like a little girl?"

"What happens on watch, stays on watch, miss." Constable Davies gathered his chair and left.

"That's as good as a yes." Eliza prodded Heath's thigh with the tip of her shoe.

"Tough crowd." Heath hid a yawn behind his hand then held it out to her. "Join me?"

Eliza sank next to him and played her thumb over the top of his hand. "Thank you."

"For what?"

She raised an eyebrow. "I can't imagine this floor is comfortable."

"That is where you are wrong. This carpet is very plush. At least for the first ten minutes." He hitched to a sitting position, his eyes darkening. "The job of a sidekick is to make sure the hero lives to fight another day." The playful light returned to his eyes. "Besides, I had hoped you'd wake in the middle of the night, take pity on me, and invite me in."

She swatted at him. "Maybe that can—" She sniffed. "Do you smell that?"

He wound a strand of her hair around his finger. "Smells like Mrs. Bankcroft is luring you away from me to her kitchens."

"And it's working." She planted a smacking kiss on his lips. "Race you."

"But I have to shower and—"

"Not my problem," she singsonged as she raced through the house and into the kitchens.

"Good morning, Miss Eliza." Mrs. Bankcroft lifted a regal brow as Eliza slid onto a barstool and stared at the empty baking tins.

"Mrs. B, it seems you have found my secret weakness." Eliza dipped her finger into a mound of caramelly goo left over in a baking tin.

The cook lightly whacked at her fingers with a wooden spoon. "Don't go spoiling your breakfast."

"This is my breakfast." She gave her best cheeky grin and snuck another gooey drop to her mouth.

Mrs. Bankcroft's ample bosom heaved a sigh, and she slid a bowl over to Eliza, its insides dripping with caramel. "Here." She thrust a spatula in Eliza's face. "It's a good job I'm in a giving mood this morning."

A whine filtered from the closed pantry.

"I take it Gizmo's back."

"And in time-out too. Causing all that ruckus. Naughty mongrel." Mrs. Bankcroft slid the last of the caramel rolls to a china platter covered in peonies and set it next to a steaming bowl of scrambled eggs. "Jonas—" Her face reddened. "Oh dear. I didn't... oh dear..."

"Sit, Mrs. B, before you faint."

Mrs. Bankcroft shooed Eliza away with a towel but plopped in the offered chair. "I'm not the fainting sort, and I don't intend to start that habit now." A sheen of sweat beaded on her top lip, and under the crimson stains of a blush, her peach skin faded to bone white.

Eliza offered her a glass of orange juice. "Drink this."

"Got anything stronger?"

"You sound like me last night after finding a knife in my shoe." At Mrs. Bankcroft's raised eyebrow, Eliza retold the evening's events.

"There, there, what a to-do, I tell you." Mrs. Bankcroft wiped at her forehead with her apron. "What's this world comin' to?" She rubbed her hands together and wobbled to her feet. "No need for murder and mischief to make breakfast cold now, is there? Poppy!"

Seconds later, Poppy scooted into the kitchen. "What do you want?"

Mrs. Bankcroft gave her the eye. "I'll remind you of your station, girl."

Poppy set her chin higher.

"Get breakfast on the table." Mrs. Bankcroft heaved a sigh and narrowed her gaze at Poppy's retreating form. "I don't know what's got into that girl. Surly. Bad-mannered as ever I saw."

Before Eliza could comment, Mrs. Bankcroft called out several other names. Over the next few minutes, staff scampered here and there, taking trays and dishes laden with food from the kitchen to the dining room.

Emptied of staff and food, the kitchen settled into a quiet punctuated with the scratching and whining of the doggie prisoner. "That's the last of it. Go on with you now, Miss Eliza, and enjoy your last breakfast with the family."

Eliza paused, one foot out of the door. "What?"

"Just like you young people nowadays. Only listening with half an ear. Most of the family leaves today."

"But how? Where? With the investigation still going, I thought—"

"That's your problem. You think too much. Going to get you in trouble someday."

Eliza worried her bottom lip between her teeth. Mrs. Bankcroft would be very disappointed in how much thinking she really did and the very real trouble she had gotten into.

"Some of your relations, sorry for speaking out of turn, threw a mighty temper tantrum, I tell you. Thought they'd be next." Mrs. Bankcroft wiped her damp forehead with her apron. "Don't say as I blame them. Anyhow, Wentworth snagged their passports and such to keep them from running, but he gave the order they could leave. The inns and pubs in Lambton will sure make out well with the mass exodus of relations." She waved her hands at Eliza. "Now shoo, girl. Out of my kitchen." A wink took away the sting of the words.

In a trance, Eliza left the kitchen and shivered at the thought of the vast quietness descending upon Pemberley.

"There you are." Heath, freshly showered, grinned and swiped his thumb under her bottom lip. "You've had your breakfast, I see."

She wiped her mouth. "Nothing to see here."

"Oh, I disagree. Very much." He kissed her. "I can taste the evidence on you. Now, let's see if any of Cook's breakfast is left."

"We weren't that late." Eliza pouted at a few crumbs of caramel rolls, a dot of scrambled egg, and a burnt edge of bacon left on the buffet table. Her stomach grumbled, unhappy with only two finger licks of caramel.

"We could go into the village."

"Eliza, Heath, over here." Joy yodeled across the room, Great-Aunt Iris at her side. "We've saved some for you." She dropped her voice. "Vultures. All of them."

Eliza dove into a plate covered in breakfast-y goodness. Hunger at bay, she relayed her night to Joy and Aunt Iris.

Joy's jaw dropped. Aunt Iris pushed it shut for her with a crooked index finger. "And such a pretty pair of shoes. 'Tis a shame. I had a pair almost just like those. Your great-uncle had a thing for—"

"Aunt, did you miss the part about the knife?"

"I'm not senile. Of course I heard the bit about the knife."

Heath grinned, and Eliza kicked his shin under the table. "Yes, Aunt. This means we continue on. We are getting close. I can smell it."

"You're just smelling Wentworth." Joy looked over Eliza's head. "Miss Darcy."

Eliza spun in her chair. "Wentworth. How are you this morning?"

"May I have a word?" When Heath's chair scooted along the floor, Wentworth pinned him with a gaze. "Alone."

"Yeah. Sure." Eliza followed Wentworth into the hall and out the main door. The fountain, cleaned and filled with fresh water, spouted and gurgled away as if death hadn't floated in it just days ago.

"I need advice." He scratched at the stubble on his face.

"From me?"

"No, the ghost behind you."

"Not funny."

Wentworth shrugged, an odd look on the formidable man's face. "You want to play at cops and robbers, you need to get the sense of humor of one."

"A robber?" At his glare, she wagged her finger. "What were you saying about a sense of humor?"

His white teeth flashed in a grin against his dark skin. "Touché, Miss Darcy. Touché."

Eliza sank to sit on the edge of the fountain then jumped up again. She eyed the edge. "What's the advice you need?"

"Nancy hired herself a fancy barrister and is rolling over on Garrison. Claims it was all him. That she knew nothing about the fake ledgers and thieving staff."

"What did she say about being a Wickham?"

He snorted. "Claimed she never told Fitz because she didn't want him to hate her." He tucked his arms behind him and paced the flower-lined walkway. "Doesn't sit right in the old cop gut. If she's just an innocent bystander, she'd have blown the whistle on Garrison as soon as she'd found out."

"We need to find Garrison."

"Trust me, we're looking." He sank to the edge of the fountain. "Here's the rub. Do I tell your uncle I suspect his wife of murder?"

"Do you have enough evidence?"

"Not yet." He rubbed the back of his neck. "All the evidence points to Giles, but blimey if I don't think he's innocent. But the fingerprints, motive, means, opportunity point to him." He pierced her with a look. "Is Nancy capable of murder?"

"I'm not sure her hands have blood on them, but she could be the puppet master behind it all. She's capable of doing everything possible to keep her station in life." Eliza's stomach twisted. "It will destroy him. More than he already is."

"Do you want to destroy him, or should I?" He waved away her unspoken retort. "Needs must, I say. I'll give it a go." His cell phone chirped. He glanced at it, flicked his fingers across the screen, then stashed it in his pocket. "We had to release Greta a couple of hours ago. We had nothing to hold her on. And she recanted. She'll be back, I gather. Watch her, will you?"

"This better earn me that cool-looking hat you promised."

"Promised?" Obviously not willing to point out Eliza's exaggeration, he sighed. "I can only give you the hat if you don't get dead."

Eliza hoped the same as she trudged to her room, terrified of what she would find waiting for her.

ELIZA'S BEDROOM DOOR was ajar again. She pulled up short, tiptoed to it, and peered through the opening, her heart thundering.

The door swung open. Eliza clutched the doorjamb to keep from tumbling into the room.

"Miss Darcy?" Greta slammed a hand to her chest. "You gave me a fright."

"I gave you a fright?" Eliza unclenched her fists. "What are you doing in my room?"

Greta blinked at her tone. "Making your bed, miss."

Eliza slid a glance at her made bed. "Thank you." She cleared her throat. "Sorry about that. With all that's been going on, I'm a little jumpy."

Greta skimmed by her.

"Wait. Please."

Greta paused in the doorway, her arms folded across her chest.

"I'm sorry I couldn't help you with your dad."

Greta jutted her chin out.

"I don't believe he did it."

Greta eyed her. "You expect me to believe that load of rubbish?"

"Yes. And I want to prove his innocence. But I could use some assistance."

"I don't know how I can help you."

"You know more things about this house and the people in it than I ever will."

"I don't eavesdrop."

Eliza caught the fleeing Greta's arm. "I didn't mean that." She sat the trembling woman in a tulip-covered chair. "There are secrets in this house. Which ones do you know?"

"I'm not supposed to talk about the family."

"I'm part of the family. Talk."

Greta straightened her uniform and stared out the window for several seconds.

"What's wrong with this place?" Eliza prodded.

Greta shivered. "Nancy."

"What do you mean?"

"Two years ago..." She swallowed then blinked tears away. "I needed a few more bob, you know? I had worked here for a couple of months and knew the expensive bric-a-brac just lying around. No one would notice a few pieces missing here and there. So I nicked a few. Just to get me by, you know?"

"What happened?"

"Nancy caught me red-handed."

"She didn't fire you?"

"In hindsight, I wish she had. I wish she had given me a redundancy, reported me to the police. Anything but what she did."

Eliza squeezed Greta's trembling hand. "Go on."

"She blackmailed me. Threatened to turn me in. Said she'd make it seem like I'd stolen a lot more. All I needed to do was keep stealing now and then when she ordered it, but this time, she kept the money."

"Do you have any proof?"

"I knew you wouldn't believe me."

"It's not me you have to convince. It's the police."

Greta hung her head. "Yes. I have proof, but I suppose it will hurt me before it hurts Nancy." She pawed at her throat. "Remember seeing me at the bank?"

Eliza nodded, afraid anything more than that would startle the girl into silence.

"I was depositing money Nancy gave me. It's my account, my name on all the transactions, but Nancy gets the cash."

"Is that why you kept the—" Eliza snapped her mouth shut and waved away Greta's questioning look. "Keep going."

She hesitated. "I kept the"—a blush mottled her cheeks—"bank receipts. As proof. Of what, I can't say. It will all fall back on me, anyway. Stupid, stupid! It's just my word against Nancy. Who will believe me?" Greta jumped from the chair. "Poppy!" She paced the room. "She knows it all. Nancy was blackmailing her too. And Jonas." She swallowed. "But he didn't get out either. He had gone on about cutting ties, getting away from this place, but"—tears tracked down her face—"it's too late for him, isn't it? It's too late for me too."

"But why are you scared now?" Eliza handed Greta a tissue. "Nancy's been arrested. She's gone. There's nothing to be afraid of anymore."

"Nancy's not the one. Look, I even tried to warn Piers. He was getting too mouthy. I had to tell Theo, somebody, or we'd all be caught. And look what happened to him."

A squeaky floorboard outside the door sounded an alarm. Poppy sauntered into the room. "Thought I heard Greta's voice. Mrs. Underhill is looking for you. Sent me to find you." Poppy snapped her fingers at Greta. "Chop-chop. She wanted you ten minutes ago."

As soon as Poppy sailed from the room, Greta hugged her arms to her stomach. "Oh Lord, I shouldn't have said anything." She clutched at her throat. "Please. I need to go." She stumbled from the room, the door banging against the tulip wallpaper.

Eliza massaged the back of her neck. If only she could massage away the queasiness swimming in her gut. She whipped out a text to Heath: *Run-in with Greta and Poppy. Need you.*

Library. Five minutes. Which parts of me do you need?

Eliza replied with a tongue-sticking-out emoji.

Five minutes later, she found her sidekicks assembled in the library.

"I thought we needed the whole team." Heath handed Eliza a cup of steaming tea.

She took a tentative sip. "Good idea."

"I have those every once in a while." He whispered in her ear, "I have a few other good ideas when you have time to give them consideration."

Great-Aunt Iris tutted from a high-backed chair, her white-tennis-shoe-clad feet dangling inches from the floor. "That's enough, young man. No time for a prelude to some how's-your-father."

Joy sputtered and choked on her tea at the octogenarian's reference to sex. "Aunt Iris!" Joy wiped at the tea dribbling down her chin. "That's not... appropriate."

"I'm long past the age where that still applies." Aunt Iris clucked her tongue and wiggled farther back in her chair. "I never thought I'd say this, but I miss all the barmy relatives. They were entertaining."

"Good riddance, I say." Joy sent Aunt Iris a sideways glance. "I couldn't convince Mum to stay a few more days. There's only so much of Nancy she can take. She just rang me. Said she and dad had booked the cutest B and B near the village. But you're all stuck with me. I'm not going anywhere. At least until this case is solved."

"You could be here for a while." Eliza perched on the armrest of Heath's chair.

"That's the beauty of being an author. I get to work wherever I am."

Eliza drummed her fingers on Heath's arm. "I just can't wrap my head around it all. Nancy is as guilty as the day is long. But the way Greta was talking just now in my room, someone else is pulling the strings. Maybe even killing. And she knows who it is. We need something where we can write all this down. Keep track of things."

"The old nursery will have a chalkboard. At least it did years ago." Aunt Iris scooted to the front of her chair and waved off a helping hand from Heath. "I'm not that old."

"Yes, ma'am."

"Come on." On her squeaking sneakers, Aunt Iris led them out and up the three flights of stairs to the nursery. In spite of the diligent dusting and cleaning by the staff, age and disuse coated the room. Eliza peeked under the dust covers. Some chairs, a few desks, and a cradle littered the room. A box contained crayons, markers, bits and pieces of paper, and some chalk. After taking a pink piece, she wrote on the board:

Greta Winfield — got caught stealing by Nancy — forced to steal from the estate on Nancy's behalf.

Poppy — last to see Piers alive — terrified maid — also stealing — has keys she shouldn't — could she know who the killer is?

Nancy — secret aunt to Garrison — blackmailer and embezzler.

"If they aren't afraid of Nancy, who are they afraid of?" Joy drew a large question mark in yellow chalk next to Nancy's name.

"It would have to be someone in the house." Eliza drew lines on the board. "Who else, excepting present company and Uncle Fitzwilliam, works here?"

"Tash?"

"Aunt Iris, Tash was the one attacked. He wouldn't whack his own head." Eliza wrote his name on one of the lines and drew a large *X* through it.

"What about the gardeners? Giles had nothing positive to say about any of them. And wasn't Piers killed with a hoe?" Heath took the chalk from Eliza's fingers and wrote *gardeners* on a line.

"But the outdoor staff wouldn't have the same access to the house and the family as the indoor staff and probably had no idea the secret tunnel existed." Eliza snatched the chalk back and wrote the name *Theodore* on a line. "He's always given me the creeps with all his creepy creeping."

"That's his job." Great-Aunt Iris tutted.

"There are other footmen, Jonas being one of them, and he never crept around. Poor man." Eliza shook her head. The queasiness, which had become a norm for her since the murder, chewed a hole in her middle. "Greta mentioned how he wanted out in the worst way." Eliza circled Theodore's name. Twice. She stood back and tapped the chalk against her palm. "That's it. All we have for suspects are a various assortment of groundsmen and a hobbity footman. Great. Just great."

"Maybe Nancy is the killer too." Joy scribbled the word *murderer* after Nancy's name.

"Greta was clear there was someone else. And Poppy does seem overly scared of Theodore."

"But Eliza, what could a footman of Theodore's standing—"

Eliza snorted and earned a glare from her great-aunt. "Sorry, Aunt Iris. Continue."

"—of Theodore's standing gain from murder?"

"What if he's not a footman?" Joy asked.

"Joy, if you want to be taken seriously, you must not say foolish things." Great-Aunt Iris emphasized her point with a wagging finger.

"Wait, Aunt Iris." Eliza snapped her fingers for the chalk. "Joy has a point. I remember Giles saying something about the grounds-men not being good at groundsmanning."

"I don't think that's a word." Heath wiped a smudge of chalk off her nose.

"If Shakespeare could make up over a thousand words, so can I."

"Touché."

"And we also know Nancy was blackmailing some of the staff in-to stealing from the estate. I wish Greta hadn't run off like a scared little rabbit." Eliza clutched the chalk. "She was hinting at Theodore. Which makes sense, as she always seems on edge with him."

Heath slouched against the chalkboard, smudging Nancy's name. He brushed off his shirt. "Bloody hell."

"I'm afraid things are only going to get more bloody hellish around here." Eliza plunked the piece of chalk on the table. "I'll try to find Greta later, hopefully get more information out of her."

Aunt Iris grunted a grand harrumph. "I could tuck into one of Cook's sugary delights. Shall we go see what she has lying about?"

Eliza erased the board and followed them out. "You've never had a better idea. I hope she made her gingersnap cookies."

"Biscuits," the trio of Brits reminded her.

Eliza rolled her eyes and closed the door to the nursery, speed walking to catch up with the gang instead of traversing the vast hall-ways alone while knowing a killer lurked in the corners. They had just reached the foyer when Poppy stumbled down the steps, her hair and eyes wild.

"I'm sorry... but... oh Lord... so much blood." She retched and slammed a hand over her mouth.

"There, there, Poppy. Calm down. Take a few deep breaths." Eliza took a step forward but couldn't bring herself to touch the woman.

Poppy's few deep breaths came as large gasps setting off a series of hiccups. "Greta. She's dead." She sank to the floor, a pile of wailing tears.

"Where?" Eliza stilled.

"In your room."

Heath took the steps two at a time. "Eliza, stay with Poppy."

"Nope."

He didn't bother forcing her to listen, and they raced to Eliza's room. The door swung open to a grim scene. Greta's body lay on the tulip comforter, her hands crossed in death, a piece of folded paper stuck in between her hands. She stared at the ceiling, unseeing and oblivious to the pool of blood fed by the gash in her temple and soaking through the pillow.

Eliza's world went gray and sparkly, and her legs turned to jelly. She sank to the floor, Heath's call to the police a buzzing in her ear. Knowing she shouldn't contaminate the scene but not caring, she reached up and laid her hand on Greta's shoulder, still warm through her uniform. The poor girl did not deserve such a fate. Nor had Piers or Jonas.

Strong arms lifted her from the floor. She burrowed into Heath's chest, a dam of unwept tears straining at her eyes. She knew, she feared, that Greta was not the last to share in such a fate. Eliza was next.

Chapter Eighteen
Fitted for a Coffin

Lady Catherine de Bourgh deigned to visit Pemberley. She looked as if she were sucking on a lemon the entire visit, which, thank heavens, was of short duration. She had an odd penchant for checking the curtains. I did not ask why. I had to gently remind Darcy to show forgiveness of his aunt, but his anger, once aroused, is not easily tempered. I only pray the time and distance from his aunt will heal his lost goodwill.
—Lizzy Bennet Darcy
Pemberley 1811

Morning rays streamed through a window, illuminating not tulips, as Eliza had become used to seeing, but carnations. *Drab little flowers.* She stretched, her toes touching human skin.

"Oi!" Joy yelped. "Your feet are bloody freezing."

"Sorry." Eliza curled into a fetal position and faced Joy. "Thanks for letting me sleep with you last night. I hope I didn't keep you up. I didn't sleep well."

"I'd have to be sleeping for you to disturb my sleep. Didn't get a wink either."

Eliza rubbed her eyes, trying to dispel not only the sleep from them but also the vision of the young woman whose life had come to an abrupt and unjust end. Eliza couldn't back down and would not let evil win. She would fight. Wondering whether she would win or not sent waves of doubt sloshing through her middle. She slipped from the bed and slammed her feet into her slippers. "I have a strange feeling."

"Great-Aunt Iris has those all the time. It's usually because she needs to tuck into a good meal."

For the first time in her life, Eliza didn't have an appetite. The words of the letter imprisoned in Greta's dead hands had been straightforward: *Leave or Die*. Eliza had no room for food with all the knots and tangles filling her stomach. She didn't have the heart to worry Joy about the visions of her own bloody death. Pelting people over the head with a large object seemed to be a habit of the killer, and Eliza wanted nothing to do with said head pelting but had no idea how to escape it.

She dressed behind a screen decorated with birds of paradise and ruby-red flowers and put herself together as much as her trembling hands would allow. "I'll run and see if I can find out more from Uncle."

"Didn't Heath want you to text him so he could walk you down?"

Eliza frowned. After Greta's death, Heath had cradled her, consoled her, and made her promise to always be with someone else. She had accepted that the alternative was him sleeping outside Joy's door. "Bloody nuisance," she hissed.

"Someone's getting into the English spirit. That was a good crack at the accent too."

Eliza threw her slipper at Joy's head. "Shush." She flicked her fingers over her phone screen and tapped her foot until a soft rap on the door made her heart thump in her chest.

"Good morning. How'd you sleep?" He smelled of Irish Spring soap and freshly brushed teeth.

Eliza tasted his lips. "Good."

"She's lying," Joy chirped from the bed, her blond hair jutting in a thousand different directions.

"I know." He traced the delicate skin under her eyes.

Eliza bit back a growl and sauntered away. He wrapped his hand around her upper arm, bringing her to a stop. "Eliza, please don't pretend things are okay. Don't leave me in the dark."

"Greta's death just rocked me to my core. That's all."

He smiled as if he believed her, but his hand gripped hers a little tighter than normal as they descended the stairs and walked to her uncle's study.

Wentworth rose as they entered. "Miss Darcy, Mr. Tilney, good morning." He sank back into his chair facing Uncle Fitzwilliam's desk and the man himself, grave and grim, behind the mahogany desk.

Eliza leaned a hip against the desk and gripped her uncle's hand. "What is it?"

He shook his head and motioned to Wentworth.

"Ah, some new information has come to light, I'm afraid." He flicked a glance at Uncle Fitzwilliam. "We have released Giles Winfield, as the evidence against him was not strong enough. We have, in his place, charged another."

The silence stretched until Eliza's nerves quivered. "Who?"

"Your aunt." Her uncle's eyes blinked with each word as if a gavel were pounding out those two little words in his head. He scraped back his chair and prowled the room.

Wentworth monitored the pacing for several seconds before handing Eliza a baggie with a pair of gardening gloves sealed inside. "We found these in Nancy's office. The fibers from the gloves match fibers caught in the wooden hoe handle."

Eliza stared at the gloves. The gloves had not been there when she searched Nancy's office, which meant that either she was a horrible sleuth and had missed them or someone came after her and planted them to frame Nancy. She didn't like either option.

She swallowed the bile rising in her throat. "Have you found Garrison?" Eliza feared he would say yes, buried in the garden or under her aunt's flooring. Just like in Edgar Allan Poe's short story, "The Tell-Tale Heart." Had Nancy heard it at night, thumping and pounding for justice. Had it—

"No." Wentworth broke into her daymare.

Her stomach dropped to the tips of her toes. "Is he... he..."

"Dead?" Wentworth heaved a sigh. "There has been no sign of him. Anywhere. He's either good at hiding or..." His shoulders hitched.

"I'm not saying I'd be the first to bring a casserole and a sympathy card, but he—"

"He lied." Uncle Fitzwilliam sliced his hand through the air, interrupting her. "About everything. He and Nancy connived behind my back, lied about their relationship. Come to think of it, everyone she hired seems to be in on the schemes or was blackmailed into doing her bidding." He slammed his fist on his desk. "I should just give everyone redundancies and start from scratch."

"Not Tash or Mrs. Bankcroft or..."

He pinched the bridge of his nose and sighed. "I know, Eliza. I know."

"Could Nancy have turned on Garrison? Is that the reason Piers and Jonas and Greta are dead?" Blood drained from her face. "But she can't be the killer. She couldn't have killed Greta."

"The gloves found in her possession say otherwise. We can't rule her out for the first two murders."

"But it doesn't make sense. None of this makes any sense."

Wentworth eased to his feet. "You're not telling me anything I don't already know." He shook hands with Uncle Fitzwilliam. "Miss Darcy, could I have a moment of your time?"

She stepped out into the hall with him. "Yes?"

He dug around in his suit pants pocket and handed her a paper-wrapped bundle. "Go ahead. Don't just stare at it. Open it."

She peeled back the paper and smiled. In her palm sat a souvenir of a bobby's black hat with the Union Jack flag flying freely on the brim. "What's this for?"

He gave a small salute. "You earned it. Eliza." He marched off, his boot heels clicking away.

She fisted the small tourist-y bling, her sinking heart warring with the trembling smile on her lips. She hadn't earned it. Her uncle's heart was broken, her father's betrayal still hovered over those she loved, three people were dead, and she might as well be fitted for her own coffin, as she was ninety-nine percent certain her aunt had not killed anybody.

THERE WAS ONLY ONE way to catch a rat. One needed to be sneakier than the rat. Eliza closed the door to the library, checked to see that it was empty, and slipped into the secret passageway, step stool in hand. She flicked on the flashlight, and bright beams filtered through the darkness. Her skin crawled, and she checked over her shoulder every thirty seconds. The killer knew of the secret tunnel, but she kept on, stopping at every peephole, listening and peering through the opening.

The rooms, empty of guests, rang with silence. She wanted to hear Margery's biting insults and the horrible karaoke of Callum and Jasper. She would even volunteer to have a two-and-a-half-minute conversation with Garrison. She passed the study, not wanting to snoop on her uncle. The next few peepholes opened to an empty library, an empty sitting room, and an empty dining room. Giving herself one more room to check, she scooted down the tunnel and stopped at the opening of the drawing room, slid it open, and peered through.

Poppy, in her neat uniform, dusted the drawing room furniture. The heavy curtains were open, and sunlight streamed through the windows. Poppy moved about with a duster and flicked the feathers here and there, paying no attention to the task at hand. Instead, her eyes kept scanning the room, the door, the window. She moved out of the peephole's range, and Eliza strained to hear any sound. The door clicked open, and footsteps entered the room, but the person was still out of visible range. For the first time in her life, Eliza wished she had removable eyeballs.

"Still giving the illusion you work around here?" Theodore's voice dripped with disdain.

"Theodore. You scared me sneaking up like that."

"Care for a fag?" A soft rattle of cigarettes in their carton punctured the silence.

"I'll be right there. Just have to finish the dusting."

Theodore laughed. "You don't dust. We both know that. Nancy only keeps you around for one thing."

"Shut that hole in your face. Someone could be listening."

"That's right." He snarled. "The walls have ears, don't they?"

"I warned you not to even hint at the tunnel, you dim arse," Poppy hissed. She flicked her gaze to the wall covering the secret. Eliza jerked away from the peephole, praying Poppy hadn't noticed the pinprick of dark against the embellished wallpaper.

"And wouldn't that just be the dog's bollocks if someone else knew what I knew? That sad little overlooked Poppy was nothing more than just a shirty, blackmailing slag. But Greta had figured that out, hadn't she?"

"Belt up. We both know what you've done. Best for you, you remember that. Save me a fag. Now piss off."

Theodore slammed the door.

Eliza risked another peek. Poppy stood in the middle of the room, her back ramrod straight, her body vibrating. After chucking her duster on the floor, Poppy stomped out of sight, the slamming door the only indication the room was empty. Eliza tilted her head.

Poppy had threatened Theodore. Eliza thumped her head against the cold tunnel wall in tandem with her thoughts. *Nothing. About. This. Case. Makes. Sense.*

Her brain clicked, and like little gears shifting into place, the facts, the hints, the offhanded comments slipped into order.

Afraid Poppy and/or Theodore would materialize in the tunnel, Eliza rushed out of the tunnel, into the library, and straight into Great-Aunt Iris's frown.

"Doing some sleuthing without me, I see. Hmph."

Eliza pressed a quick kiss to her great-aunt's papery-thin forehead. "No hard feelings? I'm ninety-nine percent sure who the killer is."

"Who?" Great-Aunt Iris rubbed her hands together.

"It's—no, I don't want to say without being sure. I need to check one more thing."

"Shouldn't you ring Wentworth?" her great-aunt called after her as Eliza mall-walked from the room.

"Not until I'm sure," Eliza threw over her shoulder and hoofed it to the servants' quarters. If Theodore and Poppy were out smoking, there was a good chance the wing would be emptied. Her suspicions were correct. With speed and as much efficiency as that afforded her, she tore through the men's rooms.

Finding Theodore's dresser, she rifled through the drawers in search of convincing evidence. She found nothing but a pack of smokes under his underwear and a bag of salt-and-vinegar chips on top of the scratched and worn dresser. Her hands stilled around the crinkling bag. It couldn't be that easy. Shouldn't be that easy. She tiptoed over to the unmade cot. Her foot connected with something, and it clinked against the wall. A pop can. Cherry Vimto. She stared at the can, wishing, hoping, and praying it would disappear or change into any other type of pop can. Just not be the type of pop can found in what used to be the boathouse. Double-checking for a hidden Theodore, she crept from the men's quarters to the bathroom cavernous enough for twenty men to share. The unused lockers squeaked on aged hinges. Dust filled them all.

"Dammit." Eliza moved on to the shower room. The pattern of pickle-and-olive-green-colored tiles reminded her of gym class. Shivering at the memories, she tested each showerhead. They didn't turn. On the cusp of another swear word, she stilled when the heel of her shoe clicked hollowly on a tile.

She fell to her knees and tapped on the tile. Hollow. Then she tapped on the ones surrounding it. Solid. She dug in with her fingernails and pried up the tile. A hole had been carved out, just deep enough for three cell phones. Eliza's heart stopped then thumped into overdrive. The three phones of the three victims that were never found. Until that moment. By her.

Sleuths do not hyperventilate. Eliza repeated the mantra in her head as she stowed the phones back in their hidey-hole, replaced the tile, and raced from the servants' quarters into the bright and cheery decor of the main part of the house.

The phones, the chips, the pop. All were within easy reach of a ferrety-looking footman with knowledge of the secret tunnel and in cahoots with Nancy. Forgetting her own dignity, Eliza sprinted through the house, which had gained a few rooms in her panic. She had to find Wentworth, her uncle. Heath. Somebody. She had found the killer. Instead of elation at solving the case, a lead weight settled in her stomach, stewing and communing with her resident butterflies. The murderer was—

"Theodore?" Poppy stood in the doorway leading to the servants' quarters, her back to Eliza.

Eliza skidded to a stop, darted behind a large urn filled with fake flowers, and strained to hear Theodore's reply. She couldn't make out his nasally, whining voice.

"There's been a cock-up on your shite plans. Meet me in five min-utes. Where the old boathouse used to be."

Again, no response came from Theodore. Poppy glanced up and down the hallway, a small smile ticking at the corners of her lips. Eliza tucked herself farther into the bouquet, not wanting Poppy's gaze to find her. After another set of glances, including a well-placed look at the forest of foliage Eliza hid behind, Poppy stomped off, her back ramrod straight as if a broomstick had lodged itself up her back-side.

"Would suit her right if it did," Eliza mumbled. She scampered to her room to grab her cardigan and "mackintosh," as Great-Aunt Iris called it. Eliza snatched the bright-yellow raincoat from a hook in her room. The weather had turned, and instead of late-morning sunshine, little black rain clouds spit cold rain upon the late morn-ing. *Of all the stupid places to meet.* There wasn't even any shelter from the rain there anymore. The rain pelted the windows harder. Maybe she just wouldn't go. Her inner wannabe sleuth kicked into gear. Her literary heroes never backed down due to a little rain. With a growl, she stashed her cell phone in the inner lining of her raincoat, slipped on sturdy shoes, and scampered out of the house and into the wet.

"This better be good." She tripped over a topiary rabbit. The poor creature's ear snapped off and thudded to the wet grass. She picked it up and shoved it into some twigs, but it toppled over again. After a promise of future reconstructive surgery, she abandoned the tree rabbit and sprinted to the site of the burned-down boathouse that was currently a charred mark on a beat-up old piece of cement. Nobody was there.

A twig snapped behind her. Twisting, she had only seconds to register the face of a shovel. And then she knew nothing but dark-ness.

Chapter Nineteen
The Darkest Hour

Darcy fears for my safety, and to be honest, I fear for it as well. The house was ransacked last night. Nothing of import was stolen, as our footmen scared the villain away. Darcy demands I have constant company, even on my much-loved solitary walks. Due to recent events, I am content with this arrangement but pray nightly for this mystery to resolve. I want my Darcy back. I want my Pemberley back.
—Lizzy Bennet Darcy
Pemberley 1811

A demented monkey banging cymbals was surely responsible for the clanging in her skull. Eliza clutched her head, groaning at the piercing pain stabbing her temple. Moisture seeped through her leggings, and the damp, moldy smell permeated the air. *Where in the bloody hell am I?* She peeked her eyes open only to see oily blackness. Her heart wilted in her chest. Whimpering, she curled into the fetal position.

Suck it up, buttercup. Gritting her teeth against the pain, she sat up. Her gut roiled at the movement, and her brain pounded against her skull. She rose to her feet, bit back a four-lettered curse at the pain searing through her ankle, and smashed her head on the low ceiling. She stumbled forward, her arms outstretched to keep from banging into hidden objects, and landed hard on her knees, back to the packed-earth floor.

Then she remembered. Her phone was still tucked in the inner lining of her raincoat. She yanked it out and pressed the flashlight icon, and the small room illuminated from inky blackness to dingy grayness. Cobwebs hung from the ceiling and swayed in some invisible breeze. Rickety shelves that looked a hundred years old still housed tin cans and a few odds and ends covered in decades of dust and grime. Shivers skittered over her skin like a thousand spiders. *Seriously, where am I?*

She swiped the beam of light from the ceiling and shelves to the floor and screamed. Theodore's eyes stared into her soul. His sightless eyes.

"Theodore?" she whispered and prodded him with the tip of the boot encasing her good foot. He didn't move, didn't blink. Bile erupted into her mouth. Kneeling beside him, she flicked the light beam over his body, his face. Blood pooled under his head. Biting back a scream, she reached forward, her hand entering the light, and stilled. Blood had turned her hand rusty.

Eliza Jane Darcy, you can't faint. You cannot faint. With shaking fingertips, she gently prodded her temple and the side of her head, gritting her teeth in agony. Blood. Her blood. Breathing through clenched teeth, she wiped her hand on her leggings and checked her phone. No service. Hot tears dammed in her eyes. Blinking them back, she checked out Theodore again. His white face was set in a hideous death mask. He had not died quietly or quickly. Eliza rolled him over and froze. Her head felt as if it would pop off her neck and skitter about the ceiling like a balloon. A dozen or more gash marks littered the man's head, neck, and upper back. Whoever had killed him had hated him.

And whoever had killed him had her locked in that creepy room. Meaning she was wrong about the killer. It had never been Theodore.

Heath. Joy. Uncle Fitzwilliam. She had to get to them and warn them. Her heart slid to her shoes.

After rolling Theodore's body back, she stumbled to her feet, winced, and fell to the ground. She concentrated the light from her phone on what looked like a trap door in the ceiling of the room. "Help!" Her screams echoed around her, taunting her. "Help, can anyone hear me?" Her screams turned to screeches and dissolved into whispers as she scooted as far away from Theodore's body as possible.

She would die there and wither away to nothing more than the junk on the shelves, left to rot and gather dust. If only she could tell Heath just one time that she'd come to—

The trap door swung open, and a large form fell to the dirt-packed floor with a thud and a "What the bloody, bleeding hell?" The trap door slammed shut again.

"Heath." She crawled over to him, her hands roaming his face and his hair, her lips trailing not far behind.

"Darling," Heath gasped between her roving fingers and lips. "Love, can you just... Ow, that bloody stings... can you..."

That name for her on his lips, "Love," made Eliza pant in frustration. "Why aren't you—" Her fingers stilled and came away sticky. Without direct light, she could only assume it was blood. But he was alive and warm and... alive. She smashed her lips to his but didn't give him time to reciprocate. "Are you okay? What are you doing here?" she scolded. "Why aren't you touching me?"

"First of all, if you would trail your fingers down my arms, yup, just like that"—he chuckled as she breathed a curse word—"you'll find I'm rather tied up, you see, and as for the bloody boathouse, that was your idea, which has obviously gone all sixes and sevens."

"My idea?" Eliza pulled back. "I never told you to meet me here."

"You left a note."

"No, I—"

"Poppy," they chorused. After that, they began their own individual monologues. Eliza concentrated on the fact that Poppy was probably a female dog in another life, and Heath's, well, Eliza had never heard some of his words before and assumed they were all very English and all very horrid.

Eliza's fingers fumbled for her phone and concentrated the beam on his chest. Light chased away the oily blackness, and she lost herself in Heath's eyes, so blue, so alive.

"Eliza." He tilted his body toward her and grunted in frustration. "In my front pocket is a penknife."

"You carry a pocketknife?"

"Don't I look like someone who would carry a knife?"

In spite of her wooziness, pain, and the impending sense of death and danger, or maybe because of it, a giggle burbled in the back of her throat. "They sell Swiss Army knives in the button-up shirt section of the store?"

He growled low in his throat. "A grown-ass man always carries a penknife."

"Hey, you stole my catchphrase. Well, except for the woman part."

"Imitation is the sincerest form of flattery. Now dig in my trousers and find it."

"How romantic."

"I'll make it worth your time and effort."

Eliza slipped her hand into his front pocket.

He hissed. "Hurry up."

Her fingers touched the knife. "Found it." She pulled it out and wrestled free the largest of the blades. "Here." Her fingers, numb with panic and cold, dropped the knife to the ground. A sob broke through her clenched teeth.

"Eliza?" Heath pivoted on his knees, his body swaying. "Love, listen. We are going to get out of this, you and me. But in order to make that happen, you need to cut whatever is around my wrists. Chin up. You can do this."

Eliza inhaled and exhaled, gripped the knife, and sliced through the plastic ties. Before she could pivot the blade back into place, Heath crushed her to his chest, his hands stroking her hair and her back. She winced as his fingers brushed the open wound on her temple.

"You're bleeding." Heath snatched her phone and shone the light on the side of her head. A curse word filled the small space. "I'll get you out of here. Promise." He rested his forehead gently on hers. "We couldn't find you. We searched the house, the secret tunnel. After your great-aunt claimed you knew who the killer was, my heart gave up hope. But then I found your note." He cursed again. "I should have known something didn't add up."

"What happened?" Eliza breathed in Heath's scent, latching on to it to keep from careening out of control.

"I ran to where the old boathouse used to be and wham! I came to just before being dropped in here. I heard some voices. Male and a female. They must have tied my wrists when I was out." He massaged his wrists. "If I find Theodore, I'll—"

Eliza directed the beam of light at Theodore's body. "He wasn't the one to hog-tie and drag you."

Heath hung his head in what looked like prayer before scooting to the farthest wall. He tucked her into his arms, and she rested her head on his chest and listened to his heart thumping against his rib cage. She prayed his heart would beat for the next eighty years and not the minutes or hours her gut told her were imminent. She kept the flashlight glowing, a nightlight in the dark.

"Poppy was the murderer all along?" Heath's voice rumbled deep in his chest.

Eliza's hot, welling tears finally broke free. "I'm so sorry. Sorry I got you in this stupid situation. Sorry I ever stuck my stupid nose where it didn't belong." Her voice cracked, and her tears won. Sobs wracked her body, and she was only aware of Heath's fingers on her back, making small circles and tiny figure eights.

After minutes or hours, she couldn't tell which, Heath eased her from him and wiped the tears from her cheeks with his thumb. "Don't be sorry. Ever. This is not your fault. Blame Poppy. She's the damn loon." He swiped an index finger down her nose. "And don't ever call your nose stupid. I quite like it."

She swatted his hand away. "Experts say a romance built under stressful situations is doomed and won't last."

"Lucky for you I fell in love with you before being shoved in this hole, don't you think?" He pressed a quick kiss to her lips. "Now, use that incredibly sexy mind of yours. How did we get here in the first place?"

Eliza's heart still twirled from his proclamation of love. "You... you just can't spring that on a girl and expect her to think. Rationally."

He quirked an eyebrow. "Want me to take it back, love?"

"No."

"Then let's figure this out so we can get out of here. I promise to find a romantic spot and tell you I love you all over again."

With that promise in mind—although the way his eyes darkened, it seemed more like a threat—she crinkled her nose. "Okay, it is clear Theodore was not the murderer. At least not *the* murderer. I'd bet all my money Poppy was the instigator behind all this."

"But why?"

She swiped at her eye. Fresh blood trickled from her wound and oozed down her cheek.

"Here." Heath unbuttoned his shirt, slipped it off, and tore the long sleeves from their threaded moorings. With deft fingers, he tied one sleeve around her forehead before fastening it in the back. He did the same for himself. "There, now we look the parts of vengeful victims out to destroy those who wronged us."

Eliza clutched his hand and concentrated on its warmth, then she used it as inspiration to carry her thoughts from the dingy hole of death to the bright world outside. She replayed all the moments that had never added up—the looks, the tension between staff, the odd little Poppy. Heath squeezed her hand. It all clicked.

"You figured it out, didn't you?" Heath sidled closer, his hand never leaving hers.

"I think so. It bothered me that Nancy would bring attention to her embezzlement by murdering someone. She's been sitting quietly for so long, sucking off the lifeblood of the estate like a disgusting leech. Uncle Fitzwilliam's investments alone bring in millions a year. If she continued being smart about it, she could have siphoned off a pretty little nest egg just by being a sneaking, conniving little..." Eliza closed her eyes and rubbed her temples. "Why ruin it?"

"True. You're saying someone went rogue?"

"Someone who'd come to rely on the embezzlement ring more than Nancy."

"Poppy?"

"She has far too much in her bank account to explain as just her wages as house staff. Imagine, if you will, a broke Poppy, a woman who's been overlooked her entire life, where even people she works with can't remember her name. She discovers the secret tunnel and lurks until she gets her hands on some juicy information and spies on the rest of the staff. Add a dash of crazy and a pinch of terror, and you have a mixture for a violent blackmailer." Eliza nibbled on her cuticles, thought better of it, and shoved her hand back in her lap. "She finds out that Piers wants out, is going to the cops. If the cops found out about Nancy's embezzlement, whatever Poppy had going on would dry up like the Sahara. She'd be finished."

"I bet he confided in the wrong person."

"If I were a betting woman, I'd bet he poured his soul out to Greta. And Poppy overheard. He might have even confided in Poppy." Eliza shivered. "She seemed the perfect quiet little mouse. Who'd fear her?"

Heath flicked his gaze over Theodore's body. "He learned the hard way. But what did she have over him to make him do her dirty work?"

"No clue. We need to get out of here before she comes back, though." Eliza scanned the room again with the flashlight. "Looks to be an underground cellar of sorts. The only way out is through that thing." She beamed the light up at the wooden trap door. "We're not getting out on our own."

"Oh yes we are. I have a plan. We'll be back in no time, enjoying your uncle's expensive brandy and listening to your great-aunt's crazy stories." Heath flashed her a grin so confident that Eliza was surprised they didn't teleport from the hole to her uncle's library. Her newfound family must be sick with concern. She hoped Aunt Iris wasn't taken ill with worry or that Joy wasn't three tumblers into Uncle Fitzwilliam's alcohol supply. She glanced at her phone. Eight p.m. What had seemed like days had been only hours, but she wanted out of that hole. Closing her eyes, she rested her head on Heath's chest again and listened as his rumbling voice detailed his plan.

A half hour later, the rattling of the trap door jarred her and Heath from a restless slumber.

"Ready?" he whispered into her ear and pressed a kiss behind it.

"As I'll ever be."

"Jolly good." He squirmed to where he'd been dropped before and rolled onto his back, his arms tucked behind him and his hands clasping his opened Swiss Army knife. Eliza cowered farther into the corner and clamped her jaw on her chattering teeth.

The door swung open, a ladder descended, and the small form of Poppy crawled into the dank hole. "Good. You're both here." Her face glowed eerily white in the grayness. She studied the prone figures of the two men. Her gaze finally settled on Eliza with feverish intensity.

"Didn't have any plans." Eliza shrugged with more nonchalance than she felt. Despite the cold damp, sweat beaded on her back.

Poppy gestured to Eliza's phone still pouring out light. "I see you've made your new home cozy."

"When life hands you lemons..."

Poppy stepped over Heath. "Didn't mean to whack your lover so hard on the head. I hope he fares better than Theodore." She prodded Theodore's body with the tip of her shoe. "Although Theodore got more than just one whack. Filthy wanker."

Eliza scuttled back and hid a grimace when pain shot through her ankle as Poppy approached. A rotting shelf dug into her ribs. "Why?"

"Why what? Does it matter why you're going to die? It doesn't change things. Dead is dead. Piers asked me that too. Well, more like whined it. Pitiful, really. And Theodore? He begged for his life, like it mattered. Like his life mattered." A harsh laugh grated from her throat. "A sniveling weasel like him worth sharing oxygen with? No, thank you. I did you a favor by offing him. He was the one helping your aunt suck the estate coffers dry, quid by quid. I should be the one being thanked. I was the one to figure out he was stealing from Nancy."

"You blackmailed him?"

"Why not? He had it coming, stealing from the queen herself. He made a great little front man, though. And you followed my clues so well, believed my tears."

"But I still don't under—"

"And you won't. I'm not here to monologue. I have beds to turn down and pillows to fluff. Yours." Poppy's eyes gleamed. "How sad you won't be enjoying my turndown service. I hear other guests enjoy my quality service."

Fear and rage mixed in a chemical explosion. She had to keep Poppy distracted. "I'm sure they weren't thankful after you robbed them, trinket after trinket, you thieving little bi—"

Poppy slapped her. Eliza's head ricocheted off a shelf, and stars exploded in her vision. Her wound opened again, and she was thankful for Heath's shirtsleeve wrapped tightly around her head. "I see you've added an accessory to your outfit."

Eliza fingered the sleeve. "He didn't seem to need them. I bandaged his head just in case he survived. Wouldn't want his death on my conscience."

Poppy quirked her head. "Did the lovers have a falling-out? Tragic."

"He's just a guy I met on a plane over here." Her tongue blistered at those words. He'd become so much more to her. She prayed she would survive long enough to tell him just how much. *I fell in love with you.* His words caressed her soul.

"In that case, let's get this party started." Poppy eased a pipe wrench from the waistband of her uniform. "I knew this old cellar would come in handy. Found it by accident." She tapped the iron tool against her palm. "This is all your fault. If you'd taken my threats seriously and left. Well, you didn't. If you'd just kept your nose out of it all and let the police bumble around for a while, but no, you had to stick it where it didn't belong. Ruined my little plan for a nice nest egg. Pity. I kind of liked you, but—"

Thunk!

Poppy's mouth gaped open, and her eyes bulged and rolled to gleam white. She crumpled to the ground in a heap. Heath stood over her, an old kerosene tin in hand. "I thought she'd never shut up." He checked for a pulse. "Her heart, or whatever she's got spreading her poison around, is still beating."

Eliza scrambled to her feet then caught herself as she swayed. "Heath?"

"I'm here, darling."

"I don't feel so hot." Her vision blurred, and she worried her heart was slipping into her shoes. "I can't—"

As she slipped to the floor, he caught her and whisked her into his arms. She burrowed her nose into his neck and locked her arms around him.

"Here, relax."

Heath adjusted her and carried her fireman-style toward the ladder. "Hang on. I'll get you out of here." His breathing deepened as he ascended the ladder.

"You're strong." She clung to his waist like a monkey, her head bobbing with every step he climbed. "Those damned dress shirts do you a disservice."

His only response was a chuckle, and within seconds, they broke from the cellar and stumbled to the dewy grass glistening in the moonlight. Heath laid her gently on the grass and sank beside her. "Don't look now, but I have the answer to the male voice I heard."

She disobeyed and turned her head. A man's body lay sprawled next to the cellar door. In the bright moonlight, the man's face looked oddly familiar. One of the groundsmen.

Heath crawled over to the man. "Still breathing. Barely." He sidled back to Eliza. "Call for help. We need an ambulance and—"

"Where are we?" Eliza shivered and snuggled back into Heath's embrace. Her head throbbed, her ankle pulsed, and her stomach churned. The moonlight created weird shadows over the unfamiliar territory. She fumbled for her phone, but her fingers refused to work.

Heath slid the phone from her grasp, dialed 999, and after relaying their situation and probable location, placed the phone back in her hands.

"We have to be near the estate. They dragged both of us from the old boathouse." He pressed a kiss to her forehead. "I'll investigate. Stay here."

She glanced at the man, whose shallow breathing wheezed in the quiet night. And somewhere underground, a murderer still lived. The vision of Poppy creeping out of the dark hole to finish the job had Eliza clinging to Heath. "Don't leave me. Please."

"Give me a second." He disappeared into the cellar.

Minutes passed. Eliza nearly chewed a hole through her bottom lip. She was about to slither over to the trap door when Heath reappeared, minus dress shirt and dress shoelaces. His white undershirt glowed, angelic white in the moonlight. "She's still unconscious. I tied her up for good measure."

"You're a knight in a shining undershirt."

He glanced at his outfit. "Let me finish rescuing you. I need your phone, though. For light."

Eliza handed it over. "Probably not the best time to forget yours."

"Bloody thing went missing. Can't find it anywhere." He held his hands out to her. "Can you walk?"

Eliza used Heath's support to stand on her right foot, but as soon as she shifted her weight to her left one, she cried out. "I can't. Just go. Go get help. I'll be okay."

He eyed her. "Are you sure? I don't want to leave—"

"The sooner you go, the sooner you get back." She gave him what she hoped was a reassuring smile.

Heath kissed her then darted into the darkness, taking her only source of light.

Refusing to be cowed by the dark, she set her back toward the darkest of the woods. Not knowing what was behind her was far better than knowing Poppy lay behind her, underground, tied with only laces and the remains of a shirt. She shivered and stared at the entrance to the cellar. She recalled her favorite childhood memories, the first time she saw Mount Rushmore, her first kiss—*slobbery and sloppy*—her first plane ride, her first time getting into trouble with Belle—*thank goodness juvie records are sealed*—her first year teaching—*so many names I can never name my children...* Then her mind stalled. *Will my children look like Heath or me?*

Blood coursed through her veins, warming her from her center. Never before had she experienced the rush, the tingles, the ache, the urge to share all of her, expose her inner self, her thoughts, and her future. But with Heath, she wanted it all. Wanted him to see her, every part of her, outside and inside.

A twig snapped behind her. She bolted to her feet, gasped in pain, and wobbled like a newborn fawn. A sliver of light filtered through the trees. Heath's voice called her name, and she sank to the ground in relief. The voices of others, from her uncle to Tash, made her weep.

DCI Wentworth barked orders. Uncle Fitzwilliam scooped her into a bear hug, his silence saying more than words.

Joy joined the hug, making an Eliza sandwich. "I say, Eliza, you know how to play a serious game of hide-and-seek. You even had me looking in the kitchen cupboards for you." Joy's voice cracked on looming tears. "Don't you ever do that to me again."

"It's not like she did it on purpose. Stop pawing on her."

Eliza forgot about her pain. "Aunt Iris! Are you okay? I was worried about you, worried you'd be sick with—"

"I haven't been sick a day in my life," Great-Aunt Iris tutted, but her red eyes—and arms tightening around Eliza's waist—belied her scolding.

Uncle Fitzwilliam, supporting her weight, herded them away from Eliza. "Let's get her back to the house." He placed Eliza in Heath's arms. "Mr. Tilney, if you would, please."

Eliza squeaked in protest as Heath scooped her in his arms. "You can't possibly carry me all the way back to the house."

"Ah, so you lied earlier about my dress shirts hiding the body of a Greek god."

"That's not exactly what I said."

"Let me be your hero. Just once." His words caressed her ear, sending bolts of heat through her veins.

"You already are." She relaxed in his arms and glanced over his shoulder at those she'd come to love. Uncle Fitzwilliam had Great-Aunt Iris and Joy on his arms, and Tash, the silent protector over all, was bringing up the rear.

Chapter Twenty
Only the Beginning

The intruder has been caught! Last night, just as Darcy and I were tucked up in bed, a loud commotion brought the house down. We all rushed to the entrance to find Higgins sitting upon a man reeking of liquor and stew. He is one of Wickham's men. It is apparent Wickham is out to destroy my Darcy. I struggle to understand why. I do hope this animosity can end soon. To close on a happy note, I have found a nice young man by the name of Thomas Whitechapel, a barrister, who adores Kitty and is able to overlook her naive mistake. I have warned Darcy that they will need constant chaperoning. We shall see. I hear Darcy calling my name. I believe he wants to practice a certain skill. As I often tell him, if he wants to excel at something, he must take the time to do so.

—Lizzy Bennet Darcy
Pemberley 1811

Four hours later, Heath hovered over Eliza, packaged in warm pajamas and stuffed in her uncle's chair in his study. Uncle Fitzwilliam had pulled up another chair and sat next to her, occasionally touching the back of her hand.

"I'm fine, Uncle."

"But you—"

"Are fine now. See?" She touched her head, freshly bandaged courtesy of the paramedics who'd just left, and wiggled the toes of her wrapped foot, propped up on a footstool and pillows. Once secured and iced, her ankle had quit beating out its own pulse, and she'd refused to be taken to the hospital. "I still can't believe you called my parents." Tears burned in her eyes as she recalled the hour-long phone call. She'd been chastened, congratulated, and thanked for ending years of silence and misunderstanding.

"I'm afraid my conscience wouldn't let me keep it from them. Enough secrets have come between us."

All of them? She needed to know if the rotting skeleton had finally been given a proper burial. She worried her bottom lip between her teeth. Nancy could still release her secrets from jail. Just like a poisonous vapor, and it would slowly suffocate them all and—

"Eliza." Uncle Fitzwilliam stilled Eliza's fingers drumming on her thigh and whispered, "All of them."

He had read her thoughts. She blinked. "So you know about..."

He closed his eyes as if in assent. When he opened them, they were cloudy with unshed tears. "We will talk later on this subject, shall we? For now, we have more important things to worry about."

A knock on the door kept her retort inside her head. Mrs. Bankcroft shuffled in, a tea tray in hand. With a rattle, she set the tray on the desk and stuffed a cup of steaming tea into Eliza's hands. "Here you go, dearie. Tea sets everything to rights again."

Heath, with matching bandages, kissed the top of her head and splashed a shot of brandy into her cup from his glass. "Brandy does it better."

"But I already put some in there," Mrs. Bankcroft whispered. She cupped Eliza's jaw in her warm, work-worn hands. "I'm glad you came out all right in the end, Miss Eliza. Come get a biscuit from me anytime."

"Didn't we agree to call it a cookie?"

"Not in my kitchen." She huffed and waddled out, leaving the door open.

Eliza sipped the hot beverage. "Wow. Here." She handed it to Joy, who sat by the footstool, her head resting against Eliza's good leg. "This seems more up your alley."

Joy took a sip, hummed in appreciation, and settled against Eliza's legs again. "I still can't believe you figured it all out."

"I didn't." Eliza fingered her bandage and winced. "That's how I got this."

"Remind me to punch her when I see her next."

"Get in line," Great-Aunt Iris chirped from a corner settee, her knitting needles clacking violently. She jabbed an elbow into her snoring husband's side. "Wouldn't you agree, William?"

Great-Uncle William snapped to attention. "Yes, quite right, Iris dear." He promptly fell back asleep, his neck hinging to the side.

A few snickers peppered the room, then a heavy silence descended upon them all. Eliza wedged herself farther into the chair and rested the unwounded side of her head in the corner of the headrest. She almost purred as Heath's fingers played with her hair.

The clicking of shoes announced the arrival of Wentworth. Uncle Fitzwilliam poured a glass of brandy and offered it as soon as the detective chief inspector stepped into the room. In casual clothes instead of the crisp suit and tie Eliza had become accustomed to. A cream cable-knit sweater set off his dark skin, and khaki pants trailed to his shiny brown leather shoes. Eliza pursed her lips. He looked... handsome. His craggy face still could use some anti-aging cream, but the lines added a sense of dignity and wisdom.

"Ah, just what the doctor ordered." Wentworth sipped from the crystal glass and sighed as if in deep appreciation. His eyes met Eliza's. "How is our brave detective?"

"Head hurts."

"Poppy's hurts worse." He saluted Heath with his drink. "Nice use of the paraffin can."

Heath's hand tightened on Eliza's shoulder. They both knew he had been ready to kill Poppy. He had chosen mercy at the last minute. "How's the groundsman?"

"Felix?" Wentworth puffed his cheeks. "He'll recover. Not sure how much he was involved as of yet."

"What can you tell us?" Joy sat straight. "What did that horrid Poppy have to say for herself?"

Everyone in the room pinned Wentworth with questioning eyes. He cleared his throat. "Not much more than you already know. Greed and the sick need for recognition drove her. She had discovered, courtesy of the tunnel, that Theodore was skimming from the top of Nancy's take on the estate. From the looks of it, Poppy was sucking Theodore dry until Eliza threw a 'spanner into the works.' Her words, not mine. When the rest of the staff, starting with Piers, mumbled about getting out from under Nancy's thumb, telling the authorities, Poppy saw the end of her schemes. She had to stop them from telling. If it weren't for Eliza's hunch about the embezzlement, Poppy would have got away with murder."

Uncle Fitzwilliam heaved a sigh. "I should have known. Part of me suspected something. The estate wasn't prospering as always, but I guess I needed to trust Nancy, because if I couldn't trust her, then who could I trust? That would mean everything was a lie."

Eliza wrestled out from an afghan forced on her by Great-Aunt Iris, hopped on her good foot to her uncle, and clasped his cold hands. "You have nothing to be sorry for."

"But if I'd investigated sooner, asked more questions, taken back control of what was mine, this—"

"We'll fix this. You and I." Eliza squeezed her uncle's hands and leaned into him for support. She turned to Wentworth. "What now? What happens next?"

He took a long sip of brandy. "With all the evidence, including the victims' unearthed mobiles"—he saluted Eliza with his glass and paused—"nearly forgot." He gestured to Heath with his brandy glass. "Thought you'd like to know we found your phone, Mr. Tilney."

"Dare I ask where?"

"In Poppy's room."

"Bloody hell." Heath scoured his face with his hands.

"You'll get it back soon." Wentworth sipped his brandy. "Now, where was I?"

Great-Aunt Iris spoke over her knitting needles. "You were telling us all how snappy my niece is."

"Right. Thanks to the mobiles, plus Eliza's missing shoe in Poppy's possession, plus Eliza's recording of Poppy's confession in the cellar"—he turned the full force of his smile on Eliza—"a stroke of genius, really, I'd say she has a pretty good chance of spending the rest of her life in prison. The murder charges against Lady Darcy have been dropped." He swung an apologetic look at Fitzwilliam. "But sadly, she'll spend several years in prison for embezzlement. If we can ever find the missing Garrison, he will join her."

Uncle Fitzwilliam scrubbed his hands over his face but said nothing.

Wentworth set his empty glass on Fitzwilliam's desk. "Miss Eliza, may I have a word? In private?" He held his hand out to support her.

Eliza clutched his arm and hobbled out of the study, preparing herself for the scolding she knew she deserved. "I'm sorry I didn't listen. You were right. I should have kept my nose out of it all."

He held up a hand, silencing her. "I must congratulate you." He smiled and patted her arm. "You gave it a good crack. Well done."

Eliza's heart twirled giddy somersaults. "Does that make me an official partner?"

He quirked an eyebrow. "Don't test my patience."

"What about the button?"

"The button?"

"The blue one. The one I found in the rose garden."

A smile ticked at the corners of his mouth. "Ah yes. It was nothing."

"What do you mean nothing?"

"It was just a button."

"But—" She snapped her mouth shut, a growl purring in her throat. "I thought... well, whatever."

He clapped a hand on her shoulder. "Welcome to police work, Miss Eliza. Not every molehill turns into a mountain."

She pouted. "There goes a perfectly good plastic baggie. I don't suppose I can have it to wash out and reuse?"

Heath came out into the hall.

Wentworth waved him over. "Your turn." Like the changing of the guard, Wentworth and Heath switched places.

After Wentworth went into the study and shut the door, Heath wrapped his arms around her middle, and he rested his cheek on the top of her head. "Penny for your thoughts?"

"You know I didn't mean what I said. Back in the cellar." She burrowed into his chest.

He kissed the back of her neck. "That was all part of the plan. You distracting her. Me taking her out. We work well together, don't you think?"

Oh yes. Yes, we do! She limped around in his arms and cupped his face with her hands. "You look like a dashing rogue. Pity you don't need an eyepatch or anything."

"A couple inches off and you'd be getting your wish."

"Pity." She feathered her index finger around his right eye. "Good thing for you I love you with or without one."

His fingers that had been twirling lazily on her back stilled. His cornflower-blue eyes darkened. He dipped his head to a breath away from her lips. "Someone wise once said love built around stressful situations was destined to crash and burn."

Eliza's body warmed, and her toes tingled. She licked her lips. "That wise person is an idiot. Trust me. Besides, I loved you the second I destroyed you in Battleship."

"That is where you are wrong, my love. I let you win." Before she could protest, he claimed her lips, his tongue teasing her, tasting her, branding her as his.

She sighed against his lips as the kiss simmered to a slow-burning flame. "How do you feel about helping me move?"

"I thought you liked it here. Oh, bad memories. I understand. I know of a great hotel in Lambton." He nipped her lip. "I can help get you settled."

"I'm thinking about a bigger move." She brushed a kiss across the scratch of day-old stubble on his chin. "Maybe across the pond."

He pulled from her embrace and locked eyes with her. "You're serious."

"Is it too soon to say 'deadly'?"

He ignored her comment. "What about your job? Your parents? Friends?"

She ticked off the points on her fingers. "One, my job now is to make sure Pemberley recovers from a serious case of the Nancy. It's my inheritance, and I plan to earn my keep. Two, my parents love to fly, and my father has a lot of explaining to do in person... to everybody. Three, who says I have friends?"

"Eliza, do be serious."

She snuggled into him. "I'm sure Belle would love an excuse to come flirt with your English friends."

She could feel his grin against her ear. "Who says I have friends?" His hands roamed her back, and he hooked his thumbs in the waistband of her pants. "Do you hear that strange squeaky sound?"

"Young man, I do hope you are prepared to marry my niece." Great-Aunt Iris stabbed him in the side with a knitting needle.

Eliza didn't bother extracting herself from his arms. She peered at her great-aunt. "You want to hear the good news?"

"It's about time you decided to tie the knot. If it were back in my day, you'd be married tom—"

"Aunt." Eliza wiggled from Heath's arms and hugged her. "I'm staying. For good."

"Good." Aunt Iris pinched Eliza's cheek. "I won't have to go far for the wedding." She waddled off to the study, one white-sneakered foot squeaking along the hall tile.

Heath swept her back into his arms, his chuckles rumbling in her ear. "Think of all the adventures we'll have."

Eliza laid her finger over his lips. "I hope to never have another adventure again. One was enough."

But that wasn't true. Eliza's mystery antennae quivered at the still-missing Garrison Wickham. She had at least one more adventure in her, and the idea of finding Garrison scratched at her sleuthing itch. *If he is alive, he has managed to hole himself up somewhere. And if dead...* She shoved the idea to the side. She had time to think on murder and mayhem later. Right then, she had something else to do. "I'll be back."

"Where are you going?" Heath pulled her in for a kiss.

"I need to do something. I'll be back in a jiffy. Don't worry." She pecked his bottom lip. "Go and make my great-aunt Iris like you."

"Have an easier task?"

Eliza smiled and limped to her bedroom and, not for the first time, wished Pemberley had an elevator. She no longer needed to hide Elizabeth Bennet Darcy's journals. After discarding the useful but currently unnecessary British slang book, Eliza grabbed Elizabeth's journals, sank onto the chaise lounge, and flicked the pages to the next journal entry.

I thought I would never admit to rejoicing in having my trip with Aunt and Uncle Gardiner cut short, but the Lake District has captured my heart and my imagination. We leave in a few moments for Pember-ley. Aunt Gardiner wishes to see the grounds, and I only hope to avoid seeing its master: Darcy! Oh, I hear them calling. I must go, but I shall give a faithful report on my return.

I scarce know what to write. Darcy was there. I had forgotten how handsome he is, and I daresay his disheveled look, as he was not pre-pared to receive guests, is quite becoming on him. But I digress. His manner has much changed since last I saw him. He was all kindness and gentleness toward me and my aunt and uncle. He hardly took his eyes from me. What shall I think of that? He has even invited my un-cle to fish in the stream behind the estate. And what a beautiful estate! I find it hard to catch my breath. It must be the stairs. Oh, how shall I confess to Jane when I write to her next? How shall I confess that I have fallen in love with none other than Mr. Darcy?

Eliza snapped the journal shut. Her heart hammered in her chest. Like her namesake, she had fallen in love as well. With the es-tate, with the country, and with a certain Englishman who kissed like the devil and made her feel like an angel. She pulled out a dresser drawer and tucked the journal under the lacy underwear that she couldn't wait to wear. But first things first: it was time to tell her newfound family that she, Eliza Jane Darcy, was ready to take her place as mistress of Pemberley.

Acknowledgments

To Jane Austen and Agatha Christie: my addiction to your writing may or may not be healthy.

To my sister, Sarah: I'll never forget mocking the English accents leaking through the dining room French doors. Then I sat and watched BBC's *Pride and Prejudice* with you. Things have never been the same since.

To my husband: if only Jane Austen had known you... Mr. Darcy, move over. I got myself a true hero.

To my four minions: As Jane Austen hardly mentions children in her novels, I will hardly mention you here. Just kidding. You are my beautiful, funny distractions, and quite frankly, I wouldn't have it any other way.

To my editors, Jessica A. and Angela M.: you two make up my dream team.

To my Experts on All Things English: George, Nick, and Jen, I probably cannot count the number of eye rolls over my American assumptions about England and its people. However, you were patient with me and encouraged me and helped me write a novel that I am extremely excited about. Cheers!

About the Author

Jessica Berg, a child of the Dakotas and the prairie, grew up amongst hard-working men and women and learned at an early age to "put some effort into it." Following that wise adage, she has put effort into teaching high school English for over a decade, being a mother to four children (she finds herself surprised at this number, too), basking in the love of her husband of more than fifteen years and losing herself in the imaginary worlds she creates.

Read more at https://www.jessicabergbooks.com.